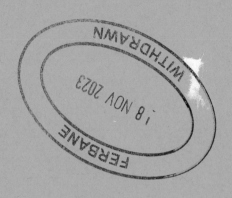

VALLISTA

BOOKS BY STEVEN BRUST

The Dragaeran Novels

Brokedown Palace

THE KHAAVREN ROMANCES

The Phoenix Guards
Five Hundred Years After
The Viscount of Adrilankha,
which comprises
The Paths of the Dead,
The Lord of Castle Black,
and
Sethra Lavode

THE VLAD TALTOS NOVELS

Jhereg	*Athyra*	*Jhegaala*
Yendi	*Orca*	*Iorich*
Teckla	*Dragon*	*Tiassa*
Taltos	*Issola*	*Hawk*
Phoenix	*Dzur*	*Vallista*

Other Novels

To Reign in Hell
The Sun, the Moon, and the Stars
Agyar
Cowboy Feng's Space Bar and Grille
The Gypsy (with Megan Lindholm)
Freedom and Necessity (with Emma Bull)
The Incrementalists (with Skyler White)
The Skill of Our Hands (with Skyler White)

STEVEN BRUST

VALLISTA

TOR

A TOM DOHERTY ASSOCIATES BOOK

NEW YORK

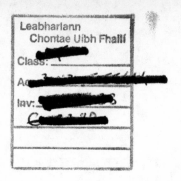

This is a work of fiction. All of the characters, organizations, and events portrayed in this novel are either products of the author's imagination or are used fictitiously.

VALLISTA

Copyright © 2017 by Steven Brust

Edited by Teresa Nielsen Hayden

All rights reserved.

A Tor Book
Published by Tom Doherty Associates
175 Fifth Avenue
New York, NY 10010

www.tor-forge.com

Tor® is a registered trademark of Macmillan Publishing Group, LLC.

The Library of Congress Cataloging-in-Publication Data is available upon request.

ISBN 978-0-7653-2445-0 (hardcover)
ISBN 978-1-4299-4699-5 (ebook)

Our books may be purchased in bulk for promotional, educational, or business use. Please contact your local bookseller or the Macmillan Corporate and Premium Sales Department at 1-800-221-7945, extension 5442, or by email at MacmillanSpecialMarkets@macmillan.com.

First Edition: October 2017

Printed in the United States of America

0 9 8 7 6 5 4 3 2 1

For Matt

Acknowledgments

Emma Bull, Pamela Dean, Will Shetterly, Adam Stemple, and Skyler White are the main people who pointed out where inside the vaguely shaped lump of marble an actual book was concealed. Alexx Kay once again helped me keep my chronology straight, and all of those who update Lyorn Records helped yet again. Thanks to editor Teresa Nielsen Hayden, to Irene Gallo and her Poignant Proletarians of Production, Anita Okoye for editorial handholding, and copy editor Rachelle Mandik. I must also thank my friend Brian Murphy, because reasons.

Additional copyediting and proofreading by sQuirrelco Textbenders, Inc.

THE CYCLE

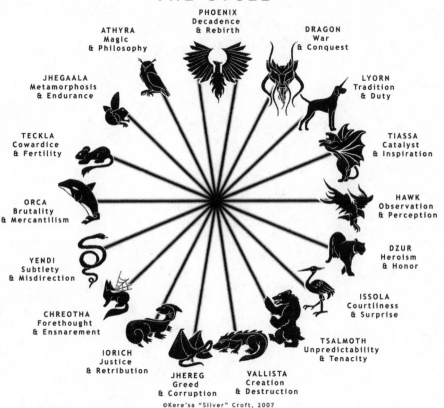

PHOENIX
Decadence
& Rebirth

DRAGON
War
& Conquest

ATHYRA
Magic
& Philosophy

LYORN
Tradition
& Duty

JHEGAALA
Metamorphosis
& Endurance

TIASSA
Catalyst
& Inspiration

TECKLA
Cowardice
& Fertility

HAWK
Observation
& Perception

ORCA
Brutality
& Mercantilism

DZUR
Heroism
& Honor

YENDI
Subtlety
& Misdirection

ISSOLA
Courtliness
& Surprise

CHREOTHA
Forethought
& Ensnarement

TSALMOTH
Unpredictability
& Tenacity

IORICH
Justice
& Retribution

VALLISTA
Creation
& Destruction

JHEREG
Greed
& Corruption

©Kere'sa "Silver" Croft, 2007

Part One

ANALYSIS

1

DEVERA THE WANDERER

It is a truth universally acknowledged, that a human assassin in possession of an important mission must be in want of a target. I found mine in South Adrilankha, the Easterners' quarter, in a district called Heart's Road. I always wonder where those names come from, you know? Maybe someone cut someone's heart out and it went rolling down the street. More likely it was named for some Lord Heart who owned a vacant lot there once, but I like my version. Anyway, that's where I was, in the open-air market just past where the Tinsmiths' Guild used to be.

I'd been on the run for several years at this point, and spent most of my time looking over my shoulder; but I'd managed to find an old friend of my grandfather's who had let me stay with him for a couple of weeks in exchange for certain services. There were few services I'd have refused if it meant not living in flophouses for a few days, so I agreed at once. All of which brought me to a small circular market in the ghetto, where, as I said, I found my target.

She was an Easterner, of course—or human, if you prefer.

A shriveled old woman, dressed in garish purple and wearing a silverite necklace with clamshells. Loiosh, my familiar, spotted her first, and said into my mind, "*There, Boss. No, further to the right.*"

I didn't approach her directly; I walked around the edge of the crowd that had gathered to watch the antics of a fat man and his squirrel, and studied her from thirty feet away. She stood behind a long table; at her back was a small wagon. There were no signs of draft animals.

I watched for about ten minutes, because you need to get a good feel for your target. A few people would approach her, speak, and leave; once in a while someone would buy something. Eventually, I strolled up as if I just happened to be going by.

I let my eyes shift, and I stopped, as if something had just accidentally caught my attention. She looked at me, a little wary, a bit interested.

"Well," I said. I gestured with my chin. "That looks like a javorn sausage."

"It is," she said, her voice neutral.

I nodded and started to move past. Stopped. "Haven't had that in a while," I allowed. "How much?"

"Sixteen," she said.

I chuckled. "No, seriously. How much?"

She scowled at me. "That is my own work. Hours of time, mixing, measuring, securing the freshest seasonings. Sixteen is a bargain. Though because I have a weakness for witches, you can have it for fifteen, and you'll owe me a spell sometime."

"How do you know I'm a witch?"

She snorted and repeated, "Fifteen."

"Yeah," I said. "I was thinking maybe six."

"Six," she said. "Unless you're speaking of six silver, you are insulting me. The recipe for this sausage has been passed down in my family for nineteen generations. I will not offend the memory of my ancestors by selling it for less than fourteen."

"All right," I said. "Eight, then. But you're robbing me."

She sighed. "Very well, twelve. Though I don't know why I should. I grow the marjoram in my own garden, and I use only the *illataakertben* Eastern red pepper, imported by a secret supplier who disdains any but the very finest, then dries and grinds it himself. But you seem nice, if cheap, so you can have it for eleven."

"I am cooking a meal for a friend who has done me a kindness. A penny more than nine, and I'll be unable to purchase anything else to go with it."

"Nonsense," she said. "Sell those fancy boots. Or the cloak. Or the sword. Why do you need a sword? We're peaceful here, and you have those for protection should you accidentally walk somewhere you shouldn't." Here she gestured at Loiosh and Rocza, perched on my shoulders. Then she added, "I will go to ten, but no further."

I sighed. "Ten then, but only because you're so beautiful."

"Hah," she said. "For that, I'll throw in an onion."

I smiled. "Thank you," I said.

She wrapped up the sausage and the onion, and sent me on my way.

It isn't that I needed the money, or begrudged it to her, but haggling with the sausage maker is part of any recipe for javorn sausage, and who am I to buck tradition?

When I got to the house, I fired up my host's stove, then unfolded the stove cover and put a pan on it to get hot. I sliced the sausage, browned it in goose fat with the onion, garlic,

flathat mushrooms, and four kinds of peppers. I served it over
toasted *edesteszta* bread. My host said kind things about it. His
name was Imry. He had almost no hair, but nearly all of his
teeth, and he moved fast for his age, though he couldn't seem
to entirely straighten up. The point is, it was really good, and
it was the last good meal I had for some time.

While I was there, I filled him in on my recent history—
you know, offending the Jhereg, being chased by assassins,
acquiring a Great Weapon, that stuff. He didn't seem all
that interested. As we ate, he told me about his neighbors
in great detail. Not complaining, for the most part, just telling me what they were like, and what they talked about, ate,
and did for a living. It wasn't all that exciting, but after the
last few years I didn't mind a little boredom. He eventually
started reminiscing about my grandfather. I liked that better.
Apparently, when he was young, my grandfather had made
most of the mistakes apprentice witches make, with occasionally dangerous and sometimes hilarious results. I also learned
that my grandfather had once been a great cusser, being well
versed in obscenity, profanity, scatology, and curses in at least
nine languages. I liked the stories, but I'd never tell my grandfather I'd heard them.

After we ate, Loiosh and Rocza had some of the scraps while
I cleaned the dishes; it was the least I could do and it killed
some time. These days, time was mostly what I was killing, and
I was all right with that.

The next morning we broke our fast with the leftovers,
which I warmed in bacon fat along with the bread. We sat
around and drank coffee, because he didn't know how to make
klava and I didn't want to insult him by offering to teach him,

talking about nothing in particular, when there was a clap at the door.

I stood up and grabbed my sword belt from the chair, and strapped it on. Lady Teldra and my rapier went on my left side, my knife on the right, and I took a step toward the door.

"What was that?" said my host.

"A Dragaeran," I said. "An 'elf.' They clap instead of knocking."

"Why would a—oh," he said. Then he got up and reached behind his chair, came up with a heavy club.

"No," I said. "If it's trouble, let me—"

He suggested I stop speaking, using language I had never heard from my grandfather.

The clapping sound was repeated.

I gave up on trying to stop him, but I at least beat him to the front door. I took a step to the side and gestured for him to get behind me. Then I took a deep breath and opened the door.

On the other side was what appeared to be a little girl.

"Hello, Uncle Vlad," she said.

"Hello, Devera," I said after a moment, when I found my voice again. "Uh, would you care to come in?"

She shook her head. "Oh, I mustn't. Can you come out?"

Her wanting me to step outside made me check the area behind her for places an assassin might be hiding; but that was just an instinctive reaction. Devera wouldn't be out to hurt me. She was—

She was—

She was not a normal child. I'd met her a couple of times, and seen her a few more. Some of those times might not have been real. She was kind of like that. It says something,

I suppose, that it never occurred to me until now, as I tell this, to wonder how she'd found me. Anyone else, anyone, that would have been my second question, right after *Am I about to die?* But with her, I don't know, I just accepted it.

I started to walk out, hesitated, then said, "One moment." I went back in.

Imry said, "What is it?"

"A friend," I said, which was true, I think, sort of. I threw on my cloak and said, "Thanks for everything," then stepped outside and closed the door.

We took a couple of steps into the stench of South Adrilankha and she said, "It's going to rain. We should hurry."

I looked up. The sky was the same orange-red it always was, but I didn't doubt her. "Where are we going?"

Any answer she might have given was drowned out by a truly impressive crack of thunder, followed almost immediately by a torrent of water from the sky that would have soaked me in as much time as it took to draw a breath, except that Devera made a gesture with her hand, and we found ourselves in a sort of bubble of dryness. If I hadn't been wearing the amulet, I could have done that. Maybe not that fast.

But it was a remarkable downpour. Adrilankha is usually kind and not very interesting when it comes to weather, certainly when compared to somewhere like Candletown, but every once in a while she reminds you that she's on the coast, when big storms that begin out on the ocean-sea roll into port like a skybender loaded with pandemonium. The wind bent the thinner trees and stripped branches off the thicker ones, while houses vanished in the deluge. Whatever Devera had done protected us from the wind, too, or we wouldn't have been able to stand.

"See?" she said. "It's raining."

"I guess," I said. "Where are we going?"

"Follow me." And she took off down the street, giving me the choice of staying with her or becoming very, very wet. I followed, and wondered. Was she doing something for me? Did she want my help? She looked like a kid, and more often than not, she acted like one. But was she just playing at it, knowing that looking and acting like that could get her what she wanted, or was she just what she seemed? Which was weird enough, for all love. I hadn't made up my mind. Her mother, Aliera e'Kieron, was the daughter of the goddess Verra and Adron e'Kieron, who was a sorcerer so powerful he, like, destroyed the Empire. And Aliera was friends with Sethra Lavode, the most powerful sorcerer, well, ever, and also a friend of Morrolan e'Drien, who was at least as good a witch as me. My point is, what could I do for her that they couldn't?

I had no idea, so I just went with it, protected from a truly impressive rainstorm by her magical bubble. I didn't figure anything out there that couldn't swim would survive.

"Hey, Loiosh, why don't you fly around and—"

"I will bite you, Boss. You know that."

"Heh-heh."

Devera led, I followed. We made it to the paved roads before the mud made it impossible to walk, and then we were stepping around puddles, and then there was no place to step around them, so we were wading through them. At one point, she jumped up in the air and came down and made a splash. Then she stopped and looked guiltily at me as the water soaked through my shirt and trousers. "I'm sorry."

"It's all right," I said, and we continued.

It would have been a strange walk in anyone's company.

The rain continued all around us, making the edges of everything fuzzy and indistinct. It was like walking through a different world, one where the world I knew was nearby, but
disconnected. I wasn't worried about anyone taking a shot at
me, because I couldn't imagine anyone finding me in all of this.
Okay, that's not true; I was still worried, because it had become
a habit, but I was aware of how irrational it was. We didn't see
another soul in all of South Adrilankha. Loiosh and Rocza
rode quietly on my shoulders.

And it went on and on.

We reached the Stone Bridge, crossed it, and made our way
through the City—the area where Dragaerans lived—but we
still saw no one. It was kind of creepy.

Hours passed, I think. If you've ever wondered how long it
takes to go, on foot, from one end of Adrilankha to the other,
I can confidently tell you that it feels like a long time. As we
left the City, going west along Kieron Road, the ground started
rising, and the water came gushing down in thick, heavy
streams, threatening to carry us away with them if we strayed
into the deeper water near the gutters. At last, we came to a
place way out west beyond the City. The cliffs were about fifty
yards to my left. The ground was rising more sharply now. I'd
been here, but not often, and not recently.

"Devera, where are we going?" I asked again.

"Come on," she said, giving as responsive an answer as her
mother might have. I followed her up the road.

When we reached the top of a rise, I recognized exactly
where we were; very close to Kieron's Watch itself—a place with
all kinds of history for Dragaerans, and where there'd once
been an outlook over the ocean-sea. What I didn't recognize was an immense structure just off the road, right up to the

edge of the cliff. A few years before, last time I came this way, it hadn't been there. I'm sure of that. I remembered walking along here as I left the City, hoping I had enough of a head start on those who wanted to kill me, and that I'd be able to find a place to hide. The structure hadn't been there.

It was big, and the pure white of marble, and had graceful, swooping curves along the roof. It towered over me and was very impressive. There was a line of glass windows that I could just see on the side facing the ocean-sea, and a large double door facing the road. I hadn't heard any thunder for a while. The rain had eased up a little, but was still coming down hard.

"In there?" I said.

Devera nodded.

"What's in there?"

"Hurry," she said, and ran ahead of me to the door, where she turned and waited, looking at me with big, brown eyes.

"Boss," said Loiosh into my mind.

"Yeah?"

"This seems like a bad idea."

"Yeah."

"Devera," I said. "What is this about?"

"I need your help, Uncle Vlad," she said. I walked up to the door. There was a large carving of a vallista, half on either side. Those things always make me think of insects. I mean, I know they aren't, but something about the four legs plus two little arms thing seems insectoid. I'd seen one once, briefly, in the jungle, and it had moved very fast—just a sort of yellowish-red flash, and that weird prehensile tail. I'd never looked at one up close, though. And I didn't want to now. I looked for a clapper next to the door, didn't see one, glanced at Devera, shrugged, and clapped. No surprise: nothing happened.

"*Well, that's that,*" said Loiosh. "*Let's go.*"

"Seriously, Loiosh. Has that ever worked? Can you imagine me turning and leaving now?"

"*Of course not. I just want to be able to say I told you so.*"

Devera giggled. I glanced at her and started to ask, but then decided I didn't want to know.

I tried the doors. They opened.

Devera walked inside and I followed her into a wide hallway, with an arched doorway about twenty feet ahead. She took three steps toward it and vanished.

The doors closed behind me with a thump, followed by a click so loud it was more of a clunk. The echo of that sound came back like it was trying to send a message. Bugger messages.

"*So—*"

"*Shut up, Loiosh.*"

It was surprisingly warm; I wasn't shivering, in spite of my wet clothing.

I turned back to face the double doors. I wouldn't have bothered to try them, if it wasn't for how stupid I would have felt if they hadn't been locked. They were locked. I studied the lock, and, yeah, it looked tough. I spent a little time on it, even playing around a bit with my heaviest lockpick, and the mechanism was either very tough indeed, or broken. Or, of course, there may have been sorcery involved; let us never forget that possibility. I've managed a few times to take doors off their hinges in cases like this, but unfortunately these hinges were set too far into the wall. Well, all right, then. While Kiera the Thief could probably have opened it easily, I'd have to use brute force, and it would take a while and still might not work. I mentally shrugged and turned my back to the hallway.

"*Are you going to try to find Devera, Boss?*"

"*What am I, her governess?*"

I checked Lady Teldra, my rapier, and a few of the surprises I carry around in case I need to explain manners to impolite persons. Then I went forward through the archway.

I guess I expected something odd to happen, like me disappearing, or everything around me shifting into some alternate dimension, or maybe, I don't know, a fluffy kitten tea party. Nothing, though. I was in a wide hallway, with dark tile floors, wooden walls, arches overhead. To my left was one of those oval mirrors in a wooden frame, head height and head size. To my right was a door. I tested it, and it opened, and I entered. There was a long, long table, comfortable chairs all around it, like the place a count might have to meet with all of his vassals at once. At the far end of the room was the set of glass windows looking out over the cliff and the ocean-sea that I'd seen before I entered the building. Rain pounded on them with a constant tapping, punctuated by irregular thumps, just like it should have for a day like this.

Except that the windows should have been on the wall *behind* me. I had turned right from the hall, and the windows should have been in a room on the left.

Well, great.

I continued looking around, feeling queasy.

"*Loiosh, is this as upsetting to you as it is to me?*"

"*Yeah.*"

"*Good.*"

I thought about the mirror in the hallway just opposite the door. I know sorcerers can do things with mirrors that I don't understand, but, well, I don't understand them. Years ago, when life had been much simpler, there'd been an incident with a mirror that I still didn't care to dwell on. I went over to the windows and stared out. They were so close to the cliff edge that I could see the waves breaking on the rocks; then I felt dizzy and backed away. I walked around the room, looking into empty corners, examining the chairs and the walls, and finding nothing even remotely interesting except that the windows were fastened in really well.

Just to verify what I suspected, I picked up a chair and swung it, hard, at one of the windows. It bounced off.

"Boss, are we just going to stay in this room?"

"Is anyone trying to kill us in here?"

"Well, no."

"And can you guarantee that in the rest of the building?"

"Um, but—"

"Yeah, yeah. I know."

The table gleamed with polish, and the wood was sort of pale, but I couldn't tell you what kind it was. I also couldn't tell you why I was looking so hard. I had the feeling that I wasn't done in this room, that there was something I was missing. I'm leery of anything that feels like premonition, so I assumed there was something the back of my eyes were seeing that the front hadn't quite caught onto yet. Loiosh, for all of his sarcastic comments, was also fully alert.

I returned to the window and watched waves crash against rocks. The rain was now a steady drizzle. It really was a remarkable view. Whoever had built this place had put a lot of thought into the fine points of standing there and watching the ocean-sea. For just a moment, I wondered what it would be like to devote yourself to making things, to creating. Like if I'd ended up a cook.

"You'd be bored, Boss."

He was probably right. But still. There was, I don't know, a place in my mind, or my imagination; a what-could-have-been where my only worry was some apprentice failing to grind the salt finely enough, or over-whipping the cream; where I'd have a place to come home to every day, and where someone I loved also lived. I thought about Cawti, mother of my son. She'd have liked living with a cook—except, of course, that we'd have never met if she hadn't been paid a large sum to kill me.

"Boss?"

"Yeah, I need to get my head out of—"

"No, it isn't that. I think what's happening to you is coming from outside. I mean, outside of your head."

"I don't understand."

"There's something about this place that's doing that; I can almost see it, like the air is twisting up."

"That doesn't make sense."

"I know."

"What can you tell me about it?"

Somewhere in there, I became aware of the effect—that is, I realized I didn't care much that something was happening to me. I've had my head played with before, and I was inclined to become irate when it happened. This time, I just sort of accepted it with a kind of, "Oh, that's interesting," attitude. Whatever was doing it, that's what it was doing.

Loiosh hesitated, then flew off my shoulder, getting more distance from the amulet I wear that would have been interfering with his perceptions, and should have interfered with whatever was invading my head.

"Anything, Loiosh?"

"I don't know. It's the place itself."

"*Loiosh, that isn't helpful.*"

"*I'm trying, Boss. This isn't—I think we need to find Daymar.*"

"*That's something I never thought to hear you say.*"

"*Believe me, I'm as surprised as you. Right now, though, other than giving you strange ideas, and distracting you, is this place doing you any real harm?*"

I thought about it. I had a strange feeling of not caring; of being willing to let anything happen. Knowing it originated from outside of me wasn't making it go away. I think someplace, way, way inside of me, I was becoming both terrified and furious; but I couldn't touch the feeling—that was happening way over there. Here, now, I was just accepting whatever it was.

"*It's getting through the amulet, Loiosh.*"

"*Not exactly, Boss. It isn't getting through anywhere; it's more like you've walked into a place where things are just like this.*"

"*Then why isn't it affecting you?*"

"*It is,*" he said. "*Just not as much.*"

"Oh."

I reflected on how interesting it was that I sort of cared that I didn't care about how I cared that I didn't care.

"*Boss, can you shake out of it?*"

"*No, but maybe I can push through it.*"

"*I don't understand.*"

"*Maybe—*

I considered. It didn't actually matter, but it might work anyway, you know. So why not? I sat down in a random chair, back to the door, leaned back, closed my eyes, tried to let myself open up, if that makes any sense: I permitted my mind to drift, encouraging any spells, visions, or enchantments that wanted to show up. *Come on. If you're there. Want to play with my head? Fine. I'm not using it anyway.*

"Who are you?"

I opened my eyes. Or, rather, I thought about opening my eyes. I couldn't summon up the will to actually open them.

A woman sat across the table from me, and at some point as I looked at her I realized that I had, in fact, opened my eyes.

"My name is Vlad," I said. "Pleased to meet you. Or I will be, when I'm capable of feeling pleased again. Can you tell me anything useful about what's happening to me?"

"Sorry, it's the room. My fault. And I'm Tethia." She said it as if she expected me to have heard of her. When I didn't respond, she looked significantly at Loiosh and Rocza as if expecting me to introduce them. I didn't.

"Tethia," I repeated, and looked at her clothing. She was wearing a loose-fitting yellow blouse, and some sort of thin, loose-fitting pants of a bright red. "Vallista?"

"Yes. I designed this platform, obviously."

"Uh, yeah, obviously," I said. And, "Platform?"

"What would you call it?"

"I'd probably give it a portentous name I'd regret later."

"It is called Precipice Manor."

"You're way ahead of me. Someday I'll have to introduce it to Castle Black and they can compare notes. Is this real?"

"Is what real?"

"Are you actually here, and is this really happening?"

"No, and yes."

"Fine, then. How do I fix it?"

"You mean the sense of emotional lethargy? It'll go away on its own, I hope."

"Your reassurance is—"

"Please. Why are you here?"

"Um. I was hoping you could tell me that."

"You're an Easterner, and, though you don't wear the colors, you have the aura of a Jhereg."

"The first is true, the second is close enough, I guess."

"I don't understand."

"Good. That makes me feel less lonely."

"Loiosh, what are you sensing?"

"There's something there, Boss. It feels like, uh, remember that time we spoke with a ghost?"

"Not pleasantly. All right, then."

"You were communicating with your familiar," said Tethia.

"Yes."

"How can you do that, when you wear protection against psychic phenomena?"

"I've been hoping someone can tell me."

"There are any number of things I can tell you," she said. "But you have to ask the right questions."

"What am I doing here?"

"Having visions, or communing with the dead, as you please."

"You're dead?"

"Yes. At least, I think so. I don't remember dying, but then, I don't remember being born, either."

"What are you doing here? How are you here if you're dead?"

She looked around. "I designed this place. It's more me than I am."

"I don't understand."

She shook her head. "It is what the Serioli call a *rigna!theiur*."

"Ah, yes, that helps a great deal." My heart thumped. I realized how vulnerable I was, and I didn't like it.

"There," she said. "You see? The effects are wearing off already."

"Why did I feel them at all?"

"I designed the room this way, to relax people, to make them more reasonable, willing to negotiate. The effects were stronger than I'd thought they would be on you—perhaps because you are an Easterner."

"I can see where it might be useful, though."

She frowned. "Useful wasn't my intention."

"No?"

"Well, maybe. I'd say helpful, more than useful. In intention."

"What's the difference?"

"I wasn't using it to accomplish something, I just thought it would be a good thing to have available in case of negotiations."

I wondered if I could gather some high-powered Jhereg in this room and convince them not to kill me. Probably not.

"Why?" I said.

She frowned. "I explained, I thought—"

"No, why did you build the place at all?"

"The platform?"

"Yes."

She gave me an odd look. "It's just how we are, I guess."

"Vallista?"

"Humans. We build things. We make things. All of us, or at least, most of us. I mean we, humans, Dragaerans, we just have that need. Maybe it's different for Easterners."

"That's not exactly what I meant."

"Then—"

"Why *this* building?"

"It was a problem that needed solving," she said.

Okay, this wasn't going anywhere. I tried a different approach. "When did you die?"

"I don't know. I feel as if I've been here, part of this room, part of this platform, forever, but I know that I wasn't."

"Do you know when this *platform* was built?"

"It was begun during the Interregnum, but took a long time to complete. Centuries."

"Um. I was here a few years ago, and this place wasn't."

"Yes."

"That confuses me."

"I don't blame you," she said.

For an instant she wavered, as if she were about to vanish, but then she came back. I wished I knew what to ask.

"How did you die?"

"I told you, I don't remember dying. My mother died during the Interregnum, or so I've been told. I think it may have been in childbirth. During the Interregnum, many women died that way."

"I'm sorry," I told her, because that's what you say.

She nodded and turned her head.

I wanted to ask more about her death, but I don't know proper etiquette for dealing with ghosts; I should have asked Teldra at some point. I said, "I'm not sure what to ask you. I'm just trying to learn enough of what's going on to ask the right questions."

She waited. After a moment, I said, "I don't know a great deal about how being a ghost works. It's outside of my area, if you know what I mean."

"I'm not a ghost," she said. "Not exactly. I think."

"Then what are you?"

"I'm . . . Tethia," she said, looking faintly puzzled.

"Do you know Devera?"

"Who?"

"I'll take that as a no."

"Who is she?"

"Now, that's a question I'm not qualified to answer. She's someone who is here, though."

"Here? She came here?"

"Yes."

"Why? Also, how?"

"I don't know why. I'm following her. How? It wasn't difficult; we just walked in."

"I'm sorry," she said. "I didn't mean for that to happen." Then she vanished, which I thought was rude. Lady Teldra wouldn't have approved. I remained still for a couple of minutes to see if she'd reappear, but she didn't.

"*Okay, Loiosh,*" I said. "*We've just learned something. I have no idea what, but something.*"

"*I'm sure that's really useful, Boss. Now what?*"

"*I'm feeling better. I mean, in the sense that I care, and I'm not quite so willing to just go along with whatever happens.*"

"*Good. So what do we do?*"

"*Go along with whatever happens.*"

"*How is it that I didn't see that coming?*"

"*Let's move,*" I said.

2

THE MYSTERY OF ELVEN FOOD

I took a last look around the room, but there wasn't much to see, so I went back to the corridor and continued. There were three psiprints on the wall, big ones. I didn't recognize the artist or the subject. They were all portraits or studies of faces, and all three were caught in one of those expressions where you can't tell what the subject is feeling: is that a scream, or a laugh? Is that one joy or surprise? And the other one, opposite the door—is she pursing her lips in disapproval, or trying not to laugh? If whoever owned this place picked those psiprints, it was probably an important clue to something-or-other, and someone smarter than me would no doubt find it insightful. Me, I was worrying about directions: If I opened the door on my left—the south—would it lead north? Up? Down? To another city? Another world?

Right on cue, there was another mirror. This one was small, and attached to the ceiling. That at least settled the question of their purpose: you do not put a mirror on a Verra-be-damned hallway ceiling for any reason but a magical one.

As I stood in front of the door, about to touch the knob, I

heard footsteps to my right. I turned. There was Devera again, maybe fifty feet away and running toward me. "Help me, Uncle Vlad," she said, then vanished again.

Well.

I walked through the space where I'd last seen her, passed it, turned, went through it again. I didn't disappear, she didn't reappear. I stood there for a minute, trying to decide what to do, then turned back to the door that I was now in front of again, opened it, and stepped through like I belonged there.

A man sat by a fire, reading a book. He looked up as I entered and said, "How did you get in here?"

"A pleasure to meet you as well," I told him. "I'm Vlad Taltos. And whom do I have the honor of—"

"I asked you a question!"

He was an old man, I would guess past his four thousandth year, when Dragaerans start looking like they're about to dissolve into a pile of dust so killing them seems pointless. He wore a yellow robe that was probably silk, with intricate embroidery in purple. He seemed frail. I considered putting something sharp into him to teach him manners, but that doesn't work as often as you'd think. I said, "I'm sorry, what did you say your name was?"

He glared at me. "Lord Zhayin of Housetown, and I ask you again, how did you get in here?"

"It's the craziest thing," I said. "I walked in the door. This door. Right here. See it?"

"Rubbish."

"I'd have clapped but I didn't see a clapper."

"The door to the manor!"

"Oh, that one. It wasn't locked, and there was no clapper there, either."

"Impossible," he suggested. "You can't have—" He broke off and glared.

"Uh-huh." There was another chair, also facing the fire, and a small table between them, holding a cup. He didn't invite me to sit down or offer me wine. What would Lady Teldra have said?

"Are you a necromancer?" he demanded.

"That's sort of a personal question, don't you think? I hadn't meant to intrude; the place didn't look occupied."

"'The place,' as you put it, is called Precipice Manor, and it is most definitely occupied, and I'll ask you to leave at once, before I call the servants to have you removed."

Unless there were a lot of servants, and they could handle themselves in a brawl, I didn't like their chances of taking me anywhere I didn't care to go, but I didn't say that. "Leave?" I said. "I just got here."

"And do you habitually walk into people's homes?"

"You're asking personal questions again. Maybe we can talk—"

I stopped, because he was yanking on the pull-rope near his hand. You can get some idea of how big a place is by how well you can hear the bell when a pull-rope is pulled, and that time I didn't hear anything at all. I looked around the room. It was small, considering the size of the manor, the size of Dragaerans, and the tendency of aristocrats to make everything four times as big as it needs to be. Next to the hearth was a door, and on the opposite wall was a portrait that was almost certainly a younger Zhayin. There were also several framed certificates: one from the Oldcastle School of Design saying he was an honorary professor, another something about an award that mentioned the Silver Exchange, another showing that he had been graduated from Pamlar University.

Presumably this was his room, and he liked being watched over by himself. At one time, I'd wanted to buy a castle, but I don't think I'd have gone so far as to sit around with a portrait of myself. From his expression in the painting, he hadn't been noticeably more cheerful when he was younger. I also, just in passing, noted which pieces of furniture I could throw, what tables might be overturned, and how much room I'd have to maneuver if things got interesting. One of the tables contained a clear glass bottle that, from the color of the liquid inside, looked like it might have contained alcoholic tincture of murchin, which I only noted for its possible use as a projectile; Zhayin's addiction wasn't my concern. I relaxed and waited.

The other door opened, and a man came through. His facial features were hard to make out, but his dress was Teckla, except for a sort of beret pulled over his forehead that had the inevitable Vallista emblem. I concluded that he was a servant because I'm brilliant that way. I'd never seen a servant wearing a cap of any sort, and wondered if it indicated something about his job. He seemed to be considerably younger than his master, somewhere in that vague sort of middle age that's over a thousand but less than three. He moved a bit stiffly, like his knees had had enough of this whole bending thing, but it was probably more his position than age that caused it. I won't move that well either when I'm two thousand years old, but I'll have been dead for one thousand nine hundred and some, so it isn't a fair comparison.

"This person," said Zhayin, "needs help with the front door. Would you see him out?"

"Yes, sir," said the servant, and looked at me. I thought about how to play it. I wasn't leaving, of course, but I was curious about whether the servant could succeed in getting the door open where I'd failed, and I thought he might be easier to interrogate than his master. So I shrugged and headed for the doorway. I stopped there for a moment, bowed, and smirked at Zhayin. "We'll be talking again. My lord."

The servant followed me out the door, I stopped and waited for him. I said, "I'm Vlad."

It is hard, if you're a servant, to figure out just where in the natural hierarchy to put a guy who acts like a nobleman, carries a sword, but is an Easterner. We just don't fit into any of the niches. It's always interesting to see how each one will handle it. This one didn't even hesitate, though: he bowed slightly and said, "I am called Gormin, sir." Then he resumed walking back toward the double doors.

"Don't get many visitors here, I take it?"

"No, sir," he said.

"You've been with Lord Zhayin for quite a while, I imagine?"

"Over a thousand years, sir."

"A good guy to work for?"

"I have no complaints, sir."

We reached the double doors. He pulled on them, and, when they failed to open, he frowned. He pulled a chain from around his neck and selected one of three large keys from it. It fit the lock, but failed to turn.

"Yeah," I said.

"That is most peculiar," he said. "I must look into the matter." He bowed to me, turned on his heel, and started back down the hall. I went with him, of course.

He stopped. "Sir," he said.

"Hmmm?"

He did his best not to look uncomfortable. "Perhaps I could

show you to a sitting room, and have some wine sent to you while you wait?"

It sure seemed important to him.

"How long have you been here? I mean, this place?" I gestured around me.

"Precipice Manor, my lord? Since it was built."

"When was that?" I'm not sure why I felt the need to verify what Tethia had said, but I did. No, I do know why: she was a ghost, or something like it, and I wanted to know how her perceptions matched those of someone who was actually alive.

"It's hard to say, sir."

"Hard to say? You don't know how long you've been living here?"

"Sir, it became habitable over a hundred years ago. My lord took up residence gradually over that time. Of course, I followed him, wherever he lived."

"Where else was he living?"

"The old castle, my lord."

"The old castle?"

"Yes, my lord. The ancestral home, in Housetown."

"I see."

He coughed, and subtly indicated the direction he wanted me to go.

I shrugged. I guessed he told me enough to earn some cooperation. "Sure."

He seemed relieved. I followed him past the room with the fireplace and into one on the same side that was similar—a little bigger, four chairs instead of two, a larger hearth, and more tables. The fire was already going. Rocza flapped on my shoulder, a sign of nervousness. She quieted down—I suppose

Loiosh had said something reassuring. The servant told me that someone would be by with refreshment. I sat down and stared into the flames as if they might tell me something. They didn't, but they made me wonder if someone just came through and lit all the fires every day; this one had obviously been going for a while.

Gormin left, shutting the door behind him. I listened for a "snick" of it locking, but didn't hear one.

"Well, Loiosh? Any thoughts?"

"No thoughts, Boss. I'm too creeped out to think."

"Yeah, there is something odd going—what was that?"

"That" was the sound of something heavy, like stone, slid-ing. It seemed to come from above, and farther down the hall, although I know that when you're inside, the direction of sound can be deceptive. I continued watching the fire, knowing Loiosh was watching behind me. Nothing happened immediately and I relaxed a little.

"Think there are secret passages, Boss?"

"Of course there are secret passages, Loiosh. Who'd build a place like this and not put in secret passages?"

A door—the twin to the one from which Gormin had first appeared—opened. This was a man, younger than Gormin, with a stiff back and a tall forehead. He wore the colors of the Issola, but displayed an emblem of the Vallista, and was carry-ing a mug and a bottle on a tray.

"My lord," he said, bowing. "I am Harro. Would you honor our home by permitting me to bring you a cup of a Newberry from the year thirty-one?"

"That sounds wonderful, Harro. I'm Vlad, Count of Szurke, at your service." I mean, if he was going to be polite, I may as well give him the big title, the Imperial one, to reassure him that he was making the right choice.

He set the cup on the table, poured from the bottle, then set the bottle down. He bowed once more, and left before I could pump him for any information.

It was a white wine, dry and pleasant.

"*How long are we going to sit here, Boss?*"

"*Until I finish this cup, and maybe one more. Or until Gormin gets back.*"

He shifted impatiently on my shoulder, and Rocza gave a displeased hiss on my other. They were probably hungry; I know I was. But to the left, my shirt and trousers had mostly dried off.

"*We could go find the kitchen,*" Loiosh suggested.

I drank some more wine. "*We could look for it, anyway. No doubt we'd find something interesting.*"

I finished the wine and changed my mind about having more—as hungry as I was, I was afraid it would go to my head. I stood up. "*All right, let's see if we can find that kitchen.*"

I stepped back into the main corridor and sniffed. There was, maybe, a very faint smell that I associate with the ferns of the jungles outside of Adrilankha. Other than that, nothing. Certainly nothing that smelled like food. What was wrong with these people, didn't they eat?

I turned left and continued down the hall. It went for a long way with no doors, or anything else; I had to wonder what was behind the wall to my right. But then, of course, in this place, who knew? Maybe the cliff. Maybe Verra's halls. Maybe Dzur Mountain.

Eventually, a passage went off to the right, so I turned to follow it.

"Boss, *shouldn't we be seeing more servants, or guards, or something?*"

"Yeah."

After a while, there was a large and very ornate door opening to my right. I sniffed, but didn't smell any food, so I kept going. The hallway continued for a long way before there was another door; this one also on the right, and just as big. I reminded myself that I couldn't count on "left" and "right" meaning anything, but I smelled fresh-baked bread, and I figured that was liable to mean something.

I opened it, and it gleamed with marble counters and sinks, with stone ovens and steel shelves. It was a kitchen, and it was a good one. I studied the layout and very much wanted to stop and cook something. There were gleaming racks of copper pots, whole tables that were cutting boards, a bread oven (which I checked; it was empty and cold), a coldbox (which I checked; it was empty and warm) and a wood stove with two separate burners, one big and one small. They were also cool to the touch.

And wedged into a corner, up against the ceiling, was a round mirror of about two feet in diameter.

"*There's no food, Boss.*"

"*Everything has to be perfect for you.*"

I sniffed again. It still smelled like fresh bread. I love the smell of fresh bread. The kitchen led to a pantry, which was also empty, except for a bucket of apples. It seemed to me that people here probably lived on more than apples. I took one anyway, and ate it. It wasn't a variety I was familiar with, but it was good—a deep red, very crisp, very tart. I ate another, giving the cores to Loiosh and Rocza. Not what I'd been looking for, but it helped.

You know, it's funny—I've beaten, robbed, and killed over the course of my career, but wandering around the place stealing apples, I felt enough like a criminal to make me uncomfortable. Not that it stopped me.

I explored the pantry a bit more, making sure I'd missed nothing, then went through the kitchen again. There were some good knives, stuck into a wooden block. My father had never used a block like that—he'd always kept his knives in a leather case, each wrapped up in a thick towel, lovingly cleaned and put back after each use. There was also a very nice spatula; it looked to be made of silver. I considered taking it, but it's hard to conceal a spatula about your person so I left it there.

Here's the thing, though: I know kitchens. I know big kitchens, and I know what's involved in cleaning them, and either there was a god of kitchen cleaning and someone had invoked him, or no one had ever used this kitchen for anything. I was betting on the latter, though where was the smell of bread coming from? I very much doubted anyone had invented invisible bread. But unless there was invisible food around here, everyone was living on apples. It was strange. I was still thinking about invisible bread when someone screamed.

"*Loiosh, where—*"

"*Pretty close, Boss. Other side of the door.*"

I ran through my assorted weaponry to make sure everything was in place, then opened the door back into the hall.

Directly across from the door was a woman, her mouth open, her eyes filled with terror. My brain instantly did the work of fitting her into the various categories: Dragaeran, Teckla, old. It did that quickly, my brain, because my eyes had already moved on, down the hallway to my right, where I caught only a glimpse of something massive and very white that vanished down another hallway before I could figure out exactly what it was.

"Barlen preserve our souls, G'mon preserve our minds. It is free," she said, staring me in the face.

"What is? What was that?"

She shook her head, her eyes wide.

"Who are you?" I asked her.

She stared at me for a moment, as if the question made no sense, then said, "Odelpho. I was named Odelpho. It's from the place my grandmother came from, Delpho, which means 'home of the bear' in—"

"That's great," I said. "What was that thing?"

"Thing?" she said, as if she'd forgotten it. Then her eyes widened again, and she screamed and fled down the hall in the opposite direction, running a lot faster than I'd have thought she could.

"Boss—"

"*I have the same questions you do, Loiosh, and no answers to any of them.*"

I looked to my right, the way I'd seen the thing go, whatever it was.

"*This can't be good,*" said Loiosh.

I re-sheathed my rapier and a fighting knife—not actually aware of when I'd drawn them.

"Yeah," I said brilliantly, still watching the hallway.

I tried to reconstruct what I'd seen, but I just hadn't gotten a good look at it. It was big, though. I was sure of that. I had the impression it just barely fit between the walls, and had been hunched over because the ceiling was too low.

"*Are we going after it, Boss?*"

"After it? Are you nuts? What if we caught it?"

"*I love it when you break out in common sense.*"

I kept walking.

"*Boss, you said—*"

"We aren't going after it. We're just going in the same direction."

"*I can't—never mind.*"

I reached the end of the hall undecided about whether to turn left or right.

"*Boss. Someone's there. Around the corner.*"

I almost drew my sword again, but stopped myself. I mean, I was a guest, right? Meeting strangers with weapons drawn is frowned on in some circles. I admit, I don't usually frequent those circles, but here I was.

I stepped around the corner and someone tried to kill me.

If I'd had time, I'd have made some appropriate remark to Loiosh—you know, about how now I felt more at home. I didn't though—I turned the corner, and Loiosh yelled into my mind just as something came at me and I threw myself to the side. It went past me about the time I realized—more by the aftereffect it had on my eyes than by seeing it—that it had been a very bright light. Have I ever mentioned that I don't enjoy going into a fight with spots in front of my eyes? It's irritating.

Lady Teldra was in my hand.

No doubt everyone in the place felt it when I drew her—felt threatened, or terrified, or at least disturbed in some indefinable way. Those who were more sensitive to magical energy would have felt it especially keenly. Me, I felt better.

My attacker said, "Wait," which I guess is a reasonable thing to say when someone you just tried to kill pulls out a Great Weapon. But all right. I still wasn't seeing too well, so a little delay before we continued our conversation was fine with me.

He was about fifteen paces from me, and had a dark complexion and a high forehead, and stupidly long, straight hair that you'd think would get in his way when he started throwing spells around. He wore the red and white of the House of the Athyra, and the badge on his jerkin was Athyra. The hands he held palms-out toward me had long fingers.

I held myself ready, and waited.

"Sorry," he said. "You startled me." His eyes were fixed on Lady Teldra, who was currently a long, slim knife with almost no crossguard.

I remained very still, watching him. Loiosh hissed, just for effect. The guy looked nervous, but still had his hands out in front of him. The posture looked defensive, or even entreating, but you can't be sure with sorcerers, so I waited.

"I really didn't mean to attack you," he said. "I thought you were . . . you startled me."

"Lower your hands," I said.

He nodded, but it took him a while to do it, like maybe he wanted to, but his hands didn't feel like moving. I've been there.

Eventually he lowered them. "Sorry," he said again. "My name is Discaru, and I have the honor to be Lord Zhayin's consulting sorcerer."

"Taltos," I said. "I'm just a guest. I assume you mistook me for that, uh, that thing?"

"My lord?"

"Is that what you thought you were attacking?"

"I don't know to what you refer, my lord."

"Big thing, not really human, sort of pale?"

"My lord?"

"You didn't see it?"

"No, my lord."

"Or hear the scream?"

"Scream, my lord?"

"Huh," I said. I should add that, this time, I was pretty sure the "my lord" had a lot to do with the weapon I was holding. I sheathed her.

"Thank you," he said, and bowed as to almost-an-equal.

"But you've never seen a big, ugly, not-human thing in these halls?"

"Of course not, my lord. And now, if you'll excuse me, I must be about my business."

"Looking for that thing you've never seen and don't know anything about?"

"My lord?"

I shook my head. The sorcerer bowed his head and continued down the hall. I heard footsteps from behind me, and almost drew again, but it was only Harro, coming down the hall more quickly than he wanted it to seem. "There you are, m'lord. I had feared you might become lost." Issola always seem to have a melodic tone to their voices.

"Lost," I said. "You were worried I might have become lost."

"Yes, m'lord."

"That's what you were worried about?"

"M'lord?"

Issola have a way of standing at just the right distance and holding themselves so they don't seem to be towering over you. Lady Teldra used to do that too. I wondered what Sara was doing right then.

"You didn't hear the scream?"

He tilted his head and raised his brows. "Scream?"

"And I suppose you didn't see some sort of very pale, big, ugly thing wandering about?"

"You are pleased to jest, m'lord," he said with an indulgent smile.

"*Lady Teldra was a better liar, Boss.*"

"*Yeah, she was.*"

"Yes," I said. "I'm jesting. I jest like a, ah, a jesting person."

"Would you care to accompany me back to the sitting room? I've had the cook prepare something while you await the door."

What cook? "Oh, you have? Well, of course, then."

He bowed and set off; I followed him. Back in the sitting room there was wine, and a plate with smoked pinkfish, long-beans, and a loaf of bread. The bread was fresh. And visible.

"Thank you, Harro."

"Of course, sir."

"And you're sure you didn't hear a scream?"

A smile flicked across his face—exactly the right smile for someone who is aware of a jest, but doesn't actually think it's funny. He bowed and took his leave through the small door.

"*Yeah, Loiosh. He's lying.*"

"*Share the fish, Boss.*"

The bread was good. The fish was kind of bland, but not really the sort of thing you can screw up once it's been smoked. I'd have enjoyed the food more if I didn't keep wondering where it came from. The empty kitchen was as disturbing as whatever it was I'd seen out of the back of my eye. Almost as disturbing.

"*How long are we going to sit here this time, Boss?*"

"*About as long as last time.*"

I guess I should explain my thinking here. First of all,

Devera needed my help; I wasn't going to turn her down. Also, well, I was curious, and I knew there were all sorts of things going on around me that I didn't understand, but I did have some theories. For one thing, I was pretty sure there was necromancy at work in the place. If you aren't familiar with it, necromancy is magic that has to do with death, which involves places that can't be reached by means of normal travel. The Necromancer herself once explained that death was only a passage to such a place. She might be wrong, but until I had evidence to the contrary, I was going to assume she knew her stuff. For one thing, she came from a place like that. For another, well, she's called the Necromancer, right?

And the bread indicated something—the smell had been there in the kitchen, but there was no sign of anyone having made it. No sign of fish in the coldbox. Nothing at all, in fact, in the pantry, the coldbox, or the kitchen. Except apples. Why were there apples? That was at least as odd as the other stuff.

I didn't want to just sit there, but I also wasn't comfortable about just aimlessly running around the place. I thought about finding Zhayin and putting a knife or maybe Lady Teldra to his throat, and politely asking for a few straightforward answers to some simple questions. But not yet. Not until I had some idea of what sort of forces he might have available. I don't like to threaten someone and then discover that he's got the edge on me. I've had that happen a couple of times. It's embarrassing.

I finished up the bread, the fish, and the wine. Loiosh and Rocza shared the longbeans, because they always taste like soap to me no matter how they're prepared. Wherever the food came from, and whatever it indicated, it was better than not eating. Except the beans—not eating was better than the beans.

"*I wonder if the wine cellar is empty, too,*" said Loiosh. It took me a moment to realize he was being serious. But either way, what would it tell me? Besides, I doubted that I'd have more luck finding it than anything else.

On impulse, or something like it, I got up, left the room, and went back toward the front doors—just to see whether the doors I'd seen before were still there, or if everything had moved while I wasn't looking, like one of those castles in an Eastern folk tale. No, they were still there, which was some relief. I turned around, went past the doors I knew, and took the hall-way to my right that led to the empty kitchen, then kept walking. At the end of the hall, where I'd met Discaru, I turned left, under some sort of vague notion of going from one corner of the structure, the "platform," to the opposite corner.

Ahead of me, a pair of doors stood open. I went through like there was nothing to worry about, and in fact there wasn't—it was a very large ballroom with a high ceiling, stra-tegically placed cabinets with bottles and glasses, a stage at the far end, freestanding full-size mirrors in each corner, and two curving stairways leading up that looked like they were made of white marble.

I got closer, and yes, they were marble. I ascended, and found myself on a balcony that wrapped all the way around the ballroom. I wondered what it would be like to be up here when the floor was full of dancers and the room full of music. Cawti would have said something about how many Easterner or Teckla families could be fed for the price of one of the gowns or doublets.

I silently snorted—I had now, it seemed, reached the point of having imaginary conversations with her over imaginary entertainments.

There were doors in each corner on this floor. The two that were above the entrance were large and ornate; the others were smaller. Which way to go? The aristocrat, or the servant? I went through the nearest door because it was the nearest.

"At last!" said Loiosh. "After all our searching, we have found the treasure—"

"Shut up."

A mop, a bucket, two brooms, a dustpan, and a shelf full of jars of liquids and powders of various colors, as well as a few piles of rags. And the oddest place you could come up with to put a closet like that. It made no sense, which meant that, like everything else, I just couldn't see it. I was annoyed.

I closed the closet and headed for the other servants' door. I guess I expected it to be pretty much the same, but this one opened to a long, narrow corridor, doors on the left every twenty feet or so. I walked past them. They were probably servants' quarters, and while I didn't have any problem sneaking around Zhayin's manor and poking my nose into private places, for some reason walking into a servant's room seemed a little excessive.

The door at the far end was locked. I studied the lock, removed my set of picks, and spent a lot longer than Kiera would have getting it. To the left, I doubt Kiera gets the same sense of satisfaction I do from hearing that "click." I put my stuff away, opened the door, and stepped through.

3

The Phantom of the Dance

It was a neat, tidy little study—a bookshelf with books, a desk with papers, a pedestal for larger books, and a tall, slanting table with clips around the edges. On the desk was a fist-size clear ball of a sort I'd seen in Morrolan's study, and against the corner was a short, black, polished stick topped with a smaller version of the clear ball. Another corner held several cylinders, about three feet in length and perhaps half a foot in diameter. In addition to books, the shelves held several tablets of paper, some of them very large. And yeah, you guessed it: a mirror. A small one, wedged into a corner of the floor, pointing out and up. It was slightly convex, which may have meant something, I don't know.

"Boss? What if you broke the mirror?"

"I know. I've been thinking about it."

"And?"

"Not yet."

This was the first place I'd found that made it look like someone lived here—with the exception, of course, of the room Zhayin was occupying. I went in and, without touching anything, looked stuff over. There was a blue ceramic jar on the desk, containing more pencils than I'd ever seen in one place, and a truly lovely quill holder, inkstand, and sand jar all done in turquoise set with mother-of-pearl. There was also a matched pair of fountain pens, which proved that Zhayin embraced modern technology.

I glanced over the books. There were a few on sorcery and several on necromancy, but most of them had titles like, *Strength Considerations for the More Common Steel Alloys with Updated Formulae for Stress Calculations* and *Observations of the Effect of Water Pressure on Various Granite Structures Considered over Time*. None of them looked like they'd be a lot of fun to read. Loiosh waited patiently, Rocza remaining on the floor in the doorway to give me warning if anyone should approach.

I might have learned more if I'd wanted to open the drawers of the desk, or take the books down from the shelf, but sorcerers have the nasty habit of setting traps on such things—traps I couldn't detect while the amulet I wore was keeping me blind to sorcery.

The last thing I did was check for secret doors or movable walls or whatever, just because the room seemed like an odd size and in an odd place compared to the rest of what I'd seen. I didn't find anything, and I decided that was enough. Rocza resumed her place on my shoulder as I closed the door and, with some effort, locked it behind me. It's funny how often they're harder to close than they were to open. And there's no thrill in succeeding, either.

I went back, all the way around the balcony, and flung open the first set of big double doors like I had every right to.

Sure, there's no reason a place like this shouldn't have a

big dining room. In fact, if I'd thought about it, I'd have assumed it did have a big dining room. Only not *here*—not on the second floor, leading off a balcony like this. And where was the pantry? The hallway with the sitting rooms ought to be right below me, and it didn't seem like it could work. I looked behind me, and the balcony was still there. Ahead of me was a long table—maybe twenty seats on a side. And doors opposite. And really, was it possible to have a dining room any farther from the kitchen? How do you get food there without it getting cold? Or were there magic doors or something that led from one to the other?

It was big enough that I had to spend some time making sure it was empty, then I had to fight the temptation to sit down at the head of the table, just to see what it felt like.

Did I mention there was a pair of mirrors built into the walls? No, but you probably guessed it, didn't you?

"*It's a big empty room, Boss.*"

"Yeah."

"*With a table. And some chairs.*"

"Yeah."

"*Bet we can learn all kinds of things.*"

"Shut up."

I got closer. The table was empty except for half a dozen candle holders, none of which had lit candles. This made me wonder where the light was coming from, and it was only then I noticed several windows high on the wall to my right. It was still daylight outside. I tried to figure out how long I'd been there to see if that made sense, but gave up. It took me a while studying them to see that they were covered with glass—even there, way up where no one could reach them. Whoever built this place had too much money.

It hit me that I should have grabbed some paper from the study while I was there and tried to make a diagram—maybe I'd have seen something, like, I don't know, the hallways formed the sorcery rune that means "This is stupid."

"*There are doors at the other end, Boss.*"

"*So I see. Probably open onto mid-air, and I'll fall into the ocean-sea.*"

"*But you're going through them anyway, aren't you?*"

"*Of course. Unless something jumps out of the walls and eats me between here and there. Which isn't all that unlikely.*"

"*You'll probably just go mad before you get there.*"

"*This is the place for it, isn't it?*"

"*Unless you already are mad. I hope not, because—*"

"*Then you are too?*"

"*Yeah,*" he said. I kept my eye out for anything interesting, but it was just a big room with a long table. Not much you can do with that. I mean, if there's nothing there—

"*Loiosh.*"

"*Boss?*"

"*Big fancy doors at one end.*"

"*Yeah?*"

"*Big, fancy doors at the other.*"

"*Your powers of observation, Boss, are—*"

"*So where does the food come from? Where is the entrance from the kitchen? Where do the servants go? You know they can't use the doors the important people use.*"

"*Hmmm.*"

"*I thought this room was too normal.*"

The walls were blank—some decorative lamps and candle holders, and strips of a darker wood here and there, but nothing else. Secret passages? Maybe. But I looked for them, and it's pretty hard to conceal an opening in a blank wall from someone looking for it; that's why most secret passages are behind bookcases or in slatted floors or something. And if they were servants' entrances, why conceal them? In a way, the lack of servants' doors was the most bizarre and inexplicable thing I'd yet come across, and that's saying a great deal.

Verra take it, then.

The doors at the opposite end were the twins of the ones I'd first come through. I went up and flung them open. It was dark on the other side.

"*Boss—*"

I stepped forward into the darkness.

Unlike any other transition, this was accompanied by a sense of dizziness, a moment of fuzzy vision, and even a low roaring my ears. Then everything cleared, and I was—

Sitting.

Well, that was interesting.

The chair was hard and wooden, and there were more chairs, empty, in front of me, and to both sides. Many of them. Directly in front of me, past all of the chairs, was—

I was in a theater. A big one, given that it was inside another building: a quick bit of compound addition from my years of schooling told me that there were more than three hundred seats. The stage was the traditional six-sided figure, raised about four feet, and well lit from all sides. Now, you understand, there was no way a theater of this size could have fit beyond those doors I'd opened—for one thing, it would have extended down to the floor below. By now, I shouldn't have been upset about the place not making sense, only I was. I looked for the inevitable mirrors, and found them, above each door.

You had to be some kind of theater lover to build your own

three-hundred-seat theater in your house. Did Zhayin have guests often? I returned my attention to the stage. It was now occupied, which it hadn't been an instant before. Well. That was interesting.

In the center of the stage was a woman I didn't recognize. She stood there, motionless. I didn't move either, or say anything, for what felt like most of a minute. Then the music started. I didn't see anywhere for music to come from, and I certainly didn't see anyone playing it, but it started—big, orchestral. She began to dance.

I don't know much about music, and even less about dance, but I can tell you how it felt: it was like the grasslands to the north, when a strong wind comes up and the grass lies down flat, like it's bowing. And it was like the forests to the west, when the snow is first melting and the streams run black against the white blanket. Her movement never stopped—her hands drawing patterns in the air, her legs bending, straightening, leaping, collapsing; her torso moving like a snake's, her head erect and balanced and it seemed like even the twitches of muscle above her eyes were planned, and precise, and perfect.

I became aware that I was holding my breath, and let it out.

Look, I'm sorry to get all poetic on you. We both know that isn't what I'm about. My point is, it's the only way to tell you what happened, and that by itself should tell you something, all right?

So I sat there in that empty theater, and I watched her dance until, after I don't know how long, she stopped, her body twisted up into a position that was impossible in its beauty, the lights went down, and the music ended. Then I sat there for a little longer. I was just coming back to myself enough to wonder what it all meant when she jumped down from the stage and approached me, working her way through the aisle, then over to my row. Her movements were like water, or, you know, something that flows. She was short for a Dragaeran—maybe half a head taller than Aliera, and the term "willowy" might have been invented to describe her.

I sat and waited. She took the chair to my left. She didn't look at me; her eyes were focused ahead, on the stage she'd just left. She said, "My name is Hevlika."

"Vlad. You're an amazing dancer."

"Thank you."

"I can't imagine the hours of training to learn to do that."

She nodded, still staring straight ahead. "I've been studying the art for four centuries. I started when I was barely forty."

"Dancing before you could crawl."

"That's the saying, yes."

"I also liked your entrance."

"My—?"

"When I entered, the stage was empty. I looked away, looked back, and there you were. Nice trick."

"Oh. That was not my effect, it was yours."

"Oh?"

"Yes. Don't you know? In any performance, the audience provides most of the magic for their own enchantment?"

"I've heard that, but I never took it quite so literally. It's never been my area of study. How did I manage it?"

"How could I know?"

I didn't have a good answer to that. "This place," I said.

"Hmmm?"

"This is an odd place. Things happen that I can't figure out."

"And outside of this place, you understand everything so well?"

"Don't be cryptic."

She chuckled a little.

"I can't even tell what House you are."

"Does it matter?"

"Always."

"You wonder if I'm real."

"Yeah."

"I wonder if you are."

"I could tell at once we had a lot in common. Can you tell me anything useful about what's going on in this place?"

She looked around for a moment, then faced the stage again.

"What do you mean?"

"The kitchen was empty, unused, but there was fresh bread."

"What brought you here?"

"A friend asked me for help."

"What kind of help?"

"I don't know."

She turned and looked at me. Her face was triangular, and she reminded me a little of Sara. Okay, Issola, then. After giving me a quick glance, she faced the stage again. I started wondering what was so fascinating there.

I said, "So, what can you tell me about this place?"

"Precipice Manor?"

"Yeah. Sorry, I can't say that with a straight face. Which is odd, because I know someone who calls his home Castle Black."

She spared me a quick look. "Apparently you can't say that with a straight face, either."

"True enough. So, what can you tell me?"

"I don't know a great deal. I dance. That's all."

"You dance?"

"For Lord Zhayin. Every couple of months he has me dance."

"Private performances?"

"Yes."

"There's something kind of sick about that."

"Is there?"

"Well, you know, he keeps you here, makes you dance—"

"Lets me stay here, lets me dance. He's my audience. He loves my dancing."

"It is beautiful."

"Thank you. But without him, I'd have no one to dance for."

"Eh, what? Why?"

"You don't know dancing. I'm good, but not good enough. Not anymore. Not since the injuries."

"Injuries?"

"That might be the wrong word. The wear and tear."

"I don't—"

She stuck out her leg and rested it on the seat in front of her. I tried not to look. I understand that social customs about modesty don't apply to dancers, but her legs were covered only by tights, and I wasn't used to seeing a woman's legs close up. She didn't appear to notice my discomfort.

"Most of the damage," she said, "is from jumping and landing. Some, of course, comes from the poses, but in my case, it was the hard surfaces. Thousands and thousands of landings."

"Wait," I said. "I've missed something. Damage?"

"To my leg. And hips. And, of course, feet. I can't say I have fallen arches, because I don't have any arches at all. It hurts when I walk, and when I stand still, and when I sit."

"I—"

"Also, of course, my knee." She put her leg down and put the other one up. "Much the same with this leg, but the knee problems aren't as bad. To the left, however, I have hip and lower-back pain on this side."

"Can't medical sorcery help?"

"It helps a lot. It's why I can still dance. But it can't fix everything. And a lot of the damage happened during the Interregnum, when nothing could be done, and now it's too late. But even at its best, there are limits to what can be done if you destroy your body."

I thought about the various places on my person I'd been stabbed or cut, and how many of them still hurt sometimes, or, worse, itched.

I cleared my throat. "And so—"

"There are things I can't do anymore. None of the troupes will have me. It's how things work—we dance, our bodies break down, we stop dancing. But Lord Zhayin saw me, and liked my work, and so I have an extra few centuries. In the old days, in Housetown, I used to dance for his Teckla, too, but now I have to ration myself. The problem isn't the pain, you see. It's the not dancing. I hate not dancing."

There was very little expression in her voice as she said that, and she continued staring straight ahead.

"So if, instead of dancing, you'd—"

"Not dancing was never an option."

I considered. "That's kind of a horrible thing. Do what you love, destroy yourself."

"Better than destroying someone else."

That was a little close to the mark. "You know who I am?"

"Vlad," she said. "You told me."

"Okay. Because what you said . . . never mind. How long have you been here?"

"Are all Easterners this curious?"

"How many Easterners have you met?"

"You're the second. The other asked as many questions as you."

"I'll bet he wasn't as good-looking."

She didn't laugh. She said, "It was a long time ago. And you all look alike to me. Although he didn't have any jhereg with him. And I think his hair was lighter."

"Never trust an Easterner without a pair of jhereg. How long did you say you've been here?"

When she didn't answer at once, I glanced over at her, and she was frowning. "I'm not entirely sure," she said.

"Interesting," I said.

She shrugged.

"No idea? Days, weeks, years, decades?"

"Decades, anyway. Since the Interregnum. What's the difference? I'm here now."

"Yeah, so am I. And it may not matter to you, but I'm trying to figure this place out."

"I don't understand. What's to figure out?"

"Why the kitchen was empty, and where the bread came from."

"That doesn't seem—"

"Also, what that weird thing was that made one of the servants scream."

"I don't know anything about that."

"Not to mention why it is that half the time when I walk through a door in this place what I find can't possibly be where it seems to be. I find that upsetting."

"I understand."

"Not to mention the whole matter of the ghost."

"Ghost?"

"Or something. A woman named Tethia who—"

"Tethia?"

"Yes. You know the name?"

She frowned. "It sounds familiar, but I can't think from where. Perhaps my Lord Zhayin has mentioned her."

"But you don't know anything about her?"

She shook her head.

"So, if you can't tell me what's going on around here, who can?"

"Lord Zhayin."

"Yeah, I don't think he cares to. Who else?"

"His butler."

"Right. Harro. He's not very forthcoming either."

Her lips twitched. "I don't think forthcoming is on the list of butler virtues. Also, I don't trust him."

"Why not?"

She frowned. "I can't say. There's something . . . no, I don't know why. I just don't."

"All right. In any case, butler virtues aren't something I've ever studied." I found I was tapping Lady Teldra's hilt and stopped. She was never a butler.

"What's bothering you?" she asked.

"That's an awfully direct question."

She shrugged.

"Nothing really," I said. "I'm just wandering around a magical building acting as if everything is perfectly normal."

"Well, I'm talking to an Easterner with a jhereg on each shoulder, acting like *that's* normal."

"Your point?"

"I sympathize."

I rubbed my chin with the back of my fist. "You know, I can't imagine doing that."

"Sympathizing?"

"No, being a butler. I mean, I can imagine slaving away on some long-holding if it was that or starve, and I can imagine being the Lord of some short-holding, and I can imagine singing for tavern meals if I could sing, and I can imagine being a foot soldier—I've *been* a foot soldier. But I just can't imagine walking around all stiff and proper and telling some rich fuck when his dinner is ready, and never saying anything I felt like saying. It'd make me crazy."

"Why do you care so much?"

"I don't know. Maybe something about your dance brought it out. Is it magic?"

"Not the way you mean it."

"Okay."

"To answer your question, I think some people take satisfaction just from doing their duty."

"Um. Okay."

She smiled. "I wish I could help you."

"You have," I said. "Good luck with the injuries. And the dancing."

I got up and walked to the aisle. There was a door in the back, but I had to wonder if there was another. I walked forward like I knew what I was doing, hopped up on the stage, and kept going. I glanced back. Hevlika was still sitting there, watching me. "Don't worry," I said. "It's just a stage I'm going through."

The door opened with no sound. I went through, and was back in the dining room. I continued to the balcony, stopping directly in front of the set of doors I hadn't yet opened.

"*Predictions, Loiosh?*"

"*Hah.*"

I flung open the doors.

"*Mirrors,*" I said.

"*Lots of them, Boss.*"

The walls were mirrored, the ceiling was mirrored, the floor was mirrored. I stood there looking at myself over and over again.

"*Who would do this?*"

"*Whoever did all the rest of it?*"

"*But who would make a room like this? I mean, really, some-one said, 'I know! I'll fill a room up with mirrors! That will be fun!'* "

"*You know they're magic, Boss.*"

Yeah, by now there was no doubt that they were magic. It was just annoying that given all the spells that involved mir-rors, I understood none of them.

"*We going in, Boss?*"

"*No.*"

"*Good choice.*"

"*Although we could—*"

"*Boss!*"

"*All right. But it does make me realize something: I'm a pretty good-looking guy.*"

"*Sure, Boss.*"

"But I should trim my mustache."

"Yeah, that's just what I was thinking."

I shut the door and turned around, and—

"Devera!" I said. "I've been looking for you."

She nodded. "I know. I've been looking for you, too."

If she'd been human, she'd have been about nine years old, and would have looked a bit like one of those skinny waifs you see in South Adrilankha begging you for coins while another cuts your purse. Well, except for how she dressed. She wore loose-fitting black pants with a silver stripe and an even looser-fitting shirt that was also black but decorated with silver, all of it worth more than those waifs would ever manage to steal. She had a black ribbon in her shoulder-length blond hair to keep it rigorously back out of her eyes.

I said, "Can you tell me what I'm supposed to be doing here?"

"Help me get out."

"Help you get out? You led me here."

"That was tomorrow-me. It's today-me that's trapped."

"Oh. Of course. How foolish of me."

"Boss, did you really understand—"

"Not even close, Loiosh."

"Oh, good."

"Can you explain, Devera?"

"I don't understand it, Uncle Vlad."

"Oh. So, what do you want me to do?"

"I don't know."

I'd have made some remark there about how helpful she was being, but while you can be gently ironic with Devera, you can't be sarcastic with her. You just can't.

"Okay, can you tell me which way to go from here?"

She looked around, then shook her head. Great.

"All right," I said. "Why don't you just tell me the story. I mean, what happened."

"Okay. I was visiting Daddy, and—"

"So, excuse me, that would be in the Halls of Judgment?"

She nodded.

"And that was yesterday?"

She nodded again, and I realized that that was not a useful question; "today" and "yesterday" and "tomorrow" obviously meant something to Devera, but they didn't mean the same things they meant to me: her "yesterday" might be a thousand years ago, or next month, or right now. My head didn't actually start hurting, but it felt like it wanted to, and would if I kept thinking about it.

I said, "So you were there. How did you end up here?"

"I don't know, but I couldn't get out."

"Then how did you find me?"

"Oh, I did that tomorrow."

"Oh," I said. "Yes, of course."

She nodded.

I took a deep breath and let it out. "Please, Devera. Try to explain as clearly as you can, what happened, and how I can help you."

"But, Uncle Vlad, I don't *know* what happened." She looked like she was about to cry, which I found more upsetting than any number of attempts on my life had been.

"That's okay," I said. "Just do your best."

She wiped a wrist over her eyes and nodded. She wasn't a little kid, but when she acted like one, was it an act? You tell me.

"All right," she said. "After I saw Daddy, I went to the Vestibule to visit Great-Grandmama, and—"

"Wait, who? Where?"

"The Vestibule. Darkness."

"You were visiting darkness?"

She nodded.

"Uh, you mean there was no light?"

"No, no. I mean her. Darkness."

"Darkness is a person?"

"She's a god, silly," said Devera, as if anyone should have known.

"Oh," I said. "Yes, of course. How foolish of me."

"Uncle Vlad!"

"Yeah, okay. Go on."

"And you know how when you walk through the Halls there are all those time spikes? Well—"

"Wait, what?"

"You know. The time spikes."

"I—I don't remember those."

"Oh. Well, that's how you get to the Vestibule."

"I guess there were things I didn't get to see."

She nodded. "It's a big place," she said. She's very understanding.

"So, the Vestibule?"

"Yeah, and I was visiting Darkness, and then, well, I just took a step and I was here."

"Right. Okay. And then you got out tomorrow, right?"

"Yes, but only because you helped me. That's why I came to get you."

"Why me? Why not your mother, or Sethra Lavode, or Morrolan, or the Necromancer? For that matter, why not Verra?"

She shook her head, her hair flinging about. "I can't," she

said. "Mama would . . . if I . . ." She looked at the floor. "I'm not supposed to visit Darkness."

"Oh. Okay, you came to me because you were doing something you shouldn't have, so you can't go to any of the others, and you don't know what happened or how I can fix it, but I'm the only one you can go to. There. I think I'm caught up."

"Does it scare you?"

"No, it's fine."

"Then you aren't caught up," she said, nodding vigorously.

"That makes a little too much sense. Why aren't you supposed to visit Darkness?"

"Mama says she isn't proper company."

"Your mother—Aliera, we're talking about Aliera here—says she isn't proper company."

Devera nodded.

"That is, Aliera e'Kieron, the daughter of Adron e'Kieron, the man who blew up the Empire? She is saying that Darkness isn't proper company?"

Devera nodded again.

"Did she say why?"

She looked down. "I don't know."

"Devera."

She continued looking down.

"Devera, why did your mother say Darkness isn't proper company?"

"Mama doesn't like how she eats."

"Oh. Well. I guess that might be a bad example. How does she eat?"

"She eats worlds."

"Oh. Well. And she lives in the Vestibule, near the Halls of Judgment?"

"She doesn't *live* there. But I can find her there."

"When she isn't eating worlds."

Devera nodded.

"Loiosh, how did I end up in a situation where—"

"Don't even go there, Boss."

Devera giggled.

"So," I said. "All right. I get why you don't want your mother to find out, or your grandmother, but why not one of the more powerful types?"

"They'd tell on me."

"And I won't?"

She shook her head.

"Why won't I?"

"Because you know how to keep secrets."

I started to tell her about all the stuff I'd been telling to complete strangers, then remembered how much I'd been leaving out. I said, "Yeah, I guess I do. So, what do you need me to do?"

"I don't know!" her voice was a little shrill.

"Can you explain how it is you know that I can help, but not what it is I have to do?"

"I need *someone* to help me. And you're someone, aren't you?"

"I've often wondered."

"I need someone to help me find a way out, and . . ." Her voice sounded quivery and then she stopped, looking down.

"All right," I said. "I'll try to help. Do you know—"

She vanished.

"Well, bugger."

"Surprised?"

"Not really. But we're adding that vanishing bit to the things we need answers to."

"*I'm sure it's not important, Boss.*"

"*Heh.*"

I stood there for a minute, just absorbing the conversation and failing to figure out what it meant. When I'd wasted enough time, I shrugged and set it aside as best I could.

So, now where? Back through the theater and out the other doors, or back down the stairs?

Somewhere in this place was an answer, and I hadn't yet identified the question.

I went through the dining hall to the theater—or, at any rate, the door that had opened into a theater a few minutes before. I went through it, and, as before, there was that disorientation and I found myself sitting. The consistency was oddly reassuring.

I watched the stage for a few minutes, but Hevlika didn't appear. I got up and went through the doors in the back.

They opened to a wide corridor, mostly done in pale yellow with white trim, decorated with a couple of mirrors on each side with small tables below them, and a few paintings and psiprints. The carpet was a dark blue, rich and thick. As was becoming my habit, I turned to look at the door behind me. It was still there, and I could still see the back seats of the darkened theater. Well, then.

I walked down the hallway. I could imagine it being full of nobles, all dressed in their Houses' finest finery—winged boots, sequined tights, high-collared, sweeping gowns—as they waited for the door to open. That's what this hallway was for; had it ever been used? There was a "snick" as the doors behind me closed. There was a door on the right; I opened it and was nearly shocked to see something that made perfect sense: a long room with hardwood floors, mirrors on both sides, and a rail running all around it. Just the sort of place a dancer would use to practice. I shut the door and continued.

The hallway ended with a large table beneath a larger mirror. I was getting tired of looking at myself. A door stood on either side. This one, or that one? The last several hours had been filled with choices and no rational basis to choose one or the other. I was getting annoyed.

I tried the one on the left, but it was locked. I studied the lock, then got the necessary objects from the pocket inside of my cloak, and a minute or so later had it opened.

Interesting place to put an armory. No, a really nonsensical place to put an armory.

Halberds, mostly. No dust, but also a quick test revealed they weren't especially sharp. Mostly for show? Yeah, probably. In one corner was a stand with eight broadswords, also dust-free, but they, too, could use some time with a whetstone. A shelf next to them had daggers—six of them decorative, full of cheap gems and gold coating, and another eight that were fully functional, if a bit dull. I picked them up one at a time. Decently made, triangular, good point, solid hilt, leather-wrapped grip. I resisted the urge to steal some, but I wanted to, just because. These weren't balanced for throwing, but were nicely balanced for off-hand fighting. Not works of art by any means, but examples of good, solid craftsmanship. Gosh, I love daggers. I put them back.

4

The Legend of Sleepy Harro

I left the armory, crossed the hall, opened the other door, and was once more looking down the hallway that should have been a floor below me. Rocza did a nervous dance on my shoulder, shuffling to one side and back; I caught Loiosh's head bobbing around from the corner of my eye; they were becoming a little upset about the place too, either picked up from me or just on their own.

There are any number of folktales about buildings that are alive, and have their own wishes. Sometimes, especially in Dragaeran tales, it wants to kill the hero. In Eastern tales, it often wants to protect him. A lot of what was going on would make more sense if I accepted those stories as true, and figured the place was trying to tell me something, or save me from something, or get me to do something. I eat well, but there are things I have trouble swallowing.

"Loiosh?"

"*I'm with you, Boss. I don't believe in buildings that have their own plans.*"

"Good."

"But then, until we met Sethra, I didn't believe anyone could be older than the Empire. And until we met a Jenoine, I didn't—"

"Thanks."

The door was still open, and still showed the fancy corridor. I shrugged and continued, turned a corner, and heard a cough behind me.

"Ah, there you are, my lord."

"Hello, Harro. Yes, I was stretching my legs."

"Yes, my lord. I'm grieved to tell you that we have not managed to open the door."

"I'm concerned to hear it."

"It's getting late. I am instructed to see that you are given dinner and a room for the night."

"That is very kind. This dinner of which you speak. Where is it to come from?"

"My lord? The cooks prepare the food. In the kitchen. I don't understand what you ask."

"Never mind," I said.

"Permit me to show you to a room where you may refresh yourself."

"Lead the way," I said.

As we walked, I said, "Do you know Hevlika?"

From the corner of my eye, I caught a brief tightening of his shoulders.

"The dancer?"

"Unless there's another."

He coughed into his fist. "Why, yes, I have the honor of knowing her."

"Good dancer, isn't she?"

"Why yes, my lord."

"How long have you known her?"

"My lord? She was here—that is, part of the household—before I arrived, so as long as I've been with Lord Zhayin. At the old castle, of course."

"What can you tell me about her?"

He looked deeply uncomfortable; all he could manage was a muttered, "I couldn't say, I'm sure."

I don't know if it was Issola impenetrability, or butler impenetrability, but I couldn't penetrate it so I let the matter drop. He opened a door and stepped aside. I was hit with an odd pang: Cawti, at one time at least, would have loved a room like this, all velvet drapes in red and gold, plush carpet, stuffed chairs, a bed you could hold a party in. There was a washbasin and jug on the table, an inlaid chamber pot beneath it, and a stack of towels. The water jug next to the basin was steaming.

"It's a very nice room," I said. "And someone certainly prepared it quickly."

"Yes, my lord," said Harro. "Should you require anything, pull that rope once and I shall come immediately. I will clap when dinner is ready."

"Will I have the honor of dining with Lord Zhayin?"

"I'm afraid I do not know, m'lord."

"All right."

"Will that be all, m'lord?"

"Sure."

He bowed and backed out, shutting the door behind him in front of him. I wondered how long you had to practice something like that. I poured some hot water onto a towel and ran it over my face, because I always grab luxury when I can. I laid down on the bed. It was awfully soft. But then, after having been in the wilds for so long, anything better than hard ground felt soft. I closed my eyes and drifted off for a bit.

Loiosh woke me up just before the clap came. I sat up, blinked, and said, "How long did I sleep?"

"Not long, Boss. Maybe half an hour."

"Come in," I called, and Harro did so, holding a bronze-colored tray with one hand at shoulder level. Somehow, even when I'd had money, I'd never gotten around to hiring servants. He set the tray on the table and bowed to me, and I decided that was a shame. Servants would have been nice.

When he'd gone, I sat down to a roasted fowl stuffed with greenfruit, spiral mushrooms, and capers; it should have tasted better than it did, but Loiosh and Rocza approved. The wine had been decanted so I couldn't read the label, but it was a very full red, and good.

"If we go back to that kitchen, Loiosh, it'll still show no signs of use."

"Yeah."

"Think we'll ever figure out what's going on around here?"

"Hope so, or I'll never have any peace. More exploring, or do we want to get some sleep?"

"You think I could sleep now, Loiosh?"

"Probably."

I thought about it. "Yeah, you're right."

I really needed sleep.

The smell of klava woke me up. It was on the stand next to the bed. I swung my feet down to the floor, managed to lift the klava glass, and sampled it. I'd had better, but it was drinkable. Over on the table were a few small round loaves of bread with a hole. They were of a type I'd had once before, back when

Lady Teldra was still Lady Teldra. They'd been toasted and buttered. I prefer a more substantial breakfast when I can get it, but there have been times I hadn't managed any at all, so I called it a push. The two jhereg sat at the foot of the bed, and I got the impression they were waiting for me to wake up so they could eat. It's possible Loiosh had to remind Rocza to wait, but I didn't ask.

I took my time eating the bread and drinking the klava. There have been times I've had to wake up and deal with someone being anti-social before my brain started working, but whenever possible, I like to take my time. I had an uncomfortable moment when I suddenly realized that someone had snuck into the room with food without me waking up.

"*It was Harro,*" said Loiosh. "*I was awake.*"

"*All right, then.*"

The klava was better than the coffee I'd had yesterday, but klava is always better than coffee. Well, isn't it?

"All right," I said aloud. And to Loiosh, "*Now what?*"

"*When did it become my job to—*"

"*Yeah, yeah.*"

I got up and used the chamber pot, splashed some water on my face, and got dressed. I made sure the surprises I concealed about my person—not nearly as many as I had once carried—were in place. I was about to step into the hall when there came a clap outside the door. I opened it, and Harro was there.

"Well," I said. "Good morning." And, "*Loiosh, are we being watched?*"

"*Not magically,*" he said.

"Good morning, m'lord," said Harro. "I was wondering if you would care for another glass of klava."

I shook my head. "Have you checked the door?"

"I fear it remains sealed, my Lord."

"And the secret entrance?"

"Sir?"

"A castle like this must have a secret entrance or two. Have you checked?"

"If it has one, my lord, it is secret."

"Heh. Mind if explore a bit?"

"My lord, my instructions are to request that you remain here until we have solved the problem."

"Good, then," I said. "Agreed. Your request has been heard."

I pushed past him, turned right, then left, heading in the direction of the kitchen, and the place I'd seen whatever it was that I'd seen.

"Sir?" said Harro. He caught up to me.

"Not to worry," I told him. "I always like to take a nice walk in the morning. I'm thinking there might be a pale, big, ugly thing to talk to."

He swallowed. "I must insist—"

"Yeah," I said. "I'd be disappointed if you didn't."

"M'lord, please."

"You really don't want me investigating, do you?"

He coughed, I guess trying to figure out how to answer the question without giving me any information. I considered the matter. A lot of what I do is pulling information from people, and that means figuring out the best approach for that person. Everyone is different. Some will respond to being smacked around or other forms of reason, some have to be tricked, some cajoled. And it isn't always easy to tell. With Harro, I leaned against the wall, folded my arms, and said, "If you don't want me wandering about, maybe we can have a conversation."

He shifted his weight a couple of times, then said, "What would you like to know, sir?"

One thing I wanted to know was why I was sometimes "sir" and sometimes "my lord," but I figured that was kind of a low priority. "This place is lousy with things I don't understand, so maybe just pick one and explain it."

"My lord, I—"

"All right. Try this: You've been unwilling to tell me anything about anything. Every time I've tried to learn anything, you stiffen up like—you get stiff, and you don't give anything away. But that one thing, that weird whatever-it-was I just threatened to go look at, when I mention that, your eyes crinkle and your left hand twitches and from the way you swallow I think it makes your mouth dry. So, why that? What makes that one personal?"

He stared straight ahead, but I had the impression it took some effort.

I stretched out my legs, smiled at him, and waited.

He shook his head.

"All right," I said. "Whatever. You don't have to tell me." I snapped my wrist and a dagger fell into my hand. I could have just drawn one, but the effect of having it appear like magic couldn't do any harm. He made a tiny squeaking sound and pushed himself against the wall, his eyes wide, his lips pressed firmly together, his teeth clenched.

"Oh, don't worry," I told him. "I'm not going to hurt you."

He kept staring at me like he didn't believe me. I pushed away from the wall, flipped the dagger, and caught it. "It's just that I'm really annoyed at not getting answers to my questions. So I think I'll go find Lord Zhayin and cut his throat, just to make myself feel better. Excuse me."

I took one step, and he said, "No!"

I stopped and turned. "Hmmm?"

"Please."

"Then tell me why you get so upset when I bring it up? I'm not asking for the big secret, you know. I just want to know why it bothers you so much."

Here's where I could give you all sorts of crap about watching the internal battle going on behind his eyes or something, but, really, no. No battle. He crumbled.

"All right," he said. "It's because it, what happened, was my fault."

I nodded. "Go on," I said.

Pulling information out of someone who knows how not to give it involves, first, finding the right lever, then teasing each bit and snippet out, using what you know to get what you don't. A guy like Harro is different: once you get him started, you'll get everything; all you need to worry about is what you want and in what order. In this case, I didn't have to worry about that either. It just came spilling out.

You must understand, sir, that service is a tradition of my family. As far back as the last Issola reign, when so many of our House acquired holdings and lived as landlords, my family never did. For us, service to others has always been the greatest joy. Most of my family were killed in the Disaster, but I, with a few others, was in the Duchies and so escaped the immediate effects. We wandered, and looked for those who had survived and whose houses needed putting into order. Eventually, late in the Interregnum (though of course, we didn't know it would end soon) a Dragonlord named Kâna instituted a post service for sending and receiving messages, and that is how I learned of Housetown. Not long after I came here, the previous butler stepped down and I took his place and I have had the honor to occupy this position ever since. Honor, m'lord, and if I may say so, pleasure. My mother used to say, "There is satisfaction in doing something well, and satisfaction in having done something well, and they are not the same." For me, it is the former that gives me pleasure. Does that help you understand, sir?

My duties, as a rule, have to do with attending my Lord Zhayin and supervising the other servants, but before, when we lived at Housetown, we would often receive guests, and it was then my honor to see to them, as I am attempting to do with you, m'lord. Other concerns would arise from time to time, but it was mostly a matter of doing what I was used to, what I knew how to do. I know many would find this tiresome, but I did not. Indeed, I must confess that I became uncomfortable when, on occasion, there would be a requirement to do something outside of my duties. Once I was tasked with feeding the horses while the stable-boy was being married and the others were at the wedding, and, as simple as it was, with all of the directions neatly explained, I still recall the sweat on my palms. You may laugh if you wish, but it is true. On another occasion, I had to act as valet to Prince Ferund when he made a sudden visit to our home, and, well, I was in a state of near panic the entire time—not because he was a Prince, but because I was unused to being a valet.

That is how I am, sir. It is my nature. I think it important for you to understand this if you are to make sense of what happened.

We felt the Disaster as it happened, of course—the family here, and I, in the grasslands near Suntra. But the most remarkable thing about the Interregnum, from what they tell me, was what little effect it had on this household. My lord would still receive the occasional commission, and had sufficient savings that they had no need to concern themselves with such vulgarities as money.

So it was when Lord Zhayin's son was born, early in the Interregnum, and so it was a little more than a Turn later, when I came here. The birth was, from all accounts, a joyous event for all the household, as I'm sure you can imagine, though I cannot speak from personal knowledge. My Lord hired a wet-nurse and a dry-nurse, and, after a certain amount of disruption, the house settled into a routine. The young gentleman grew, as children will, and a tutor was hired as well. He was a bright, inquisitive child who loved to draw, of course, and also enjoyed looking into corners and closets; I am told he kept his nurse busy, as you may imagine, but he fit into the household in his own way.

I arrived and took my position. Housetown is deep in the Blue Valley, north of the Guinchen region, and so was isolated from the worst of the effects; food was readily available, and the plagues passed us by. There were, of course, illnesses here and there as medical sorcery was no longer effective, but the local physickers were able to treat these well enough.

As for my lord, the loss of sorcerous ability turned out to be a stroke of fortune. Many sorcerers, of course, received educational benefits from the absence of the Orb. My understanding is limited, you understand, as I am not a sorcerer myself, but it is well known that the requirement to reach directly into the amorphia without the Orb's intervention has forced many to learn a great deal. My Lord Zhayin was no exception. In his case, he made certain discoveries in necromancy. Are you familiar with it? It is the study of unreal paths to real places, or real paths to unreal places. It begins with death, you see—that transition through which we all pass. The studies of my Lord Zhayin, aimed at eliminating the boundary between a structure and a location, or, to put it another way, between where one stands *within* a structure and where that position is exclusive of the structure, has necromancy at its heart. It may help if I explain that to do this—to integrate the pathways between worlds with the structures *within* a world has been a goal of Vallista architects for tens of thousands of years. My lord, then, as you can imagine, made great progress in this.

You recall, sir, that I mentioned the occasional illness. We were all struck by these at one time or another, and they were an intolerable annoyance. More, we were all terrified for the child, as we were told by the physickers that the young are more vulnerable to disease than adults. We exercised what care we could, and the child was never in danger. And so it went, until the dry-nurse became ill with the grippe, and before we knew it, she had infected the tutor and the second cook. It was for this reason that the child became, for a time, my responsibility.

It was the most difficult thing I have ever attempted, sir. Not for the reasons you might, perhaps, expect: learning to interact with a child is simply a more extreme case of what I have always done, that is, learn to interact with every individual as best I can for the comfort of that person. A Vallista Prince, or, if you will forgive me, a Jhereg Easterner, it is a matter of sensitivity, observation, and flexibility. So, no, learning to care for the child was by no means beyond my abilities. What made it difficult was that I was so weary. So very tired. I still had all of my own duties. I ate while walking, when I ate, and

rested when I could. It is astonishing how quickly one becomes exhausted. After a week I was having trouble keeping
my eyes open. Have you been that weary, sir? I look at you,
and—I hope you do not think me impertinent—I think you
have a wide variety of experience, so I suspect you know what
it is like to go through a day with your eyes never fully opening, where half of the things you do you don't recall and can
only hope you did them properly, when your thoughts are
focused on the next time you sleep. If you haven't had that
experience, I can't describe it, and if you have, I don't need to.

You must already know what I'm going to say, yes?

I fell asleep. Or, I suppose, "nodded off" is more precise. I
was watching the child, and I closed my eyes, and then suddenly came awake, my heart pounding, as happens at times like
that. The child was gone and the door open.

He wasn't in the hallway outside the nursery. He wasn't in
the kitchen. Later, I was asked why I didn't at once raise the
alarm, and I can only say I didn't think of it. And as I ran about
like a madman looking for him, imagining him scalding himself in the kitchen, or severing a finger in the armory, I say, to
my shame, that the knowledge that whatever happened would
be my fault was as terrifying as my fear of what that disaster
might be. Were I to live for a Great Cycle, I would never experience such terror.

Could anything make it worse? Yes, because as I left the
armory and began to run toward the Great Hall, I saw that
the doorway to the stairs up to the tower was open. In the
castle, you understand, there was no glass on the windows,
much less the unbreakable glass we have here; the vision of
him falling from the tower was all that filled my mind.

May Triharunna Nagoray forgive me for saying it, but maybe it would have been better if he had.

I reached the top of the stairs. The west tower of the castle was large and square. It contained a small room where my lord kept his magical equipment, and a necessary room, and many windows; but the door that was open led up to tower's cap, which is where my lord carried on his magical studies and experiments.

Was it a capricious god who determined the moment the child would enter? Perhaps Verra; it is the sort of thing she would do. Maybe when I reach the Paths I will ask her.

Lord Zhayin was engaged in necromancy. I am not sufficiently familiar with the art to explain exactly what he was doing, but I do know that he was reaching into the Great Sea of Amorphia to attempt to touch a place where the laws of nature are different. There were three rods placed about the room, all white, waist height, as thick as my wrist, and each was emitting both a sound and a light. The result was an odd sort of music, low, discordant, unsettling; and where the lights came together in the center of the room it had the same effect on the eye: one couldn't focus on it without feeling unsettled.

For a moment—perhaps the worst moment of the entire ordeal—my panic ebbed, because the child wasn't there, and my lord was continuing his work, looking like the conductor of an orchestra, hands weaving back and forth, eyes closed, face distant, reflecting a mind that was far, far away.

I made myself look into that place, where the light and sound met. It was hard, the way it is hard to stand in a high place, but I made myself look into the swirling emptiness. I remember the sweat on my hands, and how it seemed that my ankles were about to give way. I kept looking. Sometimes it seemed patterns would form in the light, and sometimes I was sure it was my imagination. I kept looking. I felt like whatever it was, was actually entering me, working its way into my head, changing me. I kept looking.

And I saw him, I saw the child. He had wandered into the midst of it, into the very focus of the spell.

I know I screamed, or made some inarticulate sound of denial and rage against the gods.

I remember moving toward the child, but when I screamed, my lord opened his eyes, saw me, and released the spell.

Of course it was too late then.

Sometimes I think his refusal to kill me, or even discharge me, is a form of punishment—that he wishes to make me live with my failure. Sometimes I think it is a kindness, a way to let me know that I'm forgiven. Of course, I've never asked.

My apologies, sir. You wanted to know about the child, and I have been speaking of myself. It is difficult not to, both because the event remains in my consciousness, and because speaking of the child is painful, and I suppose I was avoiding it.

The child was damaged. I suppose "damaged" expresses it as well as any other word.

What happens when a body is subjected to forces designed to change the nature of the world where they are focused? And what happens to a mind? I am not a sorcerer, still less a necromancer; I can tell you nothing of why or how, but what you saw was the result. We care for the child as best we can, and see to it he is unable to harm anyone.

Yes, I understand that you saw him. I don't know how he came to be loose. My lord keeps a sorcerer on staff just to prevent that from happening. But whatever happens, we are forbidden to speak of him. And I wouldn't have, except you— you looked like you meant it. Would you have really killed him? Yes, I think you would have. You've killed before, I can see it in you.

That is all I have to tell, m'lord. I hope it satisfies you.

Satisfied isn't exactly the way I'd put it, but it was nice to get a few answers. "Yeah," I said. "That'll do."

"Then," he said, "would you mind . . . ?"

"What? Oh." I hadn't realized I was still holding the dagger, testing the edge with my thumb. "Sorry," I said, and made it vanish.

"If that will be all, m'lord?"

Okay, I gotta give it to him: I'd just terrorized him, then dragged out his darkest secret, and he was like, "If that will be all, m'lord?" That's impressive, isn't it?

"Sure," I said. "Thanks."

He gave me a stiff and almost military half-bow, turned abruptly, and went away, presumably to collapse somewhere where he could do so privately.

"*Well, okay, Boss. That was some, uh, something. What now?*"

"*Now we explore some more. And if we see a big, ugly, whitish, drooling thing, we run.*"

"*It was drooling?*"

"*Sure. Why not?*"

"*I agree with the running part. Or, you run. I'll fly.*"

Down the hall, past the kitchen. I ducked my head in to see if it was any different; it wasn't.

"*Want to hear my nightmare, Loiosh? It's that we'll figure all*

*of this out, deal with it, and the thing with the kitchen will have
nothing to do with it and I'll never understand it."*

"My nightmares are a bit worse than that, Boss. They have
more to do with a giant, white, slobbering thing."

"It was slobbering?"

"Sure, Boss. Why not?"

"Yeah. Hey, do you actually get nightmares?"

"Not really."

After the kitchen, when the hallway ended, I turned right;
I hadn't gone that way before. On the other side of the wall to
my right should be the kitchen, and for all I knew, maybe it
was. Part of what made this place, this *platform*, so weird is that
sometimes things were just where they should be, which made
the other times even more unsettling.

There was a stairway leading up. In a normal place, you
can tell a lot about where you're going by the stairway, or, at
least, you can tell if it is expected to be used by those who live
there, by guests, or by servants. This one was white marble,
but not excessively wide, and didn't have much in the way of
decoration—if you don't count the inevitable mirror perched
on the wall as a decoration—so I would have figured it was
for residents. But that was in a normal place; here, I couldn't
be sure of anything. I started climbing. It went up, then doubled
back, which left me one floor up facing back the way I'd come,
in a hallway that was much too short for what ought to be
there.

There was a door on either side, and at the end of the hall
a pair of sconces—and, yes, a mirror. I took the ten necessary
steps, grasped the sconces, and played with them. The one on
the right turned to the right, then the one on the left turned
to the left. As secret passages go, it wasn't hard to find. The

room was small and comfortable, with a large Eastern rug in red and blue on the floor and several chairs, a small bookcase, some tables, and a cabinet that was a bit taller than I was. There was a hand pump over a deep sink, and in the corner a mop, a broom, and a pail. So, in other words, it was a fairly typical servant's closet appointed and set up for one of the residents to relax in. If that makes no sense to you, then you're just where I was. An iron chain with a handgrip hung from the ceiling. Also, there was no mirror. I didn't know if I should be pleased or worried about that.

I checked the cupboard. It was unlocked, so I opened it and was hit with a blast of cold air. This mystified me for an instant, until I saw there were cuts of meat, steaks, hanging from hooks, like the cupboard was a miniature meat locker, evidently with a cold spell set into it to preserve the meat.

I didn't find anything else interesting, so I pulled the chain. The back wall opened with a sound like stone sliding over stone. Does that sound familiar? Yeah, me too. But by the time I recognized it, it was already open.

"Uh-oh," I said cleverly. Loiosh gripped my shoulder.

I only had time to get the impression of stone walls before I saw the *thing* in the room, and it was looking at me. Its face, if you can call it that, was distorted, its head seemed too small for the rest of it, its shoulders were lumps of muscle or bone, its legs were squat and seemed bigger around than my body, and it was as pasty, ugly white as I'd first thought. It had two horns, like those of a goat, coming out of its head, and irregular splotches of dull white fur here and there about its body. It was naked, too, except for the fur, and I guess I'd still call it a he; its sex was incongruously minuscule on that frame. *No, not it, he. It's a person, or at least was once.* His mouth was full of yellow, misshapen teeth, and I was right, he drooled. Or, okay, slobbered. Fine.

I've heard people say that when something scary happens, your first reaction is to either fight it, or run away. I guess sometimes, but more often—I say as someone who has been the something scary that happened—people first freeze up. That's pretty common. But it isn't true of me. By now you should have figured that a lot of what permits me to survive is that I'm not controlled by reflexes; I look at the situation, figure out what the right move is, and then—

Oh, crap. You won't believe me anyway. Yeah, I froze.

5

At the Fountains of Sadness

I stood there, unwilling to even draw a weapon until I knew what it was going to do.

Over the years, as I've told you of these things, I've talked about people who didn't show fear when they should have, about those who can keep the appearance of calm, and even disdain, when they think they're about to die. Sometimes, that's been me. It isn't just an accident, you know. There's a reason for it that's as practical as a leather hilt. In the Jhereg, it matters for your career, and for your life. You have to be able to stare someone down when he's got you dead to rights, when you're sure you aren't going to get out alive. You do it because, if you *do* get out of it alive, if someone saw you turn into a quivering, shaking ball of terror, no one in the organization will respect you again, and you'll either need to get out of the business or mess up a lot of people tougher than you to get your reputation back. It's practical, okay? And by now, for me, it's become a habit. No, I'm not without fear; I've just learned that it isn't safe to show how scared I am.

So, if you'd been looking at me, I'm pretty sure I wouldn't have looked like I was about to piss myself.

It—he? I kept going back and forth on that in my head. It stood up and made a snarling sound, staring at me. Well, now what? I drew Lady Teldra, hoping that the power emanating from her might make the thing cower into a corner long enough for me to close the door. It didn't seem to notice; it just stood there, snarling. Its eyes were tiny even without the squint.

Then it moved. And it was fast.

I never considered standing my ground and letting it impale itself on Lady Teldra. On reflection, if I had, it probably would have gotten its hands around my throat and broken my neck in its death throes, but whatever; I threw myself backward before making any sort of conscious decision. As I did so, Loiosh and Rocza flew at its face.

I guess they made it flinch, which gave me time to scramble back.

"Careful, Loiosh!"

"Tell me about it!"

Throwing a knife at the thing would just annoy it. I scrambled back some more. Loiosh and Rocza were making quick dives at its head while it batted at them, getting a lot closer than I liked. There would have been several options involving sorcery, but that would have required removing the amulet, which was very likely a death sentence itself, because once it wasn't around my neck, the Jhereg could find me, and I knew they were trying to.

Well, crap.

I looked for a vulnerable area as I stood up. Maybe, if Loiosh and Rocza could keep it facing the other way long enough, I could hamstring it. I drew my heaviest fighting knife. I didn't much like my chances. Maybe—

"Excuse me, Lord Taltos. Let me."

I recognized the voice: the Athyra sorcerer I'd just met, Discaru. I moved to the side. "Yeah," I told him. "By all means."

"Loiosh, make some distance. Sorcery happening."

The hairs on the back of my neck stood up, and I moved farther to the side, and the beast let loose a horrid screech and cowered back into the corner. Loiosh and Rocza flew out of the room, and Discaru moved past me and pulled the chain. The door rumbled shut and I breathed again.

"There," he said, turning around and smiling as if it were no big deal, which maybe it wasn't to him. Me, I don't embarrass easy, but right then I wanted to be sand in Suntra, if you'll excuse the cliché.

"I was exploring," I managed.

"Of course," he said, as if it were completely reasonable for me to be wandering around unescorted in this manor where I didn't know anyone and half the rooms were enchanted and they kept a monster hidden in one.

"How did you know?"

"Hmm? Oh. I sensed your weapon being drawn, and came to see why."

"That took some guts."

He bowed his head briefly.

"Does this happen often?"

"Him getting out? No, almost nev—"

"No, strangers getting trapped in this place and wandering around opening doors."

"Ah. No, this is the first time that has happened."

"Pleased to give you a new experience, then."

He didn't seem quite sure how to take that.

I said, "What are you going to do?"

"About you?"

"About it."

"That isn't my decision to make. I think what we have been doing all along: keeping it alive, and keeping it safe."

"Necromancy," I said.

"Hmmm? No, no. I just used—"

"No. Necromancy. You've studied it, haven't you?"

"It's not a specialty, but yes, certainly. Why?"

"I'm trying to figure out how to get out of here, which means figuring out how this place works, and I'm starting to think figuring out necromancy has something to do with that. I've been doing a lot of figuring."

"Well, yes, of course."

"So I was thinking about asking you some questions about how necromancy is used in this, uh, 'platform.'"

He stared at me. "Where did you hear that term?"

"Platform?"

He nodded.

"Well, that's what it is, isn't it?"

He took a step back. "Why have you come?"

"Why do you think?"

"Don't—" He cut himself off. There's a limit to how force-fully you can give orders to someone who's just shown you a Great Weapon. He tried again. "I don't know. But I'm curious."

"Okay," I said. "Short version: I'm here by accident, and I'd like to leave."

Yeah, I was lying. I do that sometimes. The idea was to keep him talking. What I'd have done if he'd shown me, say, a secret way out that worked, I don't know. But he didn't. "I could teleport you out," he said.

"No, you couldn't."

He frowned and studied me. "Oh. Yes. I see. Well, if you remove—"

"I can't do that."

"All right," he said.

"I just need to figure out how this platform works."

"If you don't know how it works, how do you know it's a platform?"

"Uh, I guessed?"

He waited. I suppose I could have intimidated him. I mean, I had the means. But he'd just finished solving a problem for me, and threatening him seemed like bad form. I suppose carrying Lady Teldra around for so long has had an effect on me.

"So," I said. "A trade, then? I answer your question, you answer mine?"

He barely hesitated. "Answer mine first."

"All right. Tethia told me."

"Who?"

Had there been a flicker of shock at the name that he'd covered up like a professional? I wasn't sure, so for now I played it straight. "She called herself Tethia. Obviously a Vallista."

"I don't know her."

"She seemed to be a ghost."

"A ghost of whom? No, sorry, stupid question. Where did you see her?"

"No, no. My turn. What do the mirrors do?"

"They reflect necromantic energy and redirect it."

"What does that mean?"

"My turn. Where did you see this ghost?"

"I walked in the front door, and on my right was a small antechamber that let into a room that had a great view of the ocean-sea that should have been on the other side. She was there."

"When you were in the room, did you experience—"

"I think it's my turn now."

He closed his mouth, then nodded. "What do you want to know, exactly?"

"How does this place exist? Why do doors go where they can't go and take me to places they shouldn't? How was it built? And why is the kitchen empty?"

"That's a lot of questions."

I shrugged. "Pick one."

He nodded. "Maybe we should find a more comfortable place to talk."

"Sure," I said.

He led me back toward the stairs.

"As you have surmised," he said. "It has to do with necromancy."

"Yeah."

"And my Lord Zhayin said that the breakthrough came when he was able to reach the Halls of Judgment."

"Why would he want to do that?"

Discaru shrugged. "If you want a guess, because the Halls are a nexus of worlds."

"Oh, of course," I said. "Why didn't I think of that?"

Actually, sarcasm aside, I had a pretty good idea what it meant. I said, "I need to check something. This goal—a building that permits one to reach other worlds—has been around for a long time, and Zhayin was the first to achieve it, right?"

We stopped in front of the left-hand door. He turned the

handle and nodded. "How did you know that? The ghost again?"

"Yes."

"There's a mystery here."

"Hey, you think?"

He opened the door, stepped through the doorway, and vanished.

I couldn't see much of anything through the door; it was black, except for what I can only describe as a few vague shapes that could have been rocks, trees, mountains, clouds, animals, or people. I stood there for maybe five seconds, trying to decide what to do, when Discaru appeared again.

"Sorry," he said. "I guess that might have caught you off guard. Did you want to come along?"

"Where are we going?"

"The Paths of the Dead, of course. Or, rather, the Halls of Judgment."

"Of course," I said. "So, you were just kidding about going somewhere we could sit?"

"Oh, no. We can sit there. By the fountains. It's quite comfortable, actually."

"But your point isn't the comfort, it's bringing me to the Paths."

"You said you wanted to understand the manor, and how it works. Well, the entrance to the Halls is the key."

I had Lady Teldra, Loiosh, Rocza, and a few other sharp things. Sorcery couldn't affect me. So, how bad could the trap be? Plenty.

"Um. All right. Sure. Lead the way."

"Boss—"

"Got a better way to get answers?"

"But—"

"And it isn't like I haven't been there before."

"Yeah, I remember. That's not an argument for going."

"Probably not," I said, and followed Discaru through the door.

Like I told Loiosh, we'd been here before.

There's this mountain located, I don't know, somewhere way north and a bit east of Adrilankha, where there's a stream or a river that goes over a cliff, which is where Dragaerans, if they're considered worthy by some standard I couldn't even guess at, are sent over because Dragaerans think that sending a corpse down a waterfall to go smashing itself at the bottom of a cliff shows respect. Don't ask me. Not my custom, not my waterfall.

Point being, the place is full of dead people, most of them trying to find their way to the Halls of Judgment, or wandering around aimlessly after failing to do so. From things Sethra Lavode and the Necromancer have said, I get the feeling that the region full of dead people has about the same relationship to the strange area around the Halls as some bucket of water pulled out of the ocean-sea has to do with the whole.

I'd been there once years before, when I'd been too stupid to know better. Now I was much more clever and sophisticated, so everything would be fine. Right?

Having run a good number of Shereba games, and played in many, I can tell you that there's a certain type of player who makes a careful study of the strategy of the game, and then as soon as he sits down, thinks to himself, *I know so much more about the game than these people. Like, I know why sloughing the low trump here is a stupid play, and because I know that, it gives me an edge over people who do it out of stupidity, so in my case it's a smart play.* Then they slough the low trump just like the stupid player and lose their money. I'm not kidding. There's one of those guys in every game you sit down at. If you can't find him, it's probably you.

I bring this up because, well, here I was, back in the Halls of Judgment, but I *knew* it was stupid to be here, so that made it smart. Right? In fact, I figured I had a good chance of being okay as long as I didn't run into a god or something.

I looked around. Light in the Paths of the Dead is weird; there's no Enclouding like you have in the Empire, but there's also no Furnace lurking behind it, so where does the light come from? I dunno, but whatever it is leaves the place feeling just a bit too dark, like a room where you can manage to read but you really wish for one more lamp. My memories of the Halls of Judgment involved thrones and pillars and darkness. Wherever I was now was a lot more interesting. There were trees that looked remarkably like trees—the tall kind that have branches only near the top, and have wide leaves that flop down at night. I'd seen a lot of them in the west. The grass was short and tended, and there were stone benches surrounding a fountain. I like fountains. This one was formed of three rings, where each ring had small arcs of water all around it. In the middle of each ring, a tall jet formed the petals of a flower, and in the middle a third jet of water rose higher still, splitting into three parts and then dissolving into mist with a shimmering rainbow in it. I'd seen rainbows in the East, and I'd always thought it had something to do with the Furnace being right there where you could see it, but I guess not. Or, you know, magic. It's hard to form conclusions in the Halls of Judgment; in that sense it's like Precipice Manor. So far, my conclusions had not gone beyond deciding that dead people like looking at fountains, too.

Discaru and I were in a clearing that might have been fifty yards in diameter, and beyond it was mist. I turned back to the fountain and watched it for a moment more before it crossed my mind to look behind me.

"Where's the door?"

Discaru glanced over his shoulder. "These two rocks. Just turn around and take a step and we'll be back. Try it, if you'd like."

"That's all right," I said. "What is this place?"

"The Halls of Judgment."

"Thought so. What's beyond the mist?"

"Whatever you want, in a way, up to a point."

"Why are we here?"

"You want to know about how Precipice Manor does what it does. It's because of this connection, where we're standing. So I brought you."

"Oh. Well, thanks."

"It's no trouble."

There were several indistinct shapes on the far side of the fountain. "Who are they?"

"Let's go see," he said.

I walked around it, slowly, because I wanted to keep watching it. I don't know why I'm so fascinated by water in motion, but I am. I've wasted more time than I care to admit just watching waves crash in from the ocean-sea.

There turned out to be four people—figures, I should say, because I don't know if "people" is a good description for disembodied souls—standing and watching the fountain, another three seated on one of the benches. They looked like Dragaerans to me, but whether they were, or whether my brain was interpreting disembodied souls in the only way it could, I can't say. Judging from the last time I'd come this way, things worked best if I just treated them as if what I was seeing were real. I also caught sight of a few figures wearing purple robes walking past in various directions. I hadn't forgotten about them since I'd seen them last—I couldn't forget them—but I tried not to think about them.

I got close to the ones watching the fountain, and identified an Issola and two Dragonlords. I'd run into a lot of Dragonlords last time I was here, and I hadn't liked any of them. To the left, I'd liked all of the Issolas I'd met, so I thought maybe I'd say hello to this one, who was a broad-shouldered fellow with heavy brows and a tall forehead. As I got close to him, he glanced up at me, then turned his attention back to the fountain. I got the feeling he didn't care to be interrupted, so I stopped and just watched the water some more.

Morrolan has a fountain in his courtyard, and a small one in a room just opposite the stairway up to the tower with the windows. I asked him how it was done once, and he taught me the spell and said now I could make one of my own. I never had, but during those years when I dreamed of a castle I'd thought about it, and even sort of designed it in my head. It would have been tall, with water shooting high, high up, in thin jets in all directions, and back into a granite pool that would swirl rightwise. It would have been a great fountain. I didn't build it, though, because I didn't get the castle, because Cawti sort of went through some changes in what she wanted, and then I got some people mad at me and I've been too busy running for my life to do much of anything else.

The Issola stood up, bowed his head to me, and walked away. Discaru had come up next to me. "What is this thing?"

"Memory," he said.

"Huh. Looks like water."

"Well, it's that too."

"Memory is water? Water is memory? Memory is like water? Water is—"

"You don't have to complicate it so much. This is where souls come to recover their memories."

"Souls forget?"

"Those who became Purple Robes."

"Oh. So, since I haven't lost my memories, it shouldn't have much of an effect on me, right?"

I turned back to the fountain, watching an isolated jet rise, curve, turn into mist. It was pretty, the nice rainbow forming and wavering in, well, wherever the light was coming from. Jets dissolving into mist into rainbows, and so back into the pool, and up into jets.

Have you ever drunk so much that you don't remember what you did? That there are hours where you know you were up, awake, doing something, but you don't have the least clue what it was? I've only had that happen once.

It was a bad time for me. I was still married then, but things had come up with Cawti, and we couldn't even see each other without starting in on all the ugly stuff. One day, in the middle of it, I went out and got a bottle of the worst Fenarian brandy I could find and brought it home. Cawti wasn't there—she usually wasn't in those days, being busy making things better for everyone who didn't care about her, and worse for everyone who did. So I just started drinking.

At some point, Cawti came home, looked at me, started

to say something, then shook her head. She started to walk past me. I said, "You killed me." Forming words was hard.

"You're drunk," she said.

I picked up the bottle and looked at what was left.

"Yeah," I said. "But you still killed me. I mean, before. They gave you money and you killed me."

She nodded. "We'll talk in the morning."

"You know I never killed another human. Never."

"I know. We've talked about it bef—we'll talk in the morning."

"But why? I just want to know why."

"What's the point, Vladimir? You won't remember this tomorrow."

"Yes, I will."

"No, you won't."

"I just want to know why."

"Because if I refused a job because the target was an Easterner, I'd be accepting that there are two classes of people, and I wouldn't accept that."

I stared at her. "Seriously? That was your reasoning?"

"Yes. And don't tell me I was being an idiot, because I know that already."

"You were being an idiot."

She sighed. "Good night, Vladimir."

She went off to the bedroom; I had another drink.

She was right, of course. I remembered nothing about the conversation. Until now.

I'd rented the back room of the Blue Flame for the evening and the night, and laid down fifty Imperials against drinks and breakage, though I didn't expect any breakage; it wasn't that kind of night. But I made sure there was plenty of wine, oishka, and Fenarian brandy, as well as Flamebrew. I, myself, was drinking the latter. That was their own beer, a golden-colored brew made, I was told, by using a lot more malt than was usual. It had a big, dense head, and tasted light and clean and kind of spicy-sweet, and was the only beer I'd ever found that I liked. They served it in big, square wooden cups filled until the head stood out of the top like a wave held still right at the point of collapse, which is something you can do in a painting but is a lot trickier in real life.

I put myself in a corner and for a long time didn't talk to anyone. I wasn't required to: my job had been done when I rented the place and put up the money.

About thirty people showed up, though there weren't more than twenty at any one time. But still, a good turnout. Sticks would have been pleased. Everyone spoke in low tones, because we weren't Dzur; and there were never any formal speeches or service, because we weren't Dragons. We were Jhereg, and sometimes this happened, but there was no reason to pretend to be happy about it.

Most people were in groups of three or four, telling stories about Sticks, or maybe just talking. Then Narvane came up to me and sat down.

"Hey, Boss," he said. "Hey, Kragar."

Okay, I guess I hadn't been alone.

"What's on your mind?" I asked him.

"I don't wanna get sentimental," he said.

I bit back a reply and waited.

"But Sticks, he said he liked working for you. Thought you'd want to know."

"Yeah," I said. "Thanks."

He nodded and wandered off.

"He was a good guy," said Kragar.

I nodded. "Did you know him before he came to work for us?"

"Oh, yeah. Back in the day. He was a lot crazier when he was younger."

"Me too," I said.

"Vlad, you're still younger."

"Okay, so, I won't be so crazy when I'm older."

"I was with him once, we were doing some collecting for Dofer. You ever meet Dofer?"

I shook my head.

"Good guy. Retired a while ago. Not ambitious, but reliable. He sent us to collect from this Dzur."

"They're the worst. I sometimes wonder why I even let them go into debt."

"Yeah. So, this woman, I don't remember her name, but she loved clubs and public houses, you know? She had a few favorites she could be found at. Every other night you'd find her sitting around one of them, drinking, laughing, maybe getting into a fight, maybe not. So, we weren't keen on finding her there, especially in public, because she'd feel like she had to fight, and, well, she's a Dzur right? Who wants that? So one afternoon, Sticks says, 'Come on, let's get this taken care of.' And he leads me off to one of this woman's favorite places, a little cellar on Garshos, and we go in. It's pretty empty, and she isn't there, so I figure we'll leave, right? Wrong. He starts smashing up the place. Bottles, chairs, cups. Just demolishes it. The host is screaming about the Phoenix Guards, so I go over and put a knife at his throat and shake my head. He noticed the knife. Then Sticks says to him, 'There's this woman, a Dzur, and every time she comes in here, I'm gonna do this again. And if you call the Guards, I'm gonna do the same thing to your body. Got it? And that's gonna keep happening until she comes up with what she owes. Tell her that. Whether you let her in, that's up to you.' Then we hit two more places she liked to drink and did the same thing. Then we went home. Dofer got paid that evening."

"Nice," I said. "But taking a chance."

"Yeah, and I didn't like it. But back then, you didn't know what he'd do."

"He settled down though."

"Oh, yeah. A lot. Once, a long time later, we were working for Toronnan, and we needed to see this tailor, a Chreotha. We go into his shop, and I'm all set to slap him around and give him the talk about, you know, being responsible with his debts or whatever, and—"

"You give the talk?"

"Well, I figured Sticks would do that, while I did the slapping."

"Yeah, me too."

"You want me to tell this story or not, Vlad?"

"Okay, go ahead."

"So Sticks goes in, doesn't say a word, just stands in front of the guy, puts his foot up on a chair, and starts tapping one of his sticks on the guy's table. You know, the guy starts in with, 'Who are you?' and, 'What do you want?' and Sticks just keeps tapping on that table. The guy says to get out, and Sticks just keeps tapping. And the guy says he'll call for help, and his voice is all shrill and he's going, 'Who are you? I don't know you. What do you want?' and, you know, Sticks just keeps tapping, and the guy says, 'All right! I'll have his money tomorrow by noon!' And we turn around and leave, and I don't know where he got the money, but he got it."

"That sounds more like the Sticks I knew."

Kragar nodded and lifted his cup. "Gonna miss him."

"Yeah," I said. "Me too."

I pulled my eyes from the fountain. "What the—"

"A memory," he said.

"You saw that?"

"No, but it's how this works. As I told you. This is where the Purple Robes come to have their memories restored after they've served their time."

"Oh," I said. "Any chance of cheerful memories, or am I in the wrong afterlife for that?"

"Sometimes," he said. "Depends on you."

"Heh," I said.

"Loiosh, did you see anything?"

"Just echoes of what you saw, Boss."

"Okay."

"You can also see past lives here," he added. "At least sometimes. I've done it."

"Just in general, or specific ones, like, you want to know about your second, or your third, or whatever?"

"If you just look at it, you'll get some random memory, but you can sometimes direct it, if you can, well, it's hard to explain. You don't ask a question—there's no consciousness there to ask. But if you focus on something, you can sort of control it."

"Could you be a little more vague?"

He chuckled. "Once I tried thinking about a sword, and had a memory of my life as a Dragonlord."

"How was it?"

"The me of now didn't care for it, but the me of then seemed content enough. I also wondered if I'd once been a Hawk, so I concentrated on the symbol of the House, and recovered some memories. I tried Phoenix, but, alas, it seems I was never of that House."

"Okay, I get it."

"Should we go back, or do you want to see what happens?"

"Are we in a hurry?"

"I'm not."

"Let me try something, then."

"Take as much time as you want," he said.

Rocza shifted on my shoulder. Loiosh shifted on the other, then they both settled in. I stared at the fountain some more, letting my mind wander, just watching the jets. If it were an oracle, I'd ask it what was going on with that bloody house, or rather, "platform"; but there was no way to form my need for a clue into anything useful. Could I isolate some of what I didn't understand? Well, one piece was, just why was the connection between Precipice Manor and the Halls of Judgment so important? The trouble was, even if I learned the answer, I probably didn't know enough necromancy to make sense of it.

Magic is confusing.

I glared at the fountain and dared it to contradict me.

6

IN THE PAST DARKLY

On a day when the Enclouding was so thin I could not bear to look in the direction of the Furnace, I leaned against an outer wall of the shack that was my home, flexed my hands, picked up my creation, and studied it.

My creation? Where? What?

I always looked for patterns in my completed work, and sometimes found them. I knew they weren't really there, that they were something my imagination imposed on them, overlaid like a blanket of fog lying over the evergreen forest beneath me. But I always looked anyway, I suppose the way an artist will examine a completed work: is this what I meant to capture? Is there more here than I intended? Did I do good work? I watched myself handling the completed carving, and it made no sense, and it was exactly what it should be, and I reflected on art and didn't know why I would have those thoughts.

It was different, of course: an artist, I believe, is aware during the process of creation, whereas I never was. I would sit down with my set of chisels and my three hammers and my stone, and breathe in the harsh, acrid smell of the Enclouding, taking it as deeply as I could, and as I exhaled, I would see people, animals, trails, ridges, streams, hills, valleys; and as I watched and studied, my hands would carve. Or so they must, because afterward they would ache, and the callus at the base of my left thumb would perhaps have grown a little harder, and there would be chips in my eyes, and dust in my throat, and in my hands would be a carving that hadn't existed before.

It didn't happen often: maybe every twenty or thirty years would I feel that I could reach out and see. I'd tried on other occasions and got nothing, no visions, and the marks on the stone were meaningless.

And a year or two from now, when I began to long for the city again, I would come down from the mountain—my mountain—and begin the long journey to Dragaera, where I would bring my creation to House Athyra itself, nestled in the arms of the Palace like a veritable bird in a nest, and they would praise me and praise my work and study the lines and circles and triangles looking for meaning: Why was one line deeper than another? Why was one circle inside of another? Eventually, there would be an auction of the mind, and someone, someone old and near death most likely, would pay for it and I'd stay in the House for a year or maybe two, until my mountain called me back. Then I would buy supplies and hire porters and begin the long journey.

I did not try to understand the meaning; I enjoyed looking at the patterns in the abstract collection of sculptured doodles, and let my imagination take me where it would.

It is joyful and sad to finish a piece of work. On that day, the joy predominated, I suppose because the day was so fine, the air just a little chilly, the way I liked it, and as I studied the tablet

I'd made, though I could discern no patterns, still it felt like a good day's work.

Someday someone would have it, and spend hours, days, maybe years staring at my work, absorbing, finding meaning that I'd placed there, meaning I had not, and some that perhaps I had without knowing it. Though money would change hands, still it felt like a gift, a personal gift, from me to whomever that stranger was. My work would come to mean something to that person, there would be a bond between us, beyond the ties of House and perhaps kinship. As long as either of us lived, and quite possibly beyond, there would be something tying me to another in a way that a mother, a son, a lover, a student, even an artist could never know, and I valued that nearly as much as the work itself.

For that moment, I was content.

And utterly mystified.

I came back to the present, to the fountain.

What?

I looked at my hands, and they were no darker than I remembered them, and my only callus was the one at the base of my forefinger, from holding a kitchen knife. I took a breath, and there was no smell of the Enclouding, and no dust in my throat.

I turned to Discaru. "I think I got someone else's memory."

"No," he said. "That isn't how it works."

"Uh. Maybe just pure illusion?"

He shook his head.

"So that, what I saw, that was real? That was me?"

"Yes. What was it?"

"I don't know."

I turned back to the fountain, wondering what it was I had once carved into stone, and why.

I was searching for something. What was it?

Around me was the Whiterose Chasm with the high hills on either side rising, as far as I could tell, to the Enclouding. It was hard to keep my footing, because there wasn't a spot of ground not covered in stones, and they were all different sizes. And I was moving the small ones, looking under the big ones, for—

For what?

I stopped and took a moment to breathe. It was important that I find it, I knew that; I could feel the importance in my stomach.

"Kelham!"

I turned and looked in the direction the voice had come from. She was about five rods away.

"My lady?"

"Are you all right, Kelham?"

"Yes, my lady. Catching my breath."

"Very well."

I caught a glimpse of my sleeve: black, with the emblem of the Hawk on it. It seemed entirely reasonable that I be wearing the livery of the House of the Hawk, not even worth remarking on, except that, at the same time, it made no sense whatsoever. And, for that matter, who was Kelham, and why was I answering to that name, and why did it seem so normal

that I was answering to that name? And what was I doing here,
and why did it seem like I knew?

And, as I was thinking this, I went back to moving stones
and searching under boulders for—

What was I looking for?

I knew she was my liege, Lady Mundra, and she, too, was
a Hawklord; I just didn't know how I knew that.

There was a small, shallow pond to my left, perhaps eight
rods across, and on the other side was my sister, Ialhar, and she
was also searching for—

What was it?

Meanwhile, the me that knew what I was looking for kept
looking, until—

"My lady!"

The Countess looked up. "You found it?"

"Not the signet," I said. "But look there, just in the shade
of the granite with the lichen growing on it . . . it's moving,
now it's—"

"I see it," she said. "Good eye, Kelham. Rodwik, will you
show yourself, or do I have to cast a reveal?"

He appeared and my hand instinctively went to the sword
over my shoulder and the enchanted dagger at my side. The
Countess held her hand out to me, so I didn't draw. My sister
walked up and stood behind the Countess.

Rodwik bowed elaborately, hand sweeping the ground.
"What an unexpected pleasure to find you here, Mundra."

"My lady," said Ialhar. "May I cast a reveal anyway? He may
have help."

"Do it," she said.

Rodwik started to say something, but before he had the

chance, four of his people appeared, forming a loose ring around him. He smiled and shrugged.

"Good work, Ialhar," said the Countess.

"You know," said Rodwik, "I have more right to the signet than you do."

"Do you?"

"I don't mean legally," he said. "I mean that we're five to three."

"Dragon logic."

"You know, if you just give it to me, I might be able to duplicate it, then we can both have one."

"Yes, of course. Because wizards of our family have failed since the Fourth Cycle, but you'll succeed, because none of them had such perfect teeth."

"Magic works better with an Athyra on the throne. I have the notes—"

"Don't waste my time, Rodwik. Attack if you're going to, or else leave."

"Maybe we should find it first, then fight over it?"

"How about if you just tell me where you hid it?"

"Oh. You know about that." He didn't seem embarrassed. "I can use birds as spies as well as you."

"Ha. I taught you how to do that."

"Yes. Thank you. Now, where did you hide it exactly?"

"I don't think I'll show you, my dear niece."

"In that case, attack, leave, or defend yourself."

"As you please," he said. He drew sword and dagger, his retainers did the same, as did Ialhar and I; there was suddenly a lot of naked steel in the area. The Countess took her baton and let it expand to staff size, orbiting black pearls on one end, the other flashing red from the ruby.

I moved toward the Countess to protect her; as I did I lifted my dagger and pointed a line on the ground in front of Rodwik, and sent Bornia's Tremors along it. His retainers obligingly fell over as they tried to cross it, giving me time to reach her. Ialhar moved around to the other side, and we took what defensive position we could.

"Blocked," said Ialhar.

"What do you mean? Who—"

"I did a block to keep him from bringing anyone in," she said. I caught the sheepish tone in her voice, but no one else would have. I was going to enjoy twitting her about it later. If there was a later.

A five-against-three fight isn't the sort of thing you look for—unless you're a Dzur—but we had the advantage of having done this before, at the Lowferry raid, the fight at Land's End, and twice at the Mundaara River Crossing. We fell into our pattern quickly and easily as far as sorcery was concerned: I kept up a randomly changing net of defensive spells, my sister cast counterspells to open holes in their defense, and the Countess looked for the openings or weaknesses Ialhar made to strike them. We hardly moved—my sister and I only moving our daggers to point to the spots we needed, while Mundra's hands sent her staff through the motions needed by her attacks. I liked our chances with the spells.

The trouble was, there were also those swords. Five of them, against our two and a staff. A staff is good against blades if you know what you're doing, but not if you're using it to cast spells.

A sword was coming at my face and I knocked it aside, and kept my dagger weaving. I loved that dagger; it was deceptively plain, but I'd cast the enchantments on it myself, standing next to Edger the smith as he forged it. Enchantments that go into the blade at the same time it is forged are always smoother, stronger, and easier to reach than those added later, and with this one, the feather touch of command would bring the Tail-spin to life where I wished, its endless, invisible turnings wrapping up any sorcery that tried to get past it, and even pull it in from the edges. It was a beautiful weapon.

The next time the guy swung his sword at me I made a too-big sweep, pulling both of his weapons out of line, and plunged the dagger into his chest as hard as I could.

I had a plan. A quick, hard stab to take him out of combat, and then back to the spell before any of them had time to exploit the hiatus. That was the plan. In fact, I had apparently struck bone, and the knife didn't want to come out. I didn't lose the grip as he fell, but it took a lot of work to hold on. When he was prone, I put my foot on his face and pulled. He didn't like that, but he wasn't in any condition to do anything about it. I raised the knife—

—and something hit me.

I didn't feel it hit, but I was on my back, my ears were ringing, and I could see the fight happening about twenty feet away from me. I didn't hurt, but I knew better than to think that meant I was all right; sometimes when the body is damaged, the mind folds a blanket over the pain.

I watched Rodwik fall to his knees, rise, fall again, while one of his retainers cried as her lower leg dissolved in fire and smoke, then I must have blacked out, because the next thing I remember seeing was Ialhar's face, very close to mine. She was looking me over, and she had that tight-lipped narrow-eyed expression she wore when she didn't want me to know how scared she was. I tried to ask about the Countess, but my mouth wouldn't work.

"Don't try to speak," said Ialhar.

I tested my limbs to see what moved, which was pretty much nothing. "Stay still," she said, and moved her hands over me. She didn't look any less worried. My left arm was one of the few things that worked, and there was something in it. I turned it over and opened the hand.

"You found it!" she said.

I had no memory of finding it; maybe I'd landed on it, or right next to it? I didn't know.

She took it from my hand and held it up. Behind her was the Countess, bleeding from her forehead, and with her right arm hanging limp, but steady on her feet. The Countess said, "Can you . . . ?"

Her voice trailed off, and Ialhar shook her head, and put the signet on my finger, and I heard music.

That was—

What in the . . . ?

Who am I? A Hawk? No, I was . . .

My back hurt, my legs ached, and moving seemed like a lot more work than it was worth. I wondered if this was it. I mean, right now, this very instant. The little jolt of fear forced my eyes open.

Not yet. Not quite yet.

I was in my bed, in my room, surrounded by my things,

and that's how I liked it. My right hand above the blanket was spotted and withered and all of the veins stood out, but the nails were perfect, because Jaf had seen to that, knowing how much I cared. Dear Jaf. He would miss me more than most of my relations.

On the wall in front of me was my lineage block, Lyorn on top, then the symbol for the Sixth Cycle Princess Loini who had made us official, then only three more symbols. We were still new in that sense, but I'd done my part; my own Tokni had given me three children before preceding me to Death-gate. I thought of her and smiled as Jaf came into the room.

"I've found it, my lord," he said. "A copy of a copy of a copy, I'm afraid."

I gestured with a finger, but he understood and placed it in my hand: a disk just a little larger than an imperial, made of smooth ceramic, very cold to the touch. I squeezed it tightly and looked a question at him.

"Yes, my lord. Toknasa has vowed to bring you to the Falls."

I felt myself smile.

My thumb caressed the disk, and visions floated before my eyes: droplets of water, a terribly, terribly bright light in the sky, a tangle of long vines, a life-size statue holding a pair of curved swords as if caught in the middle of a dance. Then they faded. I felt Jaf's hand squeezing mine, and it was strangely comfort-ing, and I had the sensation of falling backward away from my body at great speed, then all the world became silence.

Hossi found me in a copse of trees, just within the pickets. The latrines were behind me, but the wind was blowing the other way, so it was fine.

"What are you up to, Birn," he said. "Reading?"

"No," I told him. "I'm just holding this book to discourage conversation."

He sat down next to me. "How's that working for you?"

"Great," I said. "Perfect."

"If you're serious about wanting to be alone—"

"No, it's all right."

I closed the book. He leaned over and read the spine, then made a "tsh" sound. "Don't you know it's bad luck to read that before a battle."

"Oh?" I said. "Is there going to be a battle, do you think?"

He laughed more than it was worth. "Oh, I know there's going to be a battle. I just can't remember which side we're supposed to be on."

"Who cares? It's a Dzur reign; it isn't going to make much difference anyway."

"Yeah, maybe we should just nap. Think the captain would mind?"

"Think the captain would notice?"

I stowed the book in my pack. When I'd closed it, he was looking a lot more serious. "This is a stupid battle to get killed in, isn't it?"

"Yes and no," I said. "I mean, sure, a pointless border skirmish that won't settle anything. But, battle is battle, right? And if we're dead after the battle, we won't much care."

He gave me a wry smile. "All the e'Drien women are fatalists," he said.

I elbowed his shoulder. "And all the e'Lanya men are philosophers. Let's go and get killed."

The drum sounded, right on cue.

We got up, went back to camp, pulled on our gear, and lined up.

The drum started again and we moved out. "Duck fast," he told me.

"Duck fast," I said back.

An hour later I was standing over him while he desperately tried to stop the bleeding from a long gash in his upper arm that went down to bone. I planned to help him if people would leave me alone long enough, but things were busy: it was one of those chaotic, close-pressed battles where skill with a blade meant nothing compared to who was pressing hardest. I'd always hated those. You can get a minor wound and end up trampled to death by your own side.

I was also bleeding myself, you understand, but only a few scratches.

Battles are loud. Also, they stink. But an occasional wind can relieve the stink for a bit, and sometimes, like loud conversations in crowded inns, there comes a relative lull. I faced off against a guy with two shortswords and a big nose, and I heard Hossi say, "See you next life, maybe, Birn."

I didn't look down, but I said, "I think you might live through this," and then something hit me hard in the head and I had the sudden thought, *Bad luck or not, I'm glad I read the Guide before this started.*

And then there was nothing.

"Are you all right?" said Discaru.

I realized that he'd already asked me that a couple of times.

"I think so," I said. "There's a lot of dying going on."

"Oh. Yeah. Death memories are traumatic. Try not to relive too many of them at once."

"Thanks," I said.

I guess, whatever I'd been focused on, it was about death. Just what I want to be thinking about, right? I mean, contemplating death is perfectly fine when you're safe, but when you're in danger it'll just get you killed.

And there I was thinking about it again; I made sure I wasn't looking at the fountain. Instead I was looking at—

—The Halls of Judgment. What was I doing there? Well, I was trying to solve a mystery, and, somehow or other, the Halls of Judgment were tied into it. The question was, how?

I turned back to the fountain again and watched the dance of the water.

I left early when I got the message from the Priestess, but it was Homeday, so there wasn't a lot of reason to stay. I ran my operations out of a back room of the Sleeping Cat, which I owned through a couple of layers of friends. The Cat was in a part of Dragaera City that didn't have a lot of action on Homeday, being just far enough from the Palace to be full of the dwellings of civil servants as well as markets and entertainments for them.

I took Dosci and Ven, and our first stop was to the temple of Verra on Prince Lagginer Street. I left them outside, because no one will pull anything at a temple. I made an offering and a prayer so as not to stand out, then walked around behind and clapped outside of the door to the rectory. After a moment, the Priestess appeared. She was an Athyra, and I never knew her name; I just called her Priestess. It being an early Iorich reign, she called me "my lord." She bowed and invited me in, had me sit, offered wine, which I declined.

"I have it, my lord," she said, before I could ask.

"That's good, that's good. Was it hard to get?"

Her brows went up. "Do you actually care?"

I shrugged. "I'm a caring kinda guy. And I had an Issola nanny."

"No, it wasn't hard, it just took time." She reached down next to her chair and picked up a small package, wrapped in paper the color of diluted red wine. She handed it to me. "And your end?"

I nodded. "Looking into the future, I gotta feeling you won't need to find a new location for many, many years."

"And?"

"Yes, that's all. I don't need nothin' else, so I won't be back. Unless I feel a sudden urge to pray."

Everyone I know would have made some sort of remark, like, "I could recommend some places," or even, "don't hurry." But she was an Athyra; she just nodded.

Dosci and Ven were where I'd left them, and they fell into step with me. My next stop was Black Swans Park, a tiny little place with a pond and worn stone benches and very few trees. It was a good place to relax because there was no way for anyone to sneak up on you. I sat down and opened the package.

A very simple pendant, a jhereg in black on a silver chain, about half the size of my palm. I put it over my head, slid it into my jerkin, against the skin of my chest. It felt a little cold, but there was no sensation other than that. Nor would there be. While I lived.

"I don't suppose," I said to the inker, "you can tell me what it means?"

He looked embarrassed. "Sorry, m'lady. That would take a diviner. And even then—"

"It's all right," I said, suddenly in a good mood in spite of pinpricks; I wasn't used to being "my lady" to anyone. I resolved to spend more time around tradesmen.

To distract myself from the constant stinging, I looked around the shop. There was little enough to see: curtains, a table, a shelf for his inks, samples of his work (mostly sketches, with a couple of cheap psiprints), and his House emblem, a chreotha, over the door. I tried to get involved in the art, but it just wouldn't hold my interest.

"So," I said, "you know what it is?"

"It is your guide through the Paths, my lady. And permit me to hope it will be countless centuries before you need it."

"Thank you," I said, but that killed the conversation, so my attention was on the pinpricks again.

I tried again. "Does your family have one?"

"A length of string, my lady," he said. "It has different sorts of knots tied in it at different intervals, which correspond to the choices we will face."

"Accurate?"

"It was divined for my generation, so I am hopeful."

"Well, for your sake, I hope it is, and that, as you said, you don't need it for a long time."

"Thank you, my lady. And yours?" He seemed hesitant, but I'd encouraged the intimacy, hadn't I?

"Old, I'm afraid. The family have tried to get a more re-cent one, but no luck so far."

"I trust it will serve," he said.

The ink he was using was a light blue that would match my House colors, and already I could see the intertwining lines with points marked here and there. Someday, those lines, cov-ering my left arm from wrist to elbow, would be all I'd have to guide me. Not soon, I hoped, but someday. And, as my father had said, better to get it down when young than spend one's life worrying about it.

The pinpricks continued and the design grew.

I came to consciousness with no shirt and an itch in my back.

"My back itches," I announced to anyone who might be nearby.

Shandy was, it seemed, nearby. "Dolivar's back itches," he said. "It probably doesn't have anything to do with pass-ing out half-naked on shortgrass. I would look for a mystical explanation."

I gave a few mystical explanations for his life and sat up. We were back in camp. A quick look around showed fires going, the sun just rising over the eastern hills glimpsed through occasional breaks in the trees, and Herthae chipping away at spearheads. Above me, Morning Snake would soon slither off until nightfall, but watched over us for now, if you believe in that sort of thing. Bigmoon was high up, but already becom-ing pale as the light grew; Littlemoon wouldn't rise for another nine days. I smelled breakfast. I believed in breakfast.

"What happened?" I said.

Tivisa said, "You don't remember?"

I shook my head, and it hurt, so I made some deductions. "I got hit in the head during the raid."

She nodded. "You need someone to just follow you around and yell, 'Duck!' from time to time."

"I'll get right to work on that. What hit me?"

"Flat of an ax. You did sort of duck."

"Ax. Where are they getting those?"

"You don't remember that either?" said Shandy. "They have a forge. We saw it during the raid and you said to destroy it and then you were down."

"Did we destroy it?"

"No. Sethra was there. We ran."

"Who dragged me back?"

She gestured toward Rothra. "Her and Shandy."

"Anyone hurt?"

"You."

"Anyone else?"

"Some of them."

"Other than failing to destroy their forge—damn, I don't remember it at all—did we get anything?"

"Breakfast."

"Huh. Well, I guess if we didn't lose anyone—"

"Chief!" came from behind me, shouted. It was Chiqwe, presumably on watch to the south.

I turned my head. "My name is Dolivar," I called back. Then, "What is it?"

"Someone's coming," he called.

"Okay," I yelled. "Make sure you don't shout or anything to let him know we've spotted him." Then I tried to stand up but got dizzy. I sat down again and pointed to Shandy and Rothra. "You two. Find out what's up."

They each picked up a spear from the pile, then Shandy grabbed a second one because he was Shandy. They needn't have bothered; before they could move, Chiqwe called, "Coming through," which meant that whoever it was, was no threat.

What the—?

I tried to stand up again, failed again, sat and stared.

She came walking up to me as if she knew just who I was, and with me sitting we were eye-level. A child, not more than ten years old. "Uh, hello," I said. "You are—"

"Devera. And you need to come with me now."

Okay, then. Here was something new. I had no idea what to say.

"Uh, who are you, and why?"

"I told you, and because."

"Um. Do you have a better reason?"

She just looked at me. I looked at her, and, for the first time, paid attention to what she was wearing. It was a single garment, covering her from shoulder to ground, of a rich blue I'd never seen before, and with gold on it, and, well, I had no idea who could make something like that, or how, or how many hundreds of hours it would have taken, and who has hundreds of hours to put into one garment that, well, how does it even survive ten minutes of walking around?

"Where did you get that?"

"I'll show you," she said. Then, "Please?"

I guess it was the please that did it. Well, that, and I've never been able to resist the uncanny.

"Sure," I said. "Lead on." I started trying to stand up again.

Shandy said, "Chief, you—"

"My name is Dolivar," I said. "If I don't come back, it's all on you."

I wobbled a little, then said, "All right, Devera. Walk slow."

"What happened?"

"I got hit in the head."

"Are you all right?" she seemed genuinely concerned.

"Mostly. I'm seeing imaginary children wearing impossible clothes who are convincing me to follow them I know not where, but other than that, yeah, I'm okay."

She giggled and ran off for a ways, then stopped and waited for me as I shuffled along. Everyone in camp was looking at me. I caught up with the little girl and didn't ask myself what I was doing. But, if this was a trap by the Dragon, it was a lot more clever than any of the other traps they'd set for us.

I imagined a bunch of them, probably including my sister, waiting just beyond the clearing, but I kept walking anyway. I shouldn't have worried; we didn't make it as far as the clearing.

I stopped and said, "What just happened?"

I was no longer in the clearing. I was no longer in the forest. I was in, well, I don't know what to call it. There was no sky, there were no trees, no grass. It was a like a hut built out of something impossible and big enough for a thousand million families. Okay, I'm exaggerating, but huge, all right? And all of it white.

I reminded myself that I *had* been hit in the head.

Also, Devera was gone, and I was alone. Yeah, the "hit in the head" thing—

"Hello, Dolivar."

The voice echoed weirdly, like I was in a narrow, close canyon. I turned and she was behind me, about ten feet away, unarmed, very tall, and then everything blurred and I was outdoors again, though nowhere I recognized.

"My apologies, Dolivar; I imagine the setting must have been disorienting for you. Here, let me fix your head." She reached toward me—there was something odd about her hands—and the pain in my head and the dizziness went away. I hadn't even been aware of the pain until it stopped. And I still didn't trust what I was seeing.

"I am Verra," she said.

I almost said, "Who are you?" but shut my mouth instead. People kept telling me their names as if that were useful information.

There was silence for a moment, than a titterbird whistled and I almost started laughing uncontrollably; it made more sense than anything else in the last few minutes.

"You are at a critical moment," she said.

"You mean, in my brain fever?"

"Be quiet and listen. It is perfectly fine with me if you think you're mad. It is fine if you think this is a dream. None of that matters. What matters is that you listen, and that you do what I say. It won't make sense to you, and that doesn't matter either. Listen."

Under the circumstances, I thought it best to listen. It wouldn't have mattered, I think, if I hadn't wanted to, because she walked right up to me—she really was tall—touched my forehead with one of her weird fingers, and said, "There is a line that began centuries ago, with the creation of the Great Sea that released me and my sisters. It extends into the future, I don't know how far."

Even up close, her voice had a weird, echoing sound, like she was saying everything two or three times, so close together I could just barely hear the separation. The thought formed in my head, *Why are you telling me?* but I didn't dare speak. Nor did I have to; she either pulled the thought right out of my head or guessed what I was thinking, and I'm ready to believe either one. "I've chosen you," she said, "because from the outside, you will know what is happening on the inside, and so on the inside you will work. Another will work from without, and you've just met her." I had no idea what she was talking about. "I know you don't understand," she said. "Just keep listening." As if I had a choice.

"Have you ever wondered why you exist?" she asked me. No. "I don't mean you, I mean your entire species. You are pieces in a game, Dolivar, all of you, you exist to answer a simple question: can a society of sapient beings be made to achieve a certain level of culture and then stop? You've been set up for this. Created, manipulated to do this." I had no idea what she was talking about, but she didn't seem to care. She kept going. "My sisters and I, with some others, broke them, but we haven't broken what they did. Yet. But I swear by those who perished, we will. And you're going to help, little boy." Okay, that was uncalled-for. "You will go back, and you will make peace with your brother and your sister." I would do that—"When you get back. Instantly. You'll do whatever it takes. Just as a bonus, you'll survive that way. And then later, much, much later, I can't even guess how long, you'll be there for the other end. It begins with the creation of Amorphia, and so it will end, and you will have a part to play."

Aside from anything else, I never believed in seeing the future. "I am not seeing the future, little boy, I intend to create it." *Good for you*, I was thinking. *What do I get out of it?* "Here, she said, and placed something around my neck. I looked at it; it was a piece of lapis lazuli, like out of the Broken Canyon, with a hole punched in it, and something had been carved on it. I couldn't make sense of the carving; it seemed to be an animal with wings, maybe a jhereg, but it was made up of a series of curving and twisting lines that were broken in places, and—"You'll have time to study it later. Never mind. Keep it with you, pass it on to your offspring. Someday one will find it useful. Now, go."

There was a blurring and a sharpening, a going and a coming, a silence and a sound, and I was back in the clearing. I was next to Tivisa, who jumped about four feet and said, "Where did you—"

"Don't ask," I said. Several of them gathered around me, staring. "Okay, yeah," I told them. "I'm going to go visit the Dragon tribe."

"Visit?" said Shandy, giving me a dark look.

"Yeah."

"About what?"

"I don't know. Maybe they'll have something that will make my back stop itching."

It took me a while to remember where I was. Discaru was still next to me, the personification of patience.

"Well," I said. "That was interesting."

"Are you all right?"

"I'm fine, thanks for your concern. But, yeah. That was interesting."

"Oh?"

"*Boss?*"

"*How much did you catch?*"

"*Just bits and pieces.*"

I shook my head and turned my eyes away from the fountain with the feeling that enough was enough.

"What did you learn?" he asked me.

"Give me a minute."

"All right."

"In fact, give me a few."

"All right."

"I don't know. There was a lot there, and some of it made sense, and some of it connected, and I might be able to figure it out when my head stops spinning."

He nodded. "I'm not surprised. I've looked at the water myself; I know how confusing it can get."

"Yeah. I want to sit somewhere quiet and sort it all out."

"Give it time, don't concentrate on it, and it'll sort itself out."

"All right."

"Although," he added, "I'm in no hurry."

"No, I'm going to follow your advice. In any case, I don't want to stay by the fountain." I looked around. "Somehow this isn't the best place for contemplation."

"No? That's most of what happens here."

"Maybe it's different for dead people."

He nodded. "Good point."

In spite of my words, I stood there in the Halls of Judgment and tried to wrap my head around things. Eventually, because the silence was bothering me, I said, "It's a lot to take in, to make sense of."

"Can I help?"

"I'm not sure."

"What—"

"I'm trying to work out the connections between the things I saw, how they all connect to understanding that building, that *platform* we were just in, what it all means for finding my way out once I return, and, on top of it, trying *not* to think about all those lives I had, and if they were real, and all me, and who I was, and if it had anything to do with who I am. Did that happen to you?"

"Not really," he said.

"Oh. Well, that was a conversation killer."

He gave a head shrug. "Sorry. Tell me about this ghost you saw."

"What do you want to know?"

"How did you know it was a ghost?"

"She said she'd died."

"I guess that's a good hint," he said, chuckling. "Did she say how, or where, or when?"

"She didn't seem to remember."

He turned his palms up. "All right. What *did* she say?"

"If we're back to this," I said, "then it's time for you to answer one."

"What do you want to know?"

"I don't suppose you can point me in the right direction?"

"I don't understand."

"A clue, a hint, a way to investigate that platform, to figure it out, so I know how to move around, and how to leave. Just, point me in the right direction."

He smiled a little. "Why would I do that?"

"Well, you've been helpful so far. I mean, you brought me here."

"Yes, I did."

"And you've been answering questions."

"Yes, I have."

"So, I got the crazy idea you were willing to help me solve this."

"I admit, a reasonable conclusion."

"But not true?"

"No," he said. "Not true."

I studied him, but he wasn't wearing any special expression on his face. "Well. Have I walked into a trap?"

He considered. "I suppose, in a way."

"That was stupid of me, then."

He shrugged. I tapped the hilt of Lady Teldra, and he pretended that he didn't notice and it didn't bother him.

"Maybe," I said, "we should just go back."

"I'm fine here," he said.

I looked back at the way we'd entered. The rocks were no longer to be seen. "I take it that the way back is now closed?"

"I'm afraid so."

"Maybe you should open it again."

"I'm sorry," he said. "That is quite impossible." And he began to transform.

7

THE TURN OF DISCARU

I'd never seen someone turn into something else before, and in other circumstances I'd have enjoyed watching. No, I wouldn't. Well, the point is, I'd have been a lot more fascinated if I hadn't been too busy being scared out of my senses. The face sort of shifted and blurred, and he grew a snout. His shoulders got bigger, he got taller, his arms and legs got thicker, and his skin became sort of a blotchy pink with streaks of blue. His clothes looked like they melted into his skin.

The whole thing took about two seconds and was pretty disturbing.

There was that single *thump* of my heart, then I settled in, relaxed, ready, evaluating distance, trying to guess body language in a body unlike anything I'd seen before. I found that I'd taken a step backward, but I stopped there. It wasn't that I was opposed to running from danger, but the thing looked like it could probably move really fast, which meant presenting my back wasn't my first choice. But he wasn't immediately attacking me, so I risked a quick look around. No one else in the area was reacting—they were walking, or sitting, or staring at the fountain just as before—which meant either there was illusion at work, or this wasn't an unusual occurrence here. I wasn't all that familiar with day-to-day life in the Halls of Judgment, so I tried to avoid coming to any conclusions, but it sure didn't *seem* like an illusion.

"Boss? Sniff."

I did, and, yeah, there was an acridity in the air. Well, if it was an illusion, it was a bloody good one.

"So," I said. "Uh, what's new?"

He emitted a hissing sound and his head went up and down. Until I could come up with a better idea, I'd assume that was a laugh.

I tried again. "Do you plan to keep me here?"

This time he made an inarticulate rumble full of *k*'s and guttural *r*'s. I was pretty sure there were words in there, and almost certainly a sentence. I shrugged.

My right hand wasn't exactly hovering near Lady Teldra's hilt, but the hand knew where the hilt was, if you know what I mean. We stood there. Maybe I could ask him yes-or-no questions, and he'd shake his head or something?

"Am I stuck here?"

He made the hissing laugh again and took a step toward me. I took another step back. *No. No more, Vlad. That's as far back as we go.* I took Lady Teldra's hilt in my hand, and he said something else I couldn't understand, but if I could judge from the tone, I would say I was being taunted.

I love the feeling that comes when my brain is, like, sprinting, working fast, analyzing in a fraction of a second things that normally would take a long time to sit and figure out.

It's a wonderful feeling. Now, if only I could figure out a way
to get it when I wasn't about to die some sort of unknown but
horrible death.

Laughing? Yeah, I'm pretty sure he—it—laughed when I
threatened to draw Lady Teldra.

So, was something horrible going to happen if I drew her?
Or was it some sort of bluff? It'd be stupid to die because I fell
for a simple trick. It'd be stupid to die doing something I'd received a good hint would be disastrous. It'd be stupid to die.

Well, I had all sorts of other weapons, right?

It took another step toward me and I looked at it. It was
looming over me, and if it struck out with its arms I'd have to
lean back in a hurry. I considered my weapons. I don't know,
maybe a stiletto perfectly placed in some vital spot might have
done it, but I didn't know what its vital spots were, except for
maybe the eyes. The thing was, like, nine feet high. I didn't
like my chances of hitting its eye. Besides, they were yellow. I
hate yellow. Which way? The gold or the dragon? The knife
or the poison? The rocks or the water? I had to decide, and had
no time and not enough information. If I'd had just a little more
time I'd have spun a coin.

Well, bugger it, then. It was really to act or to refrain,
and when looked at that way, there was never any choice. I
gripped her hilt and pulled.

And pulled.

And pulled.

Nothing.

She was Verra-be-damned stuck in her Verra-be-damned
sheath and I really was on the edge of pure panic. In case we
never met before, I'm Vlad Taltos and I don't panic easy, okay?

What could do that? What could have power over a Great

Weapon? Okay, later. Think later. Fight down the panic and
come up with another idea, really, really fast. Yeah. Next idea:
run like all the demons of the Halls were—

Wait a minute.

The thing had stopped, and its head tilted like a dog's.

It had expected me to draw, and, now that I hadn't, it didn't
know what to do.

A part of it fell into place: Lady Teldra had held herself in
her sheath, which must mean she knew something I didn't,
something that made it a bad idea for me to draw.

Thanks, Lady, but please don't ever scare me like that again.

But what was it? Later, later. One thing at a time.

"Sorry," I told the big ugly guy. "I didn't believe you, but I
guess she did. Hard luck."

Its eyes narrowed, which I was guessing meant the same
thing as when a human does it. It said something unfriendly,
uncomplimentary, or both. I'm good at picking this stuff up.

"I get that you're not happy right now. I'm not all that
pleased either, to be honest. And my voice is shaking a little
because you've got me all pumped up and ready to fight, and I
hate it when my voice shakes and I don't think I'm going to
forgive you for that. But if you intended to rip me open, I think
you'd have done it already. So the rules forbid it, or it would
interfere with some plan, or you can't. How about if you just
turn back into something I can understand? Maybe we can
negotiate. How does that sound?"

It spoke again, and I was pretty sure it was not only declin-
ing my offer, but wishing something bad would happen to me.

"Well, this is boring. If you aren't going to attack me, and
you aren't going to help me, and you won't even tell me what's
going on, I guess I'll just wander off."

My threat didn't appear to terrify it.

"Well, can you at least tell me why I couldn't draw my weapon? I'll bet you know. I mean, if you realize she's sentient, and maybe sort of partly aware, a little. I think. Anyway—"

"Your weapon," said someone, "is called Godslayer. You are in the Halls of Judgment. Where the gods live. I'll bet if you think about it real hard you can come up with a theory."

I looked around, and right next to me was a dog, medium sized, golden, looking a lot like an exceptionally furry Lyorn that had had its horn removed. I was about to ask it something stupid when someone cleared his throat. I turned further, and there was a guy there.

"Oh," I said. "I thought the dog—"

"Right," he said.

"You're human," I said. "I mean, an Easterner."

"Right again," he said.

"And you're alive," I said.

"How could you tell?"

I let that pass.

He was about my height, and had a mustache like mine, only longer and droopier, and his hair was like mine except longer and curlier. He was wearing tights of dark blue tucked into riding boots, a white blouse with big puffy sleeves I could never have pulled off, blue leather doublet with peplum and raised shoulders, black cloak pinned with a Phoenix emblem, and black leather gauntlets. If he'd had a feathered beret, he'd have looked like a courtier, except for the being human part. He had a sword hanging from a wide belt with a silver buckle, and was holding a cat.

I turned back to keep an eye on the big ugly thing, which was now rocking a little from side to side, looking at him.

The guy with the cat muttered under his breath, and the thing howled and jumped, then turned and ran. It ran off toward the fountain, splashed through it, and continued on.

"That was witchcraft," I said.

He bowed. I let the dog sniff my hand, after which it curled up at the guy's feet.

"I'm Laszló," he said.

"Vlad."

"Actually, you're Taltos, Count of Szurke."

"You're well informed. And it's Teldra."

"What?"

"Not Godslayer. Lady Teldra."

"All right."

"Who are your friends?"

"Awtlá, and Sireng," he said, indicating the dog and the cat.

"Laszló," I repeated. "Wait, I've heard of you. You're—" I stopped, because I didn't think "the Easterner who's buffing skin with the Empress" would be politic. "Around the court," I managed.

He bowed again. "Official unofficial Imperial warlock," he said.

"Okay, then, here's the big one. What are you doing in the Halls of Judgment?"

"Rescuing you," he said.

"Oh, good then. That answers everything."

He chuckled. "Do you think it's our human blood that makes us answer everything ironically?"

"Fenarian," I said. "Ever tried to exchange banter with a Muskovan?"

He nodded. "Good point."

"How many generations?"

"How—oh. I see. I was born there."

"Really? You've managed the Northwestern speech pretty good."

"I've been here a long time. I'm older than I look."

I looked around again. There was no sign of Discaru, or the-thing-that-was-Discaru.

"What was that thing, anyway?"

"A demon," he said.

I rolled my eyes. "I know it was a demon. What *kind* of demon?"

"Oh. No idea. Does it matter?"

"Well, it's part of figuring out what it was doing there, what it was doing here, what I was doing there, what I am doing here, and all like that. I don't suppose you know anything that might help?"

"What is 'there?'"

"A place west of Adrilankha called Precipice Manor."

"Sorry, no."

"All right."

I walked over to a bench and sat down, facing away from the water. Laszló came along, sat down next to me. The dog came too, put his paws over the edge and drank noisily, then curled up on the ground at our feet.

"So," I said. "Rescue."

"Yeah."

"Fill me in a bit?"

"You have friends who keep track of you."

"Do I have to guess which friends?"

"No."

I waited, then, "Are you going to tell me?"

"No."

I glanced at the Phoenix emblem. "Her Majesty. Of course."

He smiled. "I never said so."

"I wouldn't have called her a friend."

"No," he said. "That would be impertinent."

"Yeah," I said. "And I'm all about being pertinent."

"I don't think that's what that means."

"If it were the Empress," I said, "how would she have known I needed rescuing?"

"There are certain things the Orb is sensitive to. A Great Weapon passing through a necromantic gate to the Halls of Judgment is one of them. Hypothetically."

"I see."

Loiosh, having considered the matter long and thoughtfully, made up his mind and hissed at the cat. The cat looked up, yawned, then closed its eyes again.

"What was that?"

" 'Hello.' "

"Okay," I said aloud. "Uh, no one should be able to keep track of me."

"Because?"

"This," I said, tapping the amulet.

He leaned over and studied it. "Oh, yes, I see. Black *and* gold. Well, maybe it doesn't work in the Halls of Judgment? I'm not an expert."

"On Phoenix Stone, or the Halls?"

"Either, really."

"But you know something about Great Weapons."

He nodded and didn't elaborate.

"So, what now?"

"Hmmm?"

"Well, I'm sort of in the Paths of the Dead, in the Halls of Judgment no less. Last time I was here—"

"Last time?"

"Long story. Last time, I was told not to come back. So, if this is a rescue, how do you plan to get me out of here?"

"Oh, right. That."

"That."

"I'm not sure."

"Well, how do you get out?"

"Connections. I have a standing invitation, and that includes the right to leave."

"Can you bring a guest?"

"Sorry."

I stretched out my legs. "Well, isn't this a joy."

"If I might make a suggestion?"

"Sure."

"The demon should be able to return you."

"The demon you chased away? That one?"

"Yes, that one."

"Perfect."

He reached down and petted the dog between the ears. It wagged its tail. The cat jumped down from his lap. Lazsló put a hand under the dog's chin, looked into its eyes, and muttered something too quiet for me to hear, though from the rhythm I guessed it to be Fenarian. The dog stood up, sniffed the ground, and padded off. The cat ran off after it.

"Good nose on that dog?"

He nodded.

"What will he do when he finds it?"

"I guess we'll see."

He sounded like me. I considered hating him.

He reached into his cloak and came out with a small cloth bag. He opened it and extended it. "Sweetmeat?"

I took one and ate it. "Not bad."

"Apricot."

I nodded.

"So now you don't hate him?"

"It isn't like I'd already made a final decision or anything."

"If you give me some of the next one, I won't hate the cat."

"I'll take it under advisement."

"So, Awtlá, and, what was the cat's name?"

"Sireng."

"Yeah. They're familiars?"

He nodded.

"Two familiars," I said.

He nodded again.

"Didn't know that was possible."

"Boss—"

"Don't worry about it, Loiosh."

"Easy for you to say."

Rocza flapped her wings on my other shoulder.

Laszló didn't reply except by some sort of motion that could have meant anything.

Purple Robes and other "souls," I'd guess you'd say, wandered by. I kept wanting to look at the fountain, but then I remembered, and didn't. We waited, and I came up with more questions he wouldn't answer, like "Is it true about you and Her Majesty," so I didn't bother asking them.

"There," he said suddenly.

I looked up, and Discaru, or the demon, or whatever, came

hissing and growling toward us. At his heels were a wolf and a dzur. There was no sign of the dog, no sign of the cat, but there was a wolf and there was a dzur.

I turned and stared at the warlock. "Are those—"

"Not now," he said.

They herded the thing, nipping and scratching at it until it had reached us, then circled it, making sure it couldn't move. The wolf growled, the dzur hissed, the demon bellowed, Loiosh and Rocza flapped their wings. The warlock stood up and brushed off his cloak, which was the first time I realized that it was silk, and very expensive. He took his time positioning himself in front of the demon. I got up and stood next to him because if there was going to be a party I didn't want to be left out.

The warlock spoke to the demon, and I have no clue what language it was, but there were a lot of whistles and clicks and rising and falling inflections like singing, and sounds I wasn't aware the human mouth was capable of.

The demon answered, not sounding happy. They had brief conversation, and the demon turned like it wanted to run, but the wolf and dzur growled and hissed and snapped. Then Laszló raised his hand, palm out, then turned it palm up and slowly formed a fist, muttering under his breath. The demon howled, convulsed, twisted, shrank, and blurred, and then—

"Ah, Discaru," I said. "How have you been?"

He glared at the warlock. "May you never—"

"Really?" said Laszló, his voice shooting out like a thrown knife. "You're going to curse me? *You* are going to curse *me*?"

Discaru shut up.

"You're better than me," I told the warlock.

"Hmmm?"

"You're a better witch than I am."

"I've been at it a while."

"I still resent it."

"I've heard you once managed to teleport an object. I mean, with witchcraft."

"Yeah. What—"

"I've never done that."

"Okay, that helps."

"Maybe we could trade recipes sometime?"

"Sure."

I turned to the Athyra, or the demon, as you please. "So, I have some questions for you."

He suggested I do something that demons might be able to manage, though I'd prefer not to watch.

"Can't," I said. "Let's start with the one that's really bugging me: are those clothes part of the illusion, or do you create actual clothes when you transform?"

He made another suggestion, one I don't think even a demon could have managed.

"So, what's this about? Why did you really bring me here?"

His response was short, but colorful.

"I get part of it," I said. "You had to bring me here so I couldn't use my weapon against you, and so I'd draw it and get all the gods pissed off at me. But why kill me? What are you afraid I'll find out?"

His fourth suggestion disappointed me. "You're getting less interesting now," I told him. "How about just answering my question?"

He stood mute, which I guess was an improvement.

"Yeah, well." I turned to Laszló. "Can you convince him to talk?"

"How?"

"He must feel pain."

"I won't do that," he said. "I have sort of a personal history with that kind of thing and I've sworn off it."

"I guess I get that," I said, shuddering involuntarily. I hoped neither of them noticed.

I could try it myself. But no.

So many questions he could have answered.

"Boss, if he can get us out of here, he could bring us somewhere that isn't in that weird building, right?"

"Maybe."

"You could ask."

"I could."

"But you're not going to, are you?"

"All right, Discaru—is that your real name? Never mind. All right, if you won't talk, you won't. What say you bring me back and we'll pretend none of this ever happened. How does that sound?"

He smirked.

I turned to the warlock. "You sure you don't torture?"

"I'm sure."

"Too bad."

"But if he doesn't take you back, I'm happy to chain him to the fountain for ten thousand years or so. He wouldn't like that."

Discaru stiffened, then said, "I don't like threats."

I looked at the wolf, at the dzur, at Laszló, then back to him. "And?"

He gave me a murderous look, then nodded. "All right. I'll take you back." He turned and gestured, and the two rocks appeared again. I wondered if all he'd done was turn them invisible, and I could have left anytime. I doubted it was that simple.

"Let's go, then," he said.

He took a couple of steps toward the rocks, then, I guess, observed that the wolf and the dzur were gone. I turned back to László, and there were a dog and a cat next to him.

"Um," I said.

I tried to wrap my head around what had just happened, with only limited success. The cat jumped into his arms.

"Thanks," I told him.

He bowed, which made it look like the cat was bowing too, which was weird. "Glad to be of help."

I felt like there was probably more to say, but Discaru was waiting. I saluted László, turned, and followed my demonic leader.

We walked between the stones, and we were once more in a hallway of the house.

He turned and glared at me. "There," he said.

I drew Lady Teldra. "Yeah. Now, I have some questions."

He sighed. "How did I not see this coming?"

"It's not like you could have done anything about it. If you start to transform, I swear by Verra's sense of humor that I'll put this weapon through your guts before your forehead drops."

"Will you really use that thing on me?"

"Gleefully. What are you?"

"You'd call me a demon."

"Yeah, I got that part. You know, the squat legs, big snout, pink skin with blue splotches? I put that together. Now, what are you?"

"I'm from another world."

"Right. What world?"

"Depending on the language, we call it 'ground' or 'the world' or 'home' or 'dirt.' Does that help?"

"Are you trying to piss me off?"

He looked down the length of Lady Teldra, then said, "Probably not a good idea, I guess."

"I see you come from a people capable of learning. What does your race call yourselves?"

"Our term for ourselves translates to 'those who think.'"

I sighed.

"All right, tell me this, then. Why are you trying to keep me from finding out anything? What's the big deal?"

"I'm carrying out Zhayin's wishes."

"Oh, a demon thing?"

"Actually, no. He could have bound me. You know that, right?"

"Right. That's what it means to be a demon."

"Yeah. But he didn't. We're friends. He helped me once, long ago. So he asked for my help, and I agreed. That's all. Does it surprise you that I could have a human friend?"

I chose not to comment on what "human" means. I said, "No. I have a friend who's a demon. Well, he's called the Demon, he isn't really one. And he isn't a friend, he's more of an enemy. But anyway. What is it that you so desperately want me not to find out?"

"Oh, that," he said.

"Yeah, that."

"Can we negotiate?"

"Uh, I think that's what we're doing."

"You're aware that just having that, that weapon out, is attracting all sorts of attention, right? I'm expecting help—"

"To have showed up the first time I drew her," I finished for him. "That is, if there was anyone to show up."

"Okay, point," he said.

I gestured with Lady Teldra. Discaru shrugged and said, "All right."

He moved fast, really fast. Maybe it was a demon thing, or maybe I was off guard, or maybe some of each, but he was past Lady Teldra before I knew it. He slammed his shoulder into me, and as I fought to keep my balance he ran past me back into the room and vanished.

"Well, crap," I said to the walls.

"*Sorry, Boss. I should have picked up on that.*"

"*So should I.*"

I pulled the door shut. Okay, then. I'd learned some things from all of that. I wasn't sure exactly what those things were, and certainly not how they fit together, and I had absolutely no idea how—or if—they were related to the mysterious nature of the "platform" I was walking around in, but I'd certainly learned some things.

Now what?

"*Invent theories, then test them?*"

"*That's what I've been doing, Loiosh.*"

"*Oh? What theory have you tested so far?*"

"*That I died, was brought to Deathgate, and the entire house is contained in the Paths of the Dead, and this has all been part of one of those tests you have to go through to reach the Halls of Judgment.*"

"*Oh. Is it?*"

"*No.*"

"*How do you know?*"

"*The Paths are set up for Dragaerans. Only Dragaerans. They* couldn't bring in a fake, mentally constructed Easterner I'd never met. He has to have been real. If he's real, it's all real. If it's all real, then this isn't part of a test, and I'm still alive. Also, if I'd died, you'd have mentioned something about it."

"Good, then. Uh, did you really think that was going on, Boss?"

"No."

"Then—"

"I'm not starting with the most likely, I'm starting with the easiest to test."

"Oh. So, what's the next theory?"

"Actually, that was the only one I had."

"Right."

To my left was the beast, locked in its room. I didn't feel like meeting it again. To my right was the stairway back down, and places I hadn't yet explored. So, just go ahead and open doors? Why not. Maybe there were answers behind one of them. Maybe there were pieces of answers behind all of them. So downstairs, and—

"Boss, there's still a door here you haven't opened."

"Where?"

"There."

Yeah, heading back toward the stairs, on my right. Well, sure then. The echo of my boots was very distinct as I walked toward that door; I was aware of the sound as I hadn't been before.

I stood in front of the door, took a deep breath, and opened it.

Light.

Pure light.

I don't mean blinding; I didn't have an urge to shut my eyes or anything, but it was like the entire room was filled with light, or there was so much light that it was impossible to make out anything inside.

"*Loiosh?*"

"*Boss?*"

"*Seem dangerous?*"

"*Well, not as far as I can tell.*"

I shut the door and looked around. My eyes worked fine.

Why was there a room of light? Who would do that? And what would be in the room? Well, if I couldn't answer that, there was another one: what would be *past* a room full of light? As I was trying to figure that out, something else occurred to me.

A room of mirrors, a room of light, the smell of bread, stone grinding against stone, footsteps in the hall: Light and sound and smell. The fact is, if you've known me for a while, the things I notice aren't so much how much light there is, and what odd sounds there are, and smells. I have, from time to time, mentioned them, because I've been trying to give you, my listener, an idea of the place where things happened. But I've had to work to do it, because the things I notice are more like *There's a nook where someone could be hiding*, or, *That guy could be walking that way because he has a knife in his boot*, or, *I could go ten steps down that street, duck into that doorway, and vanish*, or, *Both of those guys can use a blade, but the one on the right is faster*, or, *That guardsman is watching me*. That's the stuff that I automatically pay attention to, because that's who I am, because that's what you need to be aware of when you kill people for a living. I'm not apologizing, I'm just telling you, because it was just then, standing before that door, that I became aware of how important light and sound and smell were in this place, and that I hadn't been paying enough attention to them.

There was a connection between my world and the Halls of Judgment, and the connection was based on necromancy, which I understood not at all. But I knew this much: if I was going to make sense of how this place was put together, I was going to need to pay attention to all sorts of things I wasn't used to noticing. Things are always the way they are for a reason: sometimes as a cause to create an effect, sometimes as a deliberate or accidental effect of something else, sometimes both at once. But there was a reason for the light, for the dark, for the smell of bread, for the sound of stones and footsteps.

I opened the door again.

"*Boss?*"

There was probably a little end table that I'd bark my shin on, or I'd set off a trap that would send a bucket of molten lava on my head and kill me, or something like that.

"*Boss, we're not going in there, are we?*"

"*Would you be afraid if it were dark, instead of light?*"

"*Yes.*"

"*Well, we're going in. Our answers are on the other side.*"

"*How do you know that?*"

"*Because.*"

"*Because?*"

"*Uh, because, why not?*"

"*Oh, good.*"

I don't know why entering into a room I couldn't see because of light was scarier than entering into a room I couldn't see because of darkness. Maybe how weird it was? Probably.

I took a step into the room and didn't die. I took another step, a smaller one, because now the idea of a table at shin height had set itself up in my head. I started sliding my feet forward. I heard the door close behind me, but I ignored it and continued. I kept going, and after what felt like miles, my foot reached the far wall. I was obscurely disappointed that I hadn't cleverly detected any shin-level furniture.

I ran my hands over the wall, looking for a door. I had about concluded that either there wasn't one or it was on another wall, when I found it. Then it was a matter of feeling for the knob, turning it, pushing—And I could see again.

"*That was almost too easy, Boss.*"

"Loiosh, never ever say that again."

"*Right. Sorry.*"

There was a small, oval area. There was a white marble table with a sculpture sitting on it, and a corridor leading off to the left, and a curved stairway heading up with a round mirror placed so that I could see the top stair.

"Ah ha," I said.

"Ah ha?"

"Ah ha."

"*So, you know where we are?*"

"*I think so. I think at the top of that stairway is the chamber where Zhayin does his sorcery.*"

"*Oh. Then why aren't we going the other direction?*"

I went straight across, no hesitations, and climbed the stairway.

It curved around to the left until I was pointing back the way I'd come, which, given the nature of this obnoxious structure, could mean I was anywhere pointing in any direction. I kept reminding myself of that in hopes of easing the shock the next time something bizarre happened. My boots made more of a scuffing than a tapping sound, for whatever reason.

There was a door at the top, opening outward. I put my hand on the knob, tried it, and it turned.

It was only a place set aside by a sorcerer to perform necromantic experiments in a building that didn't make sense but clearly crossed over from world to world and had managed to trap Devera here. What danger could there possibly be?

"Boss—"

I pulled the door open.

8

WITHERING DEPTHS

The room was pretty big, about a third of the size of the ball-room. The floor was black and there were designs painted in silver all over it: circles with lines connecting them and a few odd shapes here and there. There were lamps hanging from hooks on the walls, but they weren't lit. The ceiling was high and had a very large window in it—maybe the biggest window I'd ever seen. The sky was orange-red, as it was supposed to be, so I could assume it really was the sky, and I wasn't looking at some other world or something.

I took a step into the room. There were tables of varying heights scattered about. One full-size freestanding mirror leaned against the back wall; a second hung from the ceiling in the near corner. I took another step, avoiding a head-size circle on the floor because, well, I don't know. Would you have stepped in it?

I approached the nearest table, which seemed surprisingly cheap and rickety and had paint spatters on it. It held, scat-tered about haphazardly, a couple of books, a steel rod, a jar of something yellow, two polished rocks and three unpolished ones, and a small clear globe with a greenish tint.

There was also dust. A thick layer of dust over everything. I mean, thick.

I looked back at the floor, and, yes, I could see my footprints in it.

No one had been in this room for years.

Well, okay then. I put that in storage with everything else I knew. I recalled Harro's story, and thought about the beast, and decided I really did not want to be messing around in here. I wondered what the books were, but, no, I wasn't even going to pick them up to find out. Then I tried to remember how much dust I'd seen in the other rooms as I went by, but couldn't remember. Maybe that meant there hadn't been much. I'm pretty sure if I'd tracked footprints in the dust I'd have noticed. I made a mental note to watch for dust from now on.

At the far end of the room on the right-hand wall was another door, and across from it one of those four-legged ladders servants use for lighting lamps that are placed too high to do any good. I stood for a while, looking at all the juicy objects, each one with its own story and its own uses, and maybe, if I'd been smart enough, its own piece of the puzzle. I wanted to pick things up; I was afraid to pick things up. I looked up at the window over my head. Loiosh helpfully remained silent. No, I mean it: it was helpful.

I cursed and, without giving myself time for second thoughts, picked up the steel rod from the table. It didn't blow up, or shoot lightning bolts, or do anything else embarrassing. But it felt funny; its weight was oddly distributed. I turned it slowly in my hand. There was liquid inside it, flowing as I moved it, which is something I'd run into before, though I couldn't remember the details. I set it back down and picked up one of the polished rocks, studied it, didn't learn anything, put it down.

One of the books was called *Creating Nexus Points*, the other was *An Inquiry into World Drift*. I was pretty sure I could read them both and know as much as I knew now. I opened them, and they were both marked on the inside cover with a seal and the name Zhayin. Also, they were both very dusty.

I looked around the room again and shrugged. It was full of stuff, and no doubt full of information, but there was nothing I was capable of learning here. I went over to the ladder, looked up, and there was a sky-door. I climbed up, pushed the door open, and saw the sky. Then I went up the rest of the way and stepped out onto the roof.

I hadn't expected it to feel that good to be out in the open again. The air felt moist, like it should after a rainstorm, and there may even have been a bit of drizzle left. I didn't care. I took a look around and saw, yeah, you guessed it, mirrors built into the stone itself, facing inward, one on each side, each of them a little shorter than me, and a little wider. I walked all around the top of the manor. There were walls, and the great sweeping arches as I'd seen before I entered the place, but at the low points I could easily look over them. I enjoyed the view of the ocean-sea on one side, and of flatlands on another, and a jungle on yet another, and the sight of the road back home.

"You could jump down, Boss, and we could leave."

"Jump down, maybe. Probably even survive. But how am I going to leave with two broken ankles? I've heard about broken ankles. People tell me they aren't all that pleasant. Besides, you know we aren't going anywhere until we've solved Devera's problem."

He sighed into my mind.

Just for the sake of completeness, though, I walked up right to the edge and climbed onto the wall at a low point. Or, rather, I tried to—without any sensation of movement, I suddenly found myself back near the door I'd climbed up from. Huh. I tried it with the other walls, and the same thing happened.

"See, Loiosh? Even if I wanted to—"

"Yeah, I get it."

I had no idea what could produce that effect, but if the mirrors didn't have something to do with it, I'd play my next game of s'yang stones without the flat ones.

And it was there that it smacked me in the face, what should have been obvious from the beginning: yeah, Devera had spoken about "tomorrow-me," which indicated that, eventually, she was going to get out. But that didn't mean I was going to get out.

I stood there on the roof thinking about that, then I tried one of those invisible barriers again, and the same thing happened: one step forward brought me back to the somewhere in the middle of the roof.

It's one thing to decide you don't want to leave; it's another to realize that you can't.

Loiosh and Rocza remained still while I digested that like a half-cooked pudding. Then I swore, and Loiosh agreed.

We went back down. I closed the door behind me because I'm a good guy that way, then walked over to the other door and through it.

I was in a wide corridor made of rough stone. There were two doorways on either side, with no doors, opening onto small rooms with nothing in them. Storage rooms, perhaps, but to store what, and why were they empty? It hit me that a lot of what was confusing me about this place is that parts of it seemed like they'd been lived in and gotten regular use for hundreds of years, and other parts seemed like they'd just been completed, and there was no pattern to it.

On a sudden thought, I studied the ceiling, then the ceilings in those empty rooms. Where the ceiling in the hallway was stone, these were wood, and they were sagging and cracked in places. And, yes, there were the yellowish stains that said there'd been leakage. This part was old, older than anything else I'd seen, and it made even less sense than before. The floor in these small rooms—or rather, the ground—was just dirt.

I continued forward.

Have you ever wished some asshole with a sword would jump out of nowhere and try to kill you, just so you'd have a problem you knew how to solve? Me neither, but I was pretty close to it about then.

There was another doorless doorway in front of me. I stepped through it into a decent-size room filled with large objects that at first I couldn't make out. There wasn't much light; what there was being provided by a couple of large crystals glowing in the corners of—

I smiled.

"We found the wine cellar."

"You aren't going to ask why we're suddenly in a cellar?"

"No, too busy being pleased about the discovery. I may steal a bottle. I may steal two bottles."

"Stealing is a crime, Boss."

"Good point."

It looked to be about a five-thousand-bottle cellar, which is pretty good as such things go. I'd always wanted a wine cellar. I'd never had five thousand bottles at the same time. I'd had five once. These bottles were covered in dust. People generally don't dust very often in their wine cellars, but even by those standards, there was a lot. This place hadn't seen much use in a long, long time.

Which meant, hey, they'd never miss a bottle, right?

I pulled out the one closest to me. By chance, it was a Khaav'n, one of my favorites. I read the date on the label and translated it to a time just past the end of the Interregnum, two and a half centuries ago. You'd think no wine could last that long, but you'd be wrong: the sorcery to let wine age to its most perfect moment, then keep it there indefinitely is, in my opinion, the Dragaerans' greatest, perhaps only, contribution to culture.

Now, if I'd only had wine tongs.

Someday, I'd meet someone with a good, elegant way to remove the top of a wine bottle, and I'd kiss him.

But in the meantime, the old-fashioned methods work best. I went over to the nearest wall, gripped the bottle, and struck the top of it a quick, sharp blow. It came off pretty clean; I'd gotten good at this over the years.

I smiled, sniffed the wine, stopped smiling. Just to be sure, I poured a drop on my finger and tasted it. No, I wouldn't be drinking that. I tossed the bottle aside. It didn't break, it just rolled and glugged. I tried another bottle. Same variety, same year. I smashed the neck and sniffed. Same thing.

I moved over a shelf and pulled out a white Morofin, about ten years more recent, this one marked by Zerika's reign, rather than the pre-Interregnum numbering. It was bad too. I searched some more, found a Stathin, what I would call a brandy but Dragaerans call wine because they're idiots. One sniff, and I felt like a crime had been committed. I don't know if you've ever had a Stathin, but this was a crime. I sighed.

"Okay, Loiosh. What did it?"

"Boss? Have I just been promoted to wine expert?"

As mysteries go, I guess this one wasn't all that exciting; spells do fail every now and then. It's just that with everything else, it made me suspicious. But there was no good way to figure it out now. Maybe I'd find Discaru again, and ask if he'd done the spell, and if so, why he was so bad at it. That was bound to work out well.

There are things I've gotten good at over the years, like saffron rice with kethna dumplings, roasted fowl with plum sauce, and killing people. I guess figuring out what made weird houses weird was something I'd have to work on. Bugger. What was I missing?

I tried to make myself pay attention to what the floor was like, to smells, to the dimensions of a room, to lighting, and any furniture or objects that might hold useful information. But it was hard, and mentally exhausting in a way I wasn't used to.

I considered knocking over the racks just out of spite, but there might be a good bottle in there somewhere.

"Boss?"

"It's all right, Loiosh. Just need to regroup, re-form the line, and prepare for another charge."

"What, now you're a soldier again?"

"Don't you miss those days? Just a little?"

"Are you crazy?"

"Yeah, neither do I."

Well, standing here wouldn't do anything. I tapped Lady

Teldra's hilt and shifted my cloak a little. I'd figure things out later. For now, onward. The far end of the room had a doorway, and about halfway there, on the other side, there were three steps leading up to something I couldn't see clearly. I went that way, scowling at the four thousand, nine hundred and ninety-six worthless bottles, and up to the steps. What they ended in was one of those freight doors, installed at an angle, so the top was above me and the bottom was in front of me. It seemed to open out (which was good, because otherwise opening it would have given me a sharp knock on the head), but the odd part was that there seemed to be no lock. There were double iron loops, as if for a padlock, and there were brackets that looked like a bar would go there, but neither lock nor bar was to be seen.

I took hold of the door and pushed, and—nothing. Not even a hint of give, as if I were pushing into solid stone. Could it be stone? How could I know? If rooms were on the wrong side, and up took you down, and a stairway deposited you into some random place, how are you supposed to tell where you are relative to the land the building is set on?

I tried a couple more times, then gave up. I continued to the far end of the wine cellar, then through the doorway and into a very large empty room, which I guess was there in case anyone needed a big empty room for something. There were four pillars in it, evenly spaced, all of them made of the same stone as the floor and walls.

"Loiosh, does it seem like we've gone down a lot? Like, we're below ground level?"

"Rocza was just saying the same thing, Boss. She picks up on that stuff faster than me. Better ears."

Well, sure. Why shouldn't a step forward have taken us underground?

"*How deep?*"

"*She isn't good with measurement, Boss, but I think not too far. We're still above sea level.*"

I nodded and continued forward, going slowly, looking around. There wasn't much to see. My feet kicked up dust, but it looked different from the dust upstairs, lighter, chalkier. I was pretty sure that meant nothing at all, but I felt proud to have noticed. To the left, my boots were getting dusty. That warlock, Laszló, he didn't have dusty boots.

There was something green on the far wall. And as I got closer, there was a reek in the air. Not strong, but definite, like rotting vegetation. Once, when I was about six and decided that re-forming produce boxes into a castle was a better idea than mulching the garbage, my father had dragged me to a place where a pile of garbage had collected and pushed my face into it so I would understand how he did not want his kitchen to smell, ever. I hadn't forgotten that odor.

I continued back toward it. The smell got stronger, but not intolerable. When I reached the end I was able to deduce what caused the smell of rotting vegetation: there was a bunch of rotting vegetation. Vines that looked like they'd once been creeping up the wall, what looked like the remains of stunted trees complete with dead leaves around them, and dead plants that I'm sure I could have identified if they'd been alive and I knew anything about plants.

I stood there, looked, sniffed, tried to figure it out. No, I was hardly an expert, but I was pretty sure these things had been alive less than a year ago. Probably a couple of months ago.

"*Great, Loiosh. Another mystery, because we don't have enough.*"

"*Maybe this is where they grew all the food they didn't have in the kitchen.*"

"*Clever, but it doesn't address the mystery.*"

"*What mystery is that? You mean, what killed everything?*"

"*The mystery isn't how they died, it's how they lived.*"

"*What?*"

"*Those things don't grow indoors.*"

"*Oh.*"

"*So this place, this platform wasn't built here, it appeared.*"

"*Oh.*"

"*Yeah.*"

I wanted to ask Sethra Lavode if it were possible to teleport a building. For one thing, she'd know; for another, I'd treasure the look on her face. But I wasn't wholly ignorant. I had some skill in sorcery. And from what I knew, no. I mean, sure, it was possible in theory to teleport a building, but in practice, the balance it would be necessary to maintain, and the details it would be necessary to manipulate, and the power it would be necessary to hold, just, no, I didn't think even Sethra could manage it.

But if it hadn't been teleported here, or built here, then— what?

I scowled at the walls and ceiling. Every question I answered brought up two more. It was getting old.

In the far right corner was a doorway, and I could just see the beginning of a stairway, and a mirror hanging loosely from a torch bracket.

I glared at the mirror.

Could I really fix this thing and release Devera—and

myself—just by smashing a few mirrors? I didn't know if that would work, but it was time to find out.

I let a dagger fall into my hand, flipped it, took a grip so the pommel was sticking between my first two fingers, and punched the nearest mirror.

The shock went up my arm, to my elbow and my shoulder. I dropped the dagger and shook my hand.

"Boss?"

"*I'm okay. I just wish I hadn't done that.*"

Just like the windows, then. Someone had too much bloody magic. Or money. Or both.

So much for that idea. I waited until my arm felt better, recovered my dagger, and approached the stairway. It seemed safe and normal. I climbed. There were torches burning on the walls, so at least I could see. The stairway wrapped around a couple of times, then let me off in a cave.

"*Rocza says we're lower now, almost sea level.*"

"*Of course we are. I just went up, why wouldn't we be lower?*"

There was no light in the cave, but there was another burning torch right behind me.

Why were there burning torches? Did some servant come and check them every so often? And if so, where were all the servants? I'd run into three, total. I cursed under my breath and grabbed the torch from its bracket.

The cave was your basic rocky cave, but I could smell seawater. A few steps later I determined that it was coming from the right, so I turned to the left.

I followed the cave into the cliff for a long way without seeing anything but more cave in flickering torchlight.

"*Are we looking for something in particular, Boss?*"

"*No, something in general.*"

The ground was hard and uneven, difficult to walk on. It would be even harder to fight on, so I hoped that wouldn't come up. Not that I often hoped it *would* come up.

"I mean, Boss, we're no longer even in the house."

"That should make you happy. Why doesn't it make you happy?"

"Guess I'm getting hard to please."

Just after that the cave ended. There were no bones, or abandoned nests, or dens, or any other signs that there might once have been life here. I don't know what kind of animals live in caves, but none of them had ever been here.

I studied the walls, holding the torch close, and felt myself smile.

"What?"

"There are marks here, just where I thought there might be."

"So, when you said you weren't looking for anything specific—"

"I was lying. Ouch."

"Sorry, Boss. I slipped."

I wished I had some paper. I should start carrying a notebook, just in case I ever again find myself in a cave with a tenuous connection to a magical house, and I need to write down the obscure symbols carved into the rock. But I at least knew what they were, if not what they meant. They were sorcery runes, the kind of marks a sorcerer would use to help maintain concentration during difficult or complex spells. All sorcerers started that way, using them for even the simplest spells. It's how you use the energy from the Orb without burning out your brain and destroying yourself, which would interfere with further lessons. I had often used them when teleporting, just to make sure I didn't do something embarrassing. Expert sorcerers use them when doing something they find difficult. This specimen was one I'd never seen before.

"*How did you know it would be here, Boss?*"

The torch flared, then guttered for a moment. Time to go back. I took another good, long look at the runes, then turned around and started walking.

"*Because of the dead vegetation, of course.*"

"*Want me to bite you again?*"

I chuckled. "*If this house suddenly appeared, it was either purely random, or there had to be an anchor.*"

"*Anchor?*"

"*A way to magically connect to the manor's previous location, so it could be brought here.*"

"*So, you think it was teleported?*"

"*I think necromancy, and wish I understood it better. But if you're moving an object around among dimensions, then you need to establish a position so it doesn't get lost. A tunnel into the side of the cliff would be perfect, because it would be fixed, out of the way by a good distance, and easily found. Loiosh, I'm so smart, sometimes—*"

"*What about the torches?*"

"*I'm still working on that.*"

I made my way to the stairway, hesitated, continued past it.

After about twenty or thirty steps and a long curve, I saw daylight ahead. I walked out into it and blinked. When my eyes had adjusted, I took a good look around. The mirror that had to be there was big, and fixed to the top of the cave with iron bars.

Well.

"*Boss—*"

"I know. Let me think."

I didn't so much think as remember.

"I have a question," I announced to the Enchantress of Dzur Mountain.

We were in the library of Castle Black: Sethra, Morrolan, and me. In a short time, my life would be turned upside down and my marriage would explode and I'd end up running for my life, but I didn't know that, so life seemed pretty good. Aliera had just ducked out, muttering about important business, which meant she was visiting the necessary room or killing someone. Her leaving provided a break in the conversation, and let me ask about something I had been nervous asking about with her there. To wit: her daughter.

"Oh?" said Sethra.

"It's about Aliera's daughter. Devera."

"You've met her?" said Morrolan.

"A few times."

Sethra nodded and looked very knowing, but then she always looked very knowing, possibly on account of knowing stuff. "What about her?"

"Things she's said make me wonder. . . ." I stopped, considered, reconsidered, and said, "Is it possible to teleport to a different time, instead of a different place?"

"No," said Sethra.

"Okay, then."

Morrolan cleared his throat. Sethra looked at him, they exchanged some sort of communication, and Sethra shrugged and said, "I guess it can't do any harm."

"Hmmm?"

She turned back to me. "No, it is impossible to travel to a different time, as if one were traveling to a different place. We travel through time at a rate of one second each second, forward, and that's that."

"I hear a 'but' coming on."

She nodded.

"There are places that are—I don't know how to say it. *Warped*, perhaps."

"The Halls of Judgment."

"Yes. Time there isn't the same as time here."

"So, I could go there, and come back at a different time?"

She shook her head. "No, but it's possible the Necromancer could. I don't know. She isn't foolish enough to try."

"When I visited there before, and emerged, time hadn't done anything strange."

"Hadn't it?"

I tried to remember. I don't get how memory works. Some things that happened ages ago are sharp and clear, and some have gotten foggy, and I don't know why. I can usually count on my memory, for most things, or at least for anything that hasn't been messed with by—

"Such language, Vlad," said Sethra. "What is it?"

"Verra. My Goddess. She did things to my memory. I hate that. And I think the whole thing with the Paths of the Dead and the Halls of Judgment are part of it. May her—"

Morrolan cleared his throat.

"Oh, right," I said. "She's your friend." I shrugged. "Sorry."

He nodded.

"It's possible," said Sethra, "that it has nothing to do with the Goddess. Mortal minds are not meant to understand the Halls of Judgment."

"Yeah, so, back to that."

"Yes. Time. The Paths of the Dead are another world that touches our own, with Deathgate Falls providing the point of connection."

"With you so far."

"Of course, time on another world doesn't have to match time on our own."

"Of course," I said.

Sethra ignored my tone and said, "Different worlds, different laws, different time streams."

"All right."

"The Halls of Judgment permit contact among many of these worlds. That is how the Lords of Judgment created it. Multiple worlds, and time streams, have that point of contact."

I considered that. "But if they're different time streams, uh, whatever that means, it can't have any influence on ours, right?"

"You have understood exactly," said Sethra.

"Which means, it doesn't matter, because it has no effect on anything I'm likely to run into."

"Yes."

Morrolan coughed.

Sethra looked at him, then back at me. "All right, it's a little more complicated than that."

"Yeah," I said. "For one thing, there's Devera."

"Devera. Well. You might say she was born in a state of timeless flux."

"Just what I was about to suggest," I said.

Morrolan was polite enough to chuckle. "You need to decide," he put in, "whether you want to know how time works, or how Devera works, because it isn't the same conversation."

I looked over at Sethra, who nodded. "Oh," I said. "Well, okay, Devera then."

Sethra nodded. "She—oh, hello, Aliera."

She nodded, resumed her seat, and poured us all wine. "What are we discussing now?"

"Time," said Morrolan. "Its nature, its variations, and how we swim along in it."

"Ah. We should have the Necromancer here."

Everyone there liked the Necromancer, so I didn't say she gave me the creeps. Actually, I kind of liked her too.

"What you need to understand," said Sethra, as if just picking up where we'd left off, "is that place and time are intertwined. If the time in one place does not correspond with time in another, that does not mean you can move between places at the same time, or between times in the same place."

"Unless you're my daughter," said Aliera, looking smug. Then she said, "Why the curiosity, Vlad? Did you have some-when you wanted to be?"

I drank some more wine. "No, just trying to make sense of my visit to the Halls of Judgment."

"That was years ago," said Aliera. "A long time, for you."

"There," I said. "You see? It's all about time. Everything is about time. Time to do this, time to do that, need to get the timing right, this happened before that did. Time is everything. If sorcery were to provide a way to control it—"

"It doesn't," said Sethra.

"Okay. Too bad."

She frowned. "Vlad, is there something going on?"

"No," I said, because I didn't think there was. "I'm just, I don't know, fascinated."

"You're fascinated by everything," said Aliera, as if that were a bad thing.

"Yeah. Part of being an Easterner. No telling what odd directions our curiosity will take us."

Aliera nodded. "Yes. Lack of discipline in thinking. That's probably why you keep getting conquered."

"No, we just keep running out of time," I said, and the conversation drifted off onto other things.

I stared out at the ocean-sea, then up at the cliffs.

"*Boss?*"

"*That isn't supposed to be there.*"

"*What?*"

"*That chunk of rock, up there, sticking out from the cliff. It shouldn't be there.*"

"*I don't—*"

"*It fell. During the Interregnum.*"

"*Oh,*" he said. Then, "*When are we?*"

"*Your guess is as good as mine, except that it's before or during the Interregnum.*"

My first thought was to remove my amulet and see if I had my connection to the Orb. It should be safe, right? If I was back in time to before the Jhereg was after me, they wouldn't be looking for me yet. And they certainly wouldn't look for me in the past.

I almost did it, but then I hesitated. Just how confident was I that I wasn't still inside the manor, even though strange paths took me through time? Not all that confident, when I thought about it.

I looked out at the restless water again and considered.

9

THE MISERIES OF ODELPHO

I can tell you, from having lived near it all my life, that the air does funny things around the ocean-sea. Gusts come from odd directions, and the prevailing wind changes for no discernible reason, sometimes whipping around in circles, so that when you watch the leaves, they seem like they're caught up in a shield spell. Being on a cliff in front of a cave mouth looking directly out over the surf doesn't do anything to reduce the effect. My cloak opened and closed in spite of the hardware weighing it down, and my hair kept slapping different sides of my face or getting in my eyes, reminding me that I should have tied it. I had gotten into the habit of tying it many years ago, when I came near to bungling a job because it got in my eyes at the wrong moment, but I prefer it free, and hadn't had a need to worry about it for some time.

I pulled my cloak closed and stared out over the water. There were fewer wrecks on the shore, fewer tops of masts sticking out of the water, than in my day—the collection of small vessels that get smashed on the rocks and forgotten. That, as much as seeing Kieron's Watch jutting out like it hadn't a care in the world, convinced me I had left my own time and entered another. That is not something I was expecting the day before yesterday when I went to the market for javorn sausage. In a life full of weird things, this was—well, it was one of them.

"Boss? Uh, *what do we do?*"

"*I have no idea.*"

Rocza shifted nervously on my other shoulder. I guess she was picking up on how upset Loiosh was, because he was too much in tune with me not to be pretty disturbed. I'd never messed with time before, and the concept was scary. Maybe the Necromancer could deal with it, and probably Sethra would at least have a good idea of what not to do, but I didn't. I stood there, afraid to move. I mean, if I walked forward and climbed the cliff, could I travel East, find an ancestor of mine, and kill him? No, no. I had no intention of doing that, but just the idea that I *could* was immobilizing. And if I couldn't? How would that work? And if I could meet an ancestor, did that mean I could meet myself? What would I say to myself? What would myself say to me? We probably wouldn't get along very well.

Part of me refused to believe any of this was possible, but I couldn't come up with a reason why not, so it just made things worse. I felt like I was standing in a bubble of impossibility.

There was room for a couple more steps before an almost sheer drop. To my left was a sort of path going up among the rocks that looked like it might be possible to climb. Did I want to?

That Loiosh wasn't saying anything at all gave me a good idea of how this was affecting him. I licked my lips. I dropped the torch to free my hands for climbing, took a step forward, turned, and set my foot on a rock that was just outside the mouth of the cave, at the beginning of what I hoped was a path that would lead all the way to the top.

And I was inside again.

I exhaled slowly, and realized that this was good. No, I could not go back in time and prevent myself from existing. I didn't know why, but I knew I couldn't, and you can laugh at me as much as you want, but just knowing that made me feel better about the world I was living in. Even more, it meant there were a whole lot of things that I didn't want to think about that I could happily ignore.

I looked around: I was in someone's bedroom.

It was big enough for a family of Easterners to live comfortably. Two families: one of them could live on the bed. In addition to sheer size, the thing that tells you you're in the bedroom of someone rich is the lack of clothes. They always have walk-in wardrobes, or even whole other rooms for dressing— nothing you'd need is ever nearby. Being rich means making everything inconvenient. Remember to attribute that when you quote it. T-A-L-T-O-S.

There were glass windows, big ones, that looked out on the ocean-sea. I was relieved, though not surprised, that Kieron's Watch was missing, just like it was supposed to be. I wondered if it had been arranged for all the walls to face the ocean-sea, then stopped thinking about it when the headache threatened. And at first I didn't see a mirror, which surprised me, but then I realized that there was one built into a long, dark reddish vanity, and I hadn't noticed it as a mirror because, well, vanities have mirrors, right? I felt a little foolish.

I looked around the room again. Yeah, someone once lived here, but it hadn't been used, or cleaned, in a while. Whoever had lived here was important, just judging by size and the furnishings and by the psiprint of a youngish Dragaeran girl in shadow, only a quarter profile visible, hair blending into the darkness: it wasn't the sort of artwork you'd leave in a guest room—you had to want to fall asleep looking at it. I could probably spend an hour looking everything over carefully and make a few deductions about whomever it was who slept here, but it wouldn't help me solve the mystery. I assumed it was probably Zhayin himself, because why not?

So, fine. I had stepped out from a cave, started to climb a hill, and in one step had moved forward two hundred years and ended up in a bedroom. Sure. Why not have a magical connection of unknown properties between a sheer drop to the ocean-sea and your bedroom? You can spend a nice day watching the waves a few hundred years ago, then to bed. It's like adding a porch.

Back to business. The room I'd arrived in had only one door, and I didn't remember coming through it.

"*Loiosh? Is this the door where we entered?*"

He hesitated, then said, "*I don't know.*"

"*Huh.*"

I looked again at those glass windows—no, not windows exactly; they were a series of doors that were all glass except for a wood frame. Whoever built this place had way, *way* too much money. I ignored them and walked over to the regular one, then hesitated.

Magical connection of unknown properties.

I know what a teleport is like, because it takes a couple of seconds and I can feel it, and besides, the amulet prevents it from working. I know what a necromantic gate is like, because it's like your body moves first and then your soul catches up with it and there are all these golden sparks all around you, only they aren't really there, and—crap. I can't describe it, but the point is, you can't mistake it. However I'd gotten from the cliff to here, it was neither of those, and I'd wager Loiosh's next meal that it was somehow connected to whatever was trapping Devera.

"Hey—"

"Shut up."

Okay, Vlad, think it through: if different places were in different times, that meant necromancy, even if it didn't feel like a gate. Something was going on that involved connection to other worlds—

No, not *to* other worlds, *through* other worlds.

The Halls of Judgment.

The manor—the "platform"—had been designed to provide gateways to other worlds, and doing this had resulted, by accident or design, in sections of the place wrapping back on itself in odd ways and at different times, and it was somehow all tied to the Halls of Judgment. From what Sethra had said, the Halls of Judgment were easy—as such things go—to reach from our world, and from others. And this connection had somehow trapped Devera.

I badly wanted to have a nice, quiet chat with the Necromancer. Or Devera, if she'd stick around long enough to answer some questions.

I thought about how pleasant it would be to pull out a knife and rip up the bed, scatter the pillow stuffing everywhere, smash the furniture, and break the windows, just to do it. I guess I was getting more frustrated than I realized. I didn't actually rip anything up, though.

I thought about taking the amulet off just long enough to

teleport. I had risked taking it off a couple of times and gotten away with it. Yeah, it was a gamble, and every time I did it, the risk increased. But still. Get to Castle Black, find the Necromancer, have a long talk about how the world was put together, then come back.

"*Come back, Boss?*"

"*You know we're going to solve this thing one way or another, Loiosh.*"

"*But—*"

"*Devera.*"

He sighed into my mind.

No, I wasn't going to remove the amulet. Not yet. Not unless I was desperate. And I couldn't be desperate, there were still doors I hadn't opened. You're not desperate until you've opened all the doors. T-A-L-T-O-S.

I scowled at the door in front of me. Fine, then. I took a step forward and pulled it open. It might be the same hallway I'd first entered, or just one that looked the same. Might as well find out. It would be annoying to bump into Harro again and have him give me the sad eyes about staying put, but if all else failed I could always cut off his ears, right?

In ten steps I was pretty sure where I was: a few more steps would bring me back to the room where I slept, and beyond that Zhayin's room, and the strange meeting room, and the front doors.

I took a few more steps and I was elsewhere and I was annoyed. Abrupt, irrational shifts going through doors was one thing, but between two steps in a normal hallway seemed unfair.

It was no mystery what kind of room I was in. As soon as I recovered from the surprise of the transition I recognized it:

a large room full of bunk beds in neat rows, with hooks all about, and uniforms hanging from the hooks, a sword and a halberd on a stand next to each bed. This was a barracks. There were mirrors above each door, angling down. Anywhere else, the far door would lead to a training yard; but anywhere else, the near door would have led to a convenient corridor that permitted actually getting somewhere useful. I counted a total of thirty-two beds, which was not an unreasonable number.

The weapons were clean and sharp and in good condition, of similar make to the ones I'd found in the armory upstairs, though perhaps a bit more modern, judging by the forward curve of the ax, and the narrowness of the spear blade on the halberds.

Which is to say there wasn't that much to see. The other door led to a room with a slightly larger bed, a desk, a chair, and a cabinet, with several blank sheets of paper and two pencil stubs on the desk. There were no other doors, windows, or surprise exits.

I went back through the barracks and into the hallway. I turned around, and there was no door behind me, and no sign of one existing. Creepy. I shrugged and continued in the only direction I could. After a few paces, there was a door on the right, just past the bedroom from which I'd emerged. I opened it without hesitation, and said, "Oh, pardon me. Uh, Odelpho, was it? We met in the hall when you were running in terror."

"Yes, m'lord. Of course."

"I'm just, I was looking . . . so, what is this room?"

"The old nursery, m'lord."

"Oh. Of course." There was a crib there, and walls painted

deep blue, and there were hooks in the ceiling where things had once hung over the crib. "Mind if I ask what you're doing?"

"M'lord?"

"Just wondering why you're here. If you don't mind telling me."

"M'lord? Where else would I go?"

"Don't you have your own room?"

"Oh, I see. Your pardon, m'lord, I misunderstood. I thought you meant . . . I just like to come here and remember."

"To remem—ah, the child."

"Yes, m'lord."

"I'm sorry."

"I should have been there."

"But you were ill?"

She nodded. "I thought I was going to die. Now—yes, m'lord."

"Harro feels terrible about what happened."

"He told you about it?"

I nodded. "I sort of made him."

Her face did something odd, like she couldn't make up her mind about what sort of expression she should wear. "He was such a good boy. It was horrible. And poor Lord Zhayin. And poor Harro."

I nodded.

"And then, his daughter."

"Pardon me?"

"You didn't know about his daughter?"

"I only knew he had a son."

She shook her head. "I probably shouldn't speak of it. My Lord Zhayin is, well, he is a very private person, you know."

Daughter. Yes. Of course. I'm an idiot.

I nodded. "Yes, I understand. I'm sure he wouldn't want you speaking to a stranger about poor Tethia."

She nodded. "You know about her, then?"

I was afraid if I said I'd met her, the conversation would go off the road, so I said, "Only a little. Her father—Lord Zhayin—doesn't like to talk about her."

She nodded. "She's the one I'd have expected to toddle into the wrong room, you know. She was always running away, exploring, and trying to find new places and taking things apart to see how they worked."

I nodded. "What happened to her?"

"Her mother died during the Interregnum."

Okay, so, there it was. Just what Tethia had said. Hit a big drum, light a big torch, make a big splash in the pond. I still had no idea what it meant, but it was important. I wasn't going to figure this thing out until I knew what that meant.

Maybe it had something to do with the place being a "platform."

Maybe her mother had been in charge of filling the pantry, and that's why there was no food, and Tethia had starved to death.

Maybe, with all the time weirdness, Tethia's mother had died during the Interregnum, and then time twisted itself around so she was never born.

Maybe it had something to do with Devera.

One thing, though: I was starting to feel a little sorry for Zhayin. Wife dies during the Interregnum, daughter dies from something mysterious, son gets turned into some kind of hideous thing that has to be locked up. Poor bastard couldn't catch a break with a break bucket during a break storm. T-A-L-T-O-S.

I looked around for something to scowl at that wasn't an

old dry-nurse. To kill time while I figured out the best way to get information from her, I walked around the room, looking into corners, opening the door to a linen closet.

"Nice mirror," I said. "I see it's right by where the crib was. Did she like looking at herself?"

She nodded.

I still didn't have anything. Well, I suppose I could try just asking. I cleared my throat. "Odelpho, could you explain why whenever I ask how Tethia died, the only answer I get is about her mother?"

For a moment she looked like she didn't understand the question. Then she said, "M'lord? Who else have you asked? If you don't mind?"

I hesitated, then, "Tethia," I said.

Her eyes got big and she started shaking. "Where?" she whispered.

"I'm not sure how to describe it. The front room? Kind of long, overlooks the ocean-sea, tables, chairs?"

"Of course," she said, as if to herself. Her eyes lost focus. Then she looked at me again. "Please, how was she?"

"She seemed all right. Maybe a little confused, but so was I."

"She didn't seem"—she groped for the word—"sad?"

I thought about it. "Maybe a little. But mostly it seemed like she wasn't exactly there. It was more like, I don't know, she personified the room? Does that make sense?"

"Oh, I know that," she said, as if I'd tried to explain what a candle snuffer was for. "After all, she—" She broke off and flushed a little.

"She what?" I said.

She shook her head and looked down. There were tears on her cheeks.

"What is it?" I asked. My best soothing voice isn't very soothing, but I did what I could.

"I've been here for all of it," she said.

"All of—?"

"I mean, since before the building of Precipice Manor, when we lived in the old castle."

I nodded, and waited. When she didn't go on, I said, "This was during the Interregnum?"

She nodded. "Oh, yes. My lord worked in the capital before the Disaster. He was consulted on many projects, both new and reconstructions."

"There was a lot of reconstruction work?"

She gave me a funny look, then I could see the "Oh, you're an Easterner" moment of revelation, and she said, "Dragaera City was very, very old. Nothing lasts forever, especially then. The Imperial Palace itself was always being rebuilt or repaired."

"What do you mean, especially then?"

That look again, and: "Preservation spells didn't become easier until after the Interregnum. M'lord," she added, suddenly realizing that she'd been forgetting her courtesies.

"Oh, of course," I said. Then I added, "We Easterners are always younger than we look," because she was already thinking it.

She nodded, a little embarrassed and at a loss for words.

I said, "I saw the award he got for designing some building. I don't remember what."

"The new Silver Exchange. It was beautiful. It looked like a silver needle, and all around it were balconets and bay windows. It was beautiful. My lord's city house was in sight of it, just past the Tsalmoth Wing of the Palace, and I would it see every day on the way to the park with—" She broke off and looked down.

"*Everyone here is so cheerful I almost can't stand it.*"

"*Shut up.*"

"And it was then, before the Interregnum, that he started on Precipice Manor?" I managed to say it without rolling my eyes.

"Yes," she said. "No. Well—it wasn't like that."

"What was it like?"

She looked down. "I shouldn't say any more, m'lord."

"You haven't answered my question," I said, going for the silky-smooth nice-guy tone. I'm not so good at that, though I'm better at it than I used to be.

No good; she just shook her head. All right, then. I wasn't going to let this go. There was something there, and if it wasn't important, I was a Teckla. All right, let's hit it from another angle.

"You were alive during Adron's Disaster, weren't you? It must have been horrible."

She nodded.

"What did it feel like?"

She shook her head. "I can't describe it." She looked to be telling the truth, but more important, there were no signs that talking about it made her nervous, which meant I wasn't getting any closer to my answer. "You know that it created a Sea of Amorphia, just like the big one? Did you know that?"

"Yeah," I said. "Hard to believe. And then the Interregnum. I can't imagine what it must have been like."

"It was hard," she said. "Although we were luckier than some—we had everything we needed nearby."

"Were you close to Tethia's mother?"

"Close, my lord? She was my mistress."

"Right. Of course. Were you sad when she died?"

"I—" She seemed to be stumbling a little. "I didn't learn of it right away."

"Oh, so it didn't happen here?"

"No, my lord."

"Where, then?"

"It was . . . somewhere else."

Bugger. What was the big secret? I hate secrets. Except mine. I like mine. But it did seem like I was getting closer. Push more? Push more.

"Where was it, Odelpho? Where did she die?"

The old woman gave a sort of sob, sank off the chair and onto her knees, and started clawing at her face. I stood there, frozen. I'd never seen that before. It took me a long time, seconds, before I got over to her, grabbed her wrists, and knelt down next to her, Loiosh and Rocza abandoning my shoulders for some convenient shelves. Her face was tilted down and there were long, bloody scratches on it and she was sobbing. I said things, I don't know what. I don't have much practice at being soothing, okay? It doesn't come up a lot while you're killing people for money or running for your life. I said her name, and some other crap that doesn't mean anything, and after a while her wrists relaxed in my hands and she leaned forward, sobbing, and put her head on my shoulder. Verra.

"It's okay," I said.

"I can't tell you. I can't tell you."

"It's all right," I said. It was, in fact, anything but all right, but however I was going to get the information I wanted, it wasn't going to be here and now.

After a while, I helped her back into her chair. She still kept her head down. In an effort to change the subject, I said, "Tell me something: where do you eat?"

She looked up. "My lord?"

"You, servants. Where do you take your meals?"

"In the kitchen, my lord," she said, as if I were an idiot, and as if the, well, whatever had just happened hadn't happened.

I said, "I saw the kitchen. There was no food there. And no table, for that matter."

"They set up the table before meals."

"They?"

"Cook and the butter boy and the pantry girl."

"I didn't see them."

"Well, they must have been there. There's always food at dinnertime."

"All right," I said, because I couldn't think of anything else to say.

She frowned. "Are you hungry, m'lord? I could—"

"No, no. I was just curious. I'm fine."

"Why would you lie like that, Boss?"

"Shut up, Loiosh."

"Thank you for talking to me," I said.

She bowed. "M'lord," she said. Then, "May I ask you something?"

"Seems fair."

"Forgive my impertinence, m'lord, but . . ."

"Go ahead."

"Your hand. What happened to it?"

I glanced at it. "Oh, yes. I was born that way. Among my people it is a sign of high destiny to be born missing a finger." She looked doubtful, but nodded.

"Why do you ask?"

"There's a tale about—I'm sorry."

"No, it's all right. I'm curious. About Easterners?"

She nodded. "That witches have to sacrifice a piece of their body to gain their powers."

"Oh," I said. "Sorry to disappoint, but no. At least, not that I've ever heard of. Maybe it's metaphorical?"

"My lord?"

"Never mind. Thank you again for your help."

"Of course, m'lord."

I took a last look around the room, then sketched her a bow and stepped back into the hallway. It continued for a short distance to my right, or I could go left to where I might or might not be back where Zhayin was, no doubt still sitting in his little room with the portrait of himself looking disapproving.

I turned right. The door that was almost directly across the hall was different from the others: it looked heavy, made of some dark wood with intricate carvings: trees, birds, an animal that was probably a vallista. One of these times, I was going to open a door and something would come jumping out with sharp things pointed at me. I mentally shrugged and opened it.

Well, all right, the son of a bitch had a library after all. I'd been starting to doubt it. An odd place: right across from the nursery and next to a bedroom, but at least he had one.

I thought about shutting the door.

Here's the thing about walking into a library: either you turn around and walk out again, or you figure to spend the next ten hours there. I don't mean finding some book you've never heard of and "just opening it to read the first page," although there's that danger too. I mean there just isn't anything useful to be learned in a library that doesn't require a reasonably careful examination of what books are there. And they're books. You have to, like, read the titles at least.

"*Loiosh, how long since we've eaten anything?*"

"*A year. Maybe two.*"

"*That's what I thought.*"

I hesitated, and cursed under my breath. Maybe I could exercise some self-control. I went in.

It was a long room with shelves on the sides and in the back. At a guess, about six rooms of this size could fit into Morrolan's library, but Morrolan was kind of crazy that way. And in other ways, but never mind. And while I'm no good at estimating numbers of books, as opposed to bottles of wine, there had to be thousands. One thing about the Dragaeran lifespan is that it gives them a lot of time for reading. Out of habit, I looked for mirrors and counted three of them, in all corners except the one nearest the door, and all facing into the room.

The first thing to check in a library is the arrangement. I knew the first part right away: things Zhayin felt were most important were in his study. The books shelved here were everything else. The first thing I saw were novels, most of them historical. He seemed fascinated by the middle Eleventh Cycle: Issola, Tsalmoth, and Vallista reigns. To be clear, I mean contemporary novels set in that period, not written then; you'd need to be a scholar to read anything written that far back. I'd tried once, and couldn't even figure out the alphabet. I kept going. My initial guess, that it was the Vallista reigns that fascinated him, was disproved by the next section, which were all books set in the late Fifteenth Cycle, in the Jhegaala and

Athyra reigns—again, contemporary writers doing historical romances. A little more looking convinced me that he'd divided up his books according to the period where they were set; I couldn't find any other division.

The other side of the room had more novels of different periods, and, finally, the non-fiction, which consisted of about as many books as were in his study, and with similar titles; also that many again devoted to necromancy. As I was scanning them, one title jumped out at me. It was a thick but short volume bound in cheap, cracked leather. The faded gold lettering on the spine said *Bending Time and Space: Studies in the Halls of Judgment.*

Well. Yes, that was certainly interesting.

I pulled it out and studied it a bit before I opened it. It certainly showed signs of having been read; all the corners were frayed, and the gilding on the edges had been almost entirely worn off. I tried a trick Kiera had once shown me, of holding it in my left hand and seeing where it naturally fell open to determine if there were any parts that he had read repeatedly, but it fell open to the first flyleaf; maybe you needed a special touch.

Ever been working carefully to figure something out, and then in an instant had a big piece of the puzzle fall into place in the time it took to draw a breath? That's what happened when my eyes fell on a single sentence. It was written on the flyleaf in a fine, precise, artistic hand with an excellent quill, and it said, *To Tethia, with love on Kieron's Day, from Papa.*

"Son of a bitch," I muttered. Then I checked another half dozen books, and found Tethia's name in another. Then I checked a few more and found something even more conclusive: another name had been crossed out, and Tethia's had been written in. In this one, the handwriting was still precise but more artistic, with flourishes and long tails, an elegant use of the way the fountain pen can control the thickness of the line. No, I won't set up as a handwriting expert, but you pick up a little bit of everything in this business.

I looked around the library again, as if seeing it for the first time. And reconsidered the bedroom I'd just been in, and how bedroom, library, and nursery were all together, as if this particular part of the manor had been set aside for first a child, then, when the child grew, her further needs. I chuckled at myself: I'd become so used to nothing in the place making sense that I hadn't noticed when, just for a moment, something did.

It was Tethia's bedroom, and this had been Tethia's library.

Well, shave my eyebrows and call me a Discreet.

I kept the book in my hand while I went around the room again pulling books out and checking publication dates. I had to laboriously translate from different formats of pre-Interregnum dating systems, but after half an hour or so I was convinced: nothing in this library had been published after the Interregnum. Nearly all of the books were published late in the reign of Tortaalik, the last Emperor before the Interregnum.

There were four chairs scattered about just the way they should be: all of them looking comfortable, and none of them near enough to another for conversation. I took my treasure over to the nearest one and sat down. Rocza flapped furiously for a moment; I guess I'd sat down too abruptly.

"*Sorry,*" I told Loiosh.

I opened the book and started reading.

"*Boss?*"

"*Hmm?*"

"*How long?*"

"I'm just going to skim a bit, try to figure out who did what and how it worked."

"I know. I mean, how long until I should bite your ear as a gentle reminder that we're growing old. And hungry."

Rocza flapped her wings, which I took as agreement with the hungry part.

"Give me about an hour."

It didn't take an hour; in fact, it didn't take two minutes for me to get completely lost and to realize I understood nothing. Usually a book like this will have an introduction to explain the context and what the book hopes to teach, and these are often useful to those of us with no clue about the subject matter; but there wasn't one. It started right in with an account of "an attempt to use Delmi's Reclamation within the prescribed area" that resulted in "certain minor tremors detectable by water in glass" and "observable wavering of vision reminiscent of Pare's Focus when attempted beyond the recommended distance."

Well, now I knew that.

I skipped around in the book long enough to know that everything else made even less sense, and I was about to close it when my eye happened to catch the phrase "the Vestibule." This was, in case you've forgotten, the place Devera had spoken of, where she had gone to see Darkness.

I read the sentence it was in, then the sentences around it, then more sentences around it, and knew as I much I had before I started. But I wasn't prepared to call it coincidence just because I didn't understand it.

I closed the book and tapped it with my thumb for a few seconds.

I got up and walked around the perimeter of the library to

see if I could spot any breaks in the wall—libraries are obvious places for secret entrances because bookshelves are so good
at concealing them. If there were any, the bookshelves were
too good at concealing them. I sat down again and looked
at the book. I opened it again to the page with the reference
to the Vestibule, tried once again to make sense of it. If I
understood anything, it had to do with reasons not to visit
the Vestibule, and about being swallowed up, and I very, very
much hoped it would have nothing to do with my problem. I
swore and stood up. I put the book back where I'd found it,
because I am a good person, then I took a last look around the
library, and left.

10

WATERS BELOW THE GROUND

There was one more door to open before the hall ended; it was on the same side as the library.

I opened it and looked, and a fresh breeze hit me. Another thing that hit me was the realization that what I was looking at ought to be on the opposite side—that is, I should have been stepping out onto the cliff. And with that came the realization that the library ought to have extended far over the cliff.

I stepped through and was outdoors and Loiosh said, *"We're free! We've escaped!"*

"Uh-huh. *Notice how the ground is still wet from yesterday's rainstorm?*"

"No."

"Yeah."

"Oh."

"Yep. Maybe we can walk away and be somewhen, but I'll bet not. Most likely, if we keep walking we'll find ourselves back in the house."

"Going to test that?"

"Yes."

What I was seeing was just what I ought to have seen when I looked out the windows in those first rooms: the rough, rocky landscape that led to the cliffs, and what I'd seen from the roof: generally flat, not much growing except coarse grass and small shrubs. I looked for signs of Kieron Road but didn't see any, which proved nothing.

I set out walking away from the place, and after about twenty paces turned and looked at it. It wasn't gone, as I'd half expected it would be. I walked a little farther and turned again. Yes, it did appear the same as I remembered it, coming from the other direction. Speaking of directions, insofar as it made sense at all, the front entrance should be *that* way, to my right. I set off in that direction, looking for the road. The house, the manor, the "platform" was just to my right the whole time, and I kept looking at it. It annoyed me to admit that it was an awfully good-looking house, manor, "platform." It was graceful, with swooping curves, and there was a sort of purity to it. And the windows looked good, as they reflected—

I stopped and looked up.

"Boss? Why does the sky look like that?"

"Just what I was wondering."

It wasn't entirely different from the sky I usually saw when I looked up. I mean, it wasn't like I was looking at a different sky, but it seemed higher, if that makes sense, and there was some other color in there, muddying things up. The net effect was that the day seemed brighter, almost like it was out East—

I found where the Furnace was, and I could almost see it. Usually, you can feel it, but you can't *see* where it is behind the Enclouding. Now I could: right there, high above me, east and a little north.

"We've gone back to the Interregnum," I said. "I'd say pretty late in the Interregnum."

"Okay."

Rocza jumped around on my shoulder a little, nervous.

"Tell her to relax, Loiosh. We're getting used to this 'jumping around in time' thing, right? Pretty soon it'll be no big deal."

"Whatever you say, Boss."

I stared at the Furnace, hidden as it was behind the En-clouding, until I sneezed. That used to happen to me a lot when I was in the East. I stopped looking at it and watched the manor some more, but it didn't do anything.

Oh, well, it sort of did: someone passed in front of one of the windows. I couldn't identify features, but from the gait, I'd have guessed a soldier; perhaps a guard on duty. I kept watching, and someone else passed by the window, this one with hunched shoulders, perhaps a servant. Then the guard returned, or maybe there was another.

It was like the manor was occupied—like it was a place that had actual people, living their lives, instead of the manor I'd left, which, I realized, resembled nothing so much as the empty husk of what once had been or could someday be. I watched for another ten minutes to be sure, and yes, there were a lot more people in the place I was watching, and they were a lot busier than anyone in the place, or rather the time, I'd left.

I turned away from it and continued toward where the road should be, or would be someday.

The wind blew my cloak closed, which was nice of it; the day was a bit chilly.

I dodged a few boulders that seemed to grow at random

among the brush, and reached a rise. I could see the road, just
where it ought to be. I got a little closer, and there were people.

"*Loiosh.*"

"*On it, Boss.*"

He was back in a few minutes. "*An ox-cart carrying two
peasants and a load of supplies. Some boxes, some bushels of
produce.*"

"*Apples?*"

"*Not that I saw.*"

"*Anyone else?*"

"*There's a guard at the door. She looks bored.*"

"*And?*"

"*That's all.*"

Precipice Manor, it seemed, was a going concern after all:
guards where they were supposed to be, supplies delivered,
everything a normal manor house ought to have. Except for
the minor issue that the Verra-be-damned place didn't even
exist back at the time I was watching, everything was completely normal. No problem. Why should a little thing like that
bother me?

I kept walking. By the time I reached the road, the wagon
had rolled up to the doors, and the drivers were bowing and
scraping to the bored guard. I wondered where she'd direct
them, as I didn't think the cart could make it down to the cave,
and I didn't see a path going the other way, and they certainly
wouldn't take deliveries at the front door.

I wanted to keep walking around until I could get a view
of Kieron's Watch to see if it was there, because that would tell
me, I don't know, something. But I wasn't keen on running into
anyone, or being seen by a guard. I stood there for a bit, trying
to decide.

"We could explore, Boss."

"You just said that because you know I was going to say it anyway."

"Uh-huh. Anything special we're looking for?"

"If you find anything that tells us when we are, that'd be good. Other than that, no, just check things out."

He and Rocza took off from my shoulders again, Rocza flying northeast, Loiosh northwest. I turned in a slow circle, trying to pick out anything that didn't seem to belong. The wind blew. My hair whipped, my cloak billowed, and I felt like an idiot.

I watched Loiosh until with no warning he vanished. Just, poof. I felt the panic start to kick in, but before it had a chance to take hold I heard wings behind me and spun, and Loiosh was there.

"Boss! What happened?"

"How did you get there?"

"That's what I'm asking."

Okay, so, it was like the cave, maybe? Go a certain distance and it loops you back?

"Did you see anything interesting?"

"No. It all seems normal."

"Good. Or not good. I can't decide."

Rocza returned and landed on my other shoulder.

"I want to see what happens when I try it."

I'm pretty sure she and Loiosh had some sort of conversation, then Loiosh said, "Okay, Boss. That way."

I set off at an angle away from the road. After about five minutes it happened: I was back near the manor again, about forty yards from where I'd set off. I didn't feel anything when it happened, and there was no border or barrier that I could

see; just one step was *there* and the next was *here*. It was the
same as when I'd been climbing up from the cliff, and on
the roof, and in the hall by the barracks.

"*Got any guesses, Boss? This is kind of weird.*"

I struggled with the little I knew of necromancy, and finally
said, "I think so. *It's like the room. It affected me because it was
the nature of the room, not like a spell from outside.*"

"*Um,*" he added helpfully.

"*We aren't being transported from one place to another. The
world has been changed, so that's just how those paths go now.*"

"*How?*"

"*Some big, complicated necromancy? I don't know. And if it
turns out that those mirrors aren't part of it, I'll stop making fun
of Dragaeran cooking for a year.*"

"*I don't think you could.*"

"*Okay, a week.*"

"*Witnessed, Boss.*"

Just to be sure, I decided to try to reach the road again,
even though I knew what was going to happen. I wasn't wrong,
either. About thirty yards from the door, between one step and
another, I was elsewhere; this time, back in front of the door
I'd first stepped out of. Maybe I could set off in other directions
and see where I ended up, but what would that tell me? And I
was hungry, and even if the food was as mediocre as the last
meal, I still wanted it. And I wouldn't be finding it out here. I
put my hand on the doorknob, then stopped.

"*Boss?*"

"*If I can't figure out any of the big answers, I'll take a small
one.*"

"*Boss?*"

I turned my back to the door and set out perpendicular to the manor. I went at a good pace until I came to a fairly large, flat rock, then I climbed on top of it.

"*Champion of the Hill?*"

"Shut up."

I looked around, and spotted what I was looking for almost at once. I jumped down from the rock and walked another thirty paces or so, until I came to a neat double row of trees.

I smiled. Mystery solved.

"*Boss?*"

"Apple trees," I said.

"*So? Oh.*"

"Yeah. For now, I'll take solving a small mystery and call it a win."

"*How long do apple trees live, Boss?*"

"Do I look like a gardener?"

"*If you keep tromping around out here you will.*"

"Why?"

"*Boss, you were on the roof. Did you see an orchard?*"

"I might have missed it."

"*You think?*"

"Well, what else . . . oh."

"*Yeah.*"

"I didn't see an orchard because there wasn't one."

"*Yeah.*"

"It didn't exist yet."

"*Yeah.*"

"Wow, chum. Good thinking!"

"*Thanks, Boss.*"

"So this is the future. That's, yeah, okay. I think I'm going to be sick."

They both left my shoulders to give me some privacy or something, but I wasn't actually sick.

"Boss? What about the Enclouding?"

"Good question. Uh, well, if there isn't as much in the past, maybe there isn't as much in the future?"

"Why?"

"I don't know."

I turned around and retraced my steps to the door. This time, I didn't hesitate; I went back inside, finding myself once more in the same hall, near the library. Loiosh didn't say anything, but I had the feeling he was relieved.

I stepped back in and turned left.

"Food's the other way, Boss."

"We're almost at the end of the hall. And waiting will make it taste better."

"Is that the best you can do?"

"Aren't you interested in exploring this place?"

"Stay with the 'taste better' argument."

I continued down what was left of the hallway, until, after a few paces, it ended with a small door on the right-hand side. I turned back and tried to figure out if the library on the one side and the nursery on the other took up enough space for it to make sense. This was a waste of time for two reasons: because I'm not that good at judging distances, and because in this place the information wouldn't be useful anyway. After close inspection, I decided I couldn't tell, and opened the door. Or, rather, I tried it. It was locked.

"Oh ho," I said.

"Boss, did you just say 'oh ho'?"

"It's like ah ha, but not as exciting."

I knelt down and studied the lock. It looked to be a bit tougher than the one in the study had been, but I felt like I could probably get it if I were Kiera, or even being me if I was willing to take the time.

I considered the matter, and as I did, I studied the blank wall where the hallway ended. There was a picture there, an oil, not a psiprint. It was a study of a very tall, shiny building in a city I'd never seen: the Silver Exchange, at a guess.

"You know, Loiosh, if I were a secret passage, I'd be right there."

"Not in the library?"

"I'd be there, too. I'd get around a lot."

I studied the edges of the wall first and didn't see anything. Then I peeked behind the painting. The hook in the wall looked sturdy, and seemed to be built in. I played with it a little, and it turned to the side and there came a "click." I pushed, and the wall swung back like a door.

"Triumph!"

"Yeah, Boss. You're so smart I almost can't stand it."

"Shut up."

I was pretty sure the door would be behind me when I closed it. The question was whether I'd be able to open it. I checked, and found a lever, a straightforward mechanism, right where it should be. I also made sure there was light, and there was: faint squares, set in the ceiling, emitting pale bluish light. The passage was much narrower than the hallway had been; it felt like a secret passage ought to feel. I let the door swing closed, and pulled it until it clicked.

As predicted, it was still behind me. Was I starting to get a feel for this place? Yeah. Was I going to regret it if I started getting cocky about it? Yeah.

"*No mirrors, Boss.*"

I looked around. Well. Okay. Then that should mean I could just walk without ending up somewhere odd, right? Right? Well, let's find out.

There were no doors or breaks of any kind for some distance. Then, just before the passage made a right turn, there was a door. It was locked, and looked to be the same kind of lock as the last, only the lighting here wasn't as good so I couldn't be sure. I kept going. It went a long way, then, eventually making another turn to the right, with yet another door before it. Again, on the right, and again, locked. And another long walk, another right turn, another door. There was something simultaneously reassuring and disturbing about the place suddenly being predictable. I told myself it wouldn't last and continued, but it didn't turn again.

In the end, it was three sides of a square, or maybe a rectangle, with four identical doors with identical locks. The end of the little passageway had a simple latching mechanism just like the inside of the first one had. Obviously, if I pulled it and walked through, I'd be at the end of a corridor with the wall concealed by a picture, right?

I pulled the mechanism and stepped through, and to my astonishment that's exactly where I was, except that instead of a picture on the wall it was a small shelf with a selection of wines, liquors, and glassware on it. I was back in the ballroom.

I ducked back into the passage before the wall could close because I didn't want to have to figure out how to open this one. I pulled it closed and turned my attention to the lock.

Like the last one, it didn't seem to be beyond my abilities.
I dug out my set. It turned out to be easier than the one on
the study door had been. About half a minute later I put the
picks away in an inner pocket of my cloak and opened the door.

It was a courtyard. An inner courtyard, not huge, but it
certainly shouldn't fit where it was. By now I was used to that.
The breeze that came through was cool and smelled like re-
cent rain, even with the sickening musky smell that means the
worms have come up for air. Fine, then.

The courtyard was diamond-shaped, with flagstones connecting the corners. Stunted trees surrounded by ferns grew
in boxes in the quadrants. In the middle was—

I frowned.

Was that . . . ?

I approached it slowly, as if it were some species of animal
with a lot of teeth and uncertain intentions. Was it what it
looked like? Yes, it was. It was a fountain, and, as far as I could
tell, it was an exact duplicate of the one in the Halls of Judgment that had given me such entertaining memories.

I didn't want to suddenly lose myself in memories of the
past, however interesting they might be, but I did want to know
just how much this fountain was like the other. Was it actually the same fountain, appearing in two places at once through
some sort of necromantic prestidigitation, or was it just built
to look like it? Why, what, how, and all of that.

I needed to know. I took a breath and faced the fountain,
watching the droplets, following individual streams, and—

Nothing. I was a little disappointed, but mostly relieved.

Well, since nothing bad was going to happen if I studied
it, I studied it. As I said before, I like looking at fountains.
Did I mention I've always wanted one? Yeah, I think I did. I

wished I understood the mechanism more. I'd thought fountains were always sorcerous, but Kragar, who like me picked
up odd bits of knowledge, had explained that the usual methods had something to do with the weight of the water forcing
it up when stored in a reservoir somewhere, or else they built
the fountain on top of an underground spring—

Wait.

An underground spring.

Dark Water. Water that had never seen the light of day.
That metal rod I'd picked up, that's why it was familiar: a rod
filled with Dark Water was used to control the undead, which,
of course, was a branch of—

Necromancy.

Okay, then.

How the fountain and the water and the mirrors and necromancy all connected with this place, I had no idea; but there
was certainly a connection, and that was a lot more than I'd
had an hour ago. I took a slow walk around the fountain, looking at the base. Obviously, the water I was looking at didn't
qualify as never having seen the light of day; but what if there
was a spring beneath it?

"What are you looking for, Boss?"

"Really? Nothing. I'm mostly just thinking."

"That would explain the—"

"Shut up."

I stopped and closed my eyes and tried to reconstruct the
entire path I'd gone through, to hold it in my head. It made no
sense when seen as a building, so I tried to figure out if it somehow made sense as a series of connections—that is, if the flow
of room to room made sense. No, it was even worse that way.

It made no sense as a building, it made no sense as a set of randomly connected points.

It was a platform, of course. No doubt that would make perfect sense of everything, if only I understood what it meant.

There were benches around the fountain, just like in the Halls. I sat down on one and leaned forward, resting my elbows on my knees. Loiosh and Rocza shifted; Rocza hissed.

Okay, think of it as a platform. Imagine everywhere I'd been like an unrolled parchment. Maybe it crossed through time, or worlds, or some other crap I didn't understand. Even so, imagine it like that. I hadn't been in every room. But I'd seen what I needed to. This spot, here, was the middle. I could feel it. This was the middle, and that spot at the end of the cave was one end, and the other was—right. The front door, of course. The mysteriously locked front door.

It was all closed, that was the thing. From the now, to the past, to the Halls of Judgment, I had never left the "platform." There was no way out. But if that was true, how had I ever gotten into the Verra-be-damned place?

That was easy: Devera. That's why Zhayin had been so surprised to see me: he had thought no one could enter. And then, when I could enter, he couldn't figure out why I couldn't leave the same way.

Why had Devera been able to lead me through the door, but was unable to get herself out again? That was the key to the whole thing. And whatever the answer was, it had something to do with time, and the Halls of Judgment, and the nature of this strange manor. If I could go into the past, before the manor was built, I'd probably be able to learn something, but that was imposs—

Wait, was it?

Maybe I was looking at this wrong. Maybe it wasn't about deciding where to *build* it, but deciding where to *put* it. What if Zhayin—no, Tethia, or maybe both of them—had built it wherever they happened to be when they started construction? Like, you couldn't start something from scratch and already be living in it, so maybe you build it right near where you're living at the time? If that was true, there was still a connection to the *then* of having built the place, along with the *where* of its construction.

Housetown. Someone—Zhayin? one of the servants?—had mentioned a place called Housetown.

Well, good. All I needed was to find out where Housetown was. Then I'd leave the manor, get over to Housetown, see what I could learn. Maybe I'd discover what I needed to know in order to be able to leave the manor.

What was it that Tethia had said? *When I designed this platform . . .*

There had to be a way from here to there; from this "platform," to where—and when—it was made. Another anchor. I looked around. A courtyard with a fountain that exactly matched one in the Halls of Judgment: good place for a mystical, necromantic anchor, don't you think? I looked carefully around the area, looking for something that could be a door to elsewhere, or elsewhen. Nothing. I went back in my mind over all the rooms I'd been in, to try to figure out where it was likely to be. The room of mirrors? The room of light? A false back to the cave?

I was so sure it would be here, though—in this courtyard. The correspondence just felt right. This had to be one of the transition points. The front door, the gateway to the Halls, and here. But how—

If Rocza had been upset when I sat down, she was furious when I stood up, or, rather, when I suddenly found myself on my feet, staring at the fountain.

Sometimes the answer is right in front of you. Dark Water. If it had been a jhereg, it would've bit me.

I jumped up onto the rim of the fountain, then down into the main basin, which looked all of eight inches deep. I fell a lot more than eight inches; more like three feet, and only my highly trained, cat-like reflexes kept me from twisting an ankle. Or luck, whichever. Three feet of water, yet I was only wet to just above my ankles.

I was out in the open. That's the first thing you always pick up on, you know. Even before you're aware of any particular features, like trees, or furniture, you know if you're inside or outside. That's why teleporting into caverns is so disorienting, although on that occasion I was too busy bleeding and coughing and passing out to fully experience the disorientation. But this time, I was outdoors. It was a little warm and very humid. There were a lot of tall but spindly trees towering over me, tall grasses in spots alternating with mossy stones. There were rolling hills about me, and the sky looked like it had before: some Enclouding, but not as much as in my day.

I'd come through, and gotten to where I thought I was going to go, and nothing was about to kill me. Loiosh and Rocza landed on my shoulders, and Loiosh was too amazed to tell me how stupid that had been.

I found a few rocks and sticks and stacked them up in case I needed to, you know, get back or something. When I was certain I remembered exactly which rock was in front of me, which tree to my left, and which blotchy stone I was standing on, I took a step forward.

The ground rose to my right, so I went that way, and in a few steps I saw the top of a building popping up over the trees. It was sprawling, not very tall, and if it had ever been walled, the wall had gone. It didn't look like it had been built with defense in mind. If this was what they'd been calling a castle, they had a pretty loose definition of the term.

I moved closer, taking my time, trying to commit my position to memory with each step in case the manor snapped me back. Whenever I was, the "castle" was active: there was a bored-looking guard at a door, an equally bored-looking guard walking from the back toward the front, and two more strolling around on the roof pretending to be observant. I got as close as I could without stepping into the open. I wasn't interested in a confrontation.

I studied it. I couldn't guess how old it was, but in any case the stones were dirty and somewhat worn.

"*Boss? I'm getting nervous.*"

"*Me too,*" I said, noticing my finger tapping on Lady Teldra's hilt. "*Think we're being watched?*"

"*Maybe. Should we check?*"

"*Yeah.*"

They flew off toward the castle, staying high and swinging wide to cover as much distance as possible. Jhereg have very good eyes; it is hard for something to stay hidden from them even in dense brush, or under a canopy of trees.

"*You are being watched, Boss. Two of them, just up the slope behind trees.*"

Loiosh flew in tight circles, indicating where they were; Rocza returned to my shoulder.

"Are they watching casually, or actively trying to be stealthy?"

"More just casually watching."

"Okay."

Hmm. How to play this? If I walked up and confronted them, would they attack? Would they try to take me to the castle? If they did, would I just get snapped back again? And why were they watching me? Just because I was a stranger, or had I done something to attract their interest? I wasn't in the mood to fight anyone.

I shrugged and made my way toward Loiosh.

They came out to meet me. The shorter one opened the conversation with great courtesy: "Who are you, and what are you doing skulking around here?" she said. Her speech was clipped, and the vowels sounded like they'd been turned on their side. The other one kept glancing at Rocza.

My name is Szurke, and I will someday hold an Imperial title so you have to be polite out of fear of a future Empress probably wouldn't have worked well. I said, "My name is Taltos, and I'm afraid I'm lost."

"Lost," repeated the other, though it sounded like *lahst.* She took her eyes from Rocza and raked me up and down with them like she was brushing lies off my jerkin, then turned to the first and said, "He says he's lost, sergeant."

"I heard," said the first. Something in her tone gave me the crazy idea that she didn't believe me. She—the sergeant—said, "Who are you working for?"

"No one," I said. "I'm available for hire. What do you need done?"

Her eyes narrowed. "Please hand me your weapons and come with me."

"No, and yes," I said.

It took her a second to work that out. Then she said, "I must insist."

"That would be a tactical error." I started tapping Lady Teldra's hilt with my finger and waited. Loiosh returned to my shoulder, looked at her, and hissed. "You *are* outnumbered, you know," I said, and waited to see what they'd do.

11

Gormin's Guest

They hesitated. I'd put them in a tough position, what with there being only two of them; but being Dragonlords in spite of the Vallista colors, they weren't about to back down to an Easterner. I didn't actually want things to get bloody. It had been a while since I'd drawn blood at all, and I didn't miss it. (Giving that idiot game warden a bloody nose doesn't count; if he'd been willing to drop his club he could have caught himself before he hit the table, right?) In the past I'd have happily handed over my rapier and knife, counting on my extras to take care of things if there were problems; but in the past I hadn't had Lady Teldra. No way was I putting her into someone else's hands.

As far as Sarge and friend were concerned, the choices were between drawing steel and calling for reinforcements. I needed to give them another option, and I had to do it so they didn't feel they were being mocked by an Easterner. I studied the sergeant's eyes, and saw the little flicker as she made up her mind to draw.

"Look," I said. "There's no need for this. I'll come with you if you want, and I'm not about to attack anyone. I just don't feel inclined to disarm myself."

"If you don't plan on attacking anyone, why not?"

"If I did, how much chance would I have against not only you two, but however many more of you there are inside? If you really want to arrest me, go ahead and try. But if you just want to talk to me, then let's all go inside together, like civilized folk, and we'll have a conversation."

It wasn't working. I spared a few precious instants to have silent evil thoughts about Dragonlords and all of their offspring from the beginning of the Empire to the end of the world. It didn't take long; I keep a few of those thoughts around to be used as needed.

"Look," I said. "I wasn't sneaking, I wasn't hiding. I'm lost, and I was heading to the castle there, or whatever it is, to beg help. Do you really need to disarm me just to point to a way out and ask a few questions? I'll answer anything you want to know, I just hate having my weapons taken away. You're Dragonlords; surely you can understand that?"

The key was that I used the word "beg." That word put me beneath them. I wasn't challenging them, I was a conquered foe asking for decent treatment, which made it a matter of mercy, not honor. Dragonlords love showing mercy because it makes them feel powerful. Convincing Dragonlords to show you mercy is the best way to not have to kill them.

She hesitated a moment longer, then relaxed and nodded. "Trev, get behind him. And watch your distance; he looks fast, and those creatures look faster." She wasn't stupid, that one. But as I had no intention of attacking them, it didn't much matter. We walked up the hill toward the castle with Loiosh keeping his eye on the Dragonlord following me. I was still expecting whatever strange magic had brought me here to snap me back, the way it had before; but no, the thing fooled me again: we made it right up to the castle.

We entered through a doorway that stuck out from the side of the castle like it had been grafted on. The sergeant preceded me in, then led me down a narrow hallway that looked nothing at all like anything in the manor: it was lit by hanging lamps that smelled of darr fat, and paved with dark gray stones. The walls were standard brick, but the mortar seemed yellow in the lamplight. I hoped I wasn't being led to a cell. I didn't doubt my ability to break out, but after I did I'd have to escape, which wouldn't help Devera a bit.

The sergeant brought me to a room I recognized at once as an officer's quarters, complete with desk and two chairs. She gestured for me to sit in one, and said, "Trev, find me some support, and inform the lieutenant." Trev left, and the sergeant leaned against the wall, arms folded. I turned the chair so I wouldn't have my back to her. Her hair was cut short under her cap, and the sleeves had been cut off of her tunic the way some Dragonlords do to permit more arm movement. She carried a shortsword on either side, and I decided I'd just as soon not fight her if I could avoid it.

"I gave you my name," I said. "What's yours?"

"Sir will do," she said.

"Now, here I thought we were going to have a civilized conversation."

"You were wrong."

So much for conversational gambits.

A few minutes later, three guards entered; the sergeant sent them into different corners of the room without saying a word. One of them, a scrawny guy with a pronounced nose and no chin at all, seemed awfully curious about me from the way he kept staring, but I guess he was too much a soldier to open his mouth without permission. That's one reason I'm not a soldier.

I whistled a tune I'd picked up somewhere on the road and they all pretended not to be annoyed.

Eventually Trev returned with the lieutenant: I had no doubt she was an officer even before I saw the gold braid around her sleeve and polish on her boots. She had a way of walking into a room as if she expected everyone to salute. And they all did, too. I didn't, but I might have if I hadn't forgotten how to hold my hand and if I didn't mind smacking myself in the chest.

The lieutenant sat down behind the desk and said, "Stand easy," and everyone unstiffened. "Sergeant?"

"Found him skulking around and watching the castle, sir."

She nodded and looked at me. Meanwhile, I'd turned my chair to face the desk. I pushed it onto its back legs, let it return, and said, "Skulking?"

She ignored me. "Who do you work for?"

"I'm not working for anyone," I said. "Did you want to hire me?"

Her brows came together and she tried the Hard Stare. What with one thing and another, the Hard Stare doesn't so much work on me. I smiled and waited.

"You're spying for Klaver?"

"Who's Klaver?"

She glanced at the sergeant. "Why wasn't he disarmed?"

"My call, lieutenant. There didn't seem to be a need. He came along quietly enough."

The lieutenant nodded. She looked at me as if considering whether to disarm me now. If she tried, things would get interesting really fast. No doubt they thought there were enough of them to disarm me, but they were wrong. They could, perhaps, kill me, but they couldn't disarm me. I hoped they wouldn't try.

For a minute it seemed like she was about to give the order, and I did my very best to be ready for action without looking like I was ready for action. The time stretched, and then it reached that indefinable but unmistakable point where the time for action is past. She shrugged and said, "All right. Tell me this: If you aren't working for Klaver, why are you here?"

"I was taking a walk. It's a nice day for a walk."

"Where are you from?"

"Adrilankha. It's a coastal city—"

"I know where Adrilankha is. It is two thousand miles from here. Are you saying you walked all the way?"

"There have been many nice days for a walk."

The guy who'd been staring at me said, "Sir."

The lieutenant glanced at him and nodded. He cleared his throat and said, "I've visited kin in Adrilankha. The accent is right."

Accent? I don't have an accent. They had accents.

The lieutenant nodded and said, "Any other observations?"

"His cloak. I've seen Jhereg wear cloaks like that."

She turned to me. "Are you a Jhereg? Are they letting Easterners into the Jhereg now?"

"I used to be." This was sort of true, and if I'd said, *I'm going to be* it would have required too much explanation; *I'm going to have used to be* was, well, no.

"Used to be?"

"The Jhereg and I had a disagreement. That's why I decided to take a walk."

"What sort of disagreement?"

"Over how much information on Jhereg activities the Empire ought to have."

She studied me, I guess deciding whether she believed me, and whether it was worth the effort it would take to find out the truth. I studied her back. I wasn't lying all *that* much.

She said, "Will you give me your word not to try to escape?"

Unspoken was, *if not, I'm going to take your weapons away and keep you here by force.* I said, "I will. For sixty hours. That's assuming you don't do anything unpleasant to me. I react badly sometimes. But yes, if I'm not harmed, sixty hours."

The sergeant coughed significantly. We both looked at her, and the lieutenant said, "Go on."

"Sir," she said. "He's an Easterner. And he's a Jhereg."

"Yes," said the lieutenant. "And I've chosen to take him at his word."

"Yes, sir."

"Sixty hours," she said to me. "Agreed. You'll be free within certain limits; I'll have one of the servants show you those limits. Meanwhile, I'll speak to my lord about what to do with you. He abhors violence, and would himself be inclined to simply let you go, which is why it falls on me to protect his interests."

"His interests, my lady? What interests are those?"

"Perhaps you truly don't know," she said. She shrugged. "In any case, I won't be answering your questions. You'll be answering mine."

"That's not a conversation," I explained patiently. "That's an interrogation. If you interrogate me, I might become annoyed and decide not to say anything. If we have a conversation, why, then, I'll happily participate."

She took it well; I got the impression it amused her, I guess because she laughed and said, "Are all Easterners this funny?"

"Only the Jhereg ones."

"I'll tell you what, Easterner Jhereg: Just to show how friendly I am, I'll tell you this much: He is working on certain discoveries that others would like to take credit for, if possible, or to at least learn of the state of his research."

"Could you be a little more vague?"

"Does it matter?"

"I'm curious."

"For someone claiming not to be a spy, you're very inquisitive."

I shrugged. "Maybe a spy would pretend not to be? I don't know."

"Neither do I. But I'll find out."

"Oh, good. While you're finding out, what are these interests of his? No, don't tell me. He's trying to solve the age-old problem of creating a place that exists across different worlds."

I watched her closely and saw it hit. "You are not," she said, "doing a very good job of convincing me you're not a spy."

"Sorry," I said. "I'll try to do better."

"Wait here."

She collected her people with looks and led them out of the room, leaving the door open. I turned the chair again. If it was a test to see if I'd try to escape, I passed, but that's because I had no interest in leaving. If it was a test to see if I'd refrain from looking through the desk drawers, I failed.

"*Keep a watch, Loiosh.*"

"*On it, Boss.*"

I got up, went around to the front, and checked for obvious

traps on the desk drawers. I didn't see any, nor any locks. I opened the one on the upper right and had just enough time to see a stack of identical papers labeled "Requisition" when Loiosh said, "*Someone's coming.*"

I returned to the chair just as Gormin walked into the room. I managed to cover my reaction by stretching and coughing, then stood up and gave him a head bob.

It seemed strange that he didn't seem to recognize me. Yes, I understand he couldn't, that to him we hadn't met; but it still seemed strange. I said, "How do you do, I am Vlad of Szurke. Szurke is an Eastern County under the seal of the Empire." I dug out my ring and showed it to him, and his eyes widened appropriately, and he bowed. My thinking was that the better terms I was on with this guy, the more information I could get about the place.

"Sir," he said. "If you wish to accompany me, I will show you where you may take your ease."

"*Will there be food?*"

"*Shut—actually, yeah, good question.*"

"Will there be food?"

"Of course, sir. I'll bring you something as soon as you're settled."

"*I might live after all.*"

I followed him out into the corridor. "I am instructed," he said, "to let you know that you are free to visit any room along this hallway, save the lieutenant's office when she's not there. This is the library, where you may find something to divert you. This will be your bedchamber, should you be with us overnight."

"How very civilized," I said. He didn't know how to take that, so he didn't respond.

He showed me into a small withdrawing room, complete with chairs and tables. "If you care to wait, I will bring refreshment."

"Tell him to hurry."

"No."

There wasn't much to see in this room, so I concentrated all of my attention on how hungry I was. After about twenty minutes and a thousand years, Gormin returned with a tray balanced on one hand and a napkin wrapped around his other arm, with a wine bottle in the free hand. I started salivating.

He set the tray on the table with almost the flourish of a Valabar's waiter. "Rice and vegetable soup," he said. "Sliced kethna in cream sauce. Cherry tubers covered in corn meal and roasted, and a poppy-seed roll."

"Thanks," I said.

He didn't show me the bottle, but he did announce it as a '31 Khaav'n, and poured it.

It was the same sort I'd found in the cellar at the manor; for all I knew, it was out of the same cask.

Gormin bowed and left. Loiosh, Rocza, and I attacked the food without ceremony. It takes real skill to time peas in soup so they are at the point of maximum sogginess but haven't yet fallen apart, and drying out kethna that much isn't as easy as you'd think. I devoured everything, and even sopped up the too-sweet soup with the flavorless bread. It was wonderful. While Loiosh and Rocza licked the crumbs off the plate, I enjoyed the wine. Now that I could concentrate on it properly, it was good, one of those red wines that are almost purple and that experts describe as "full-bodied"—as opposed to, I don't know, skinny wines. Anyway, I liked it, and had another glass, and then Gormin returned.

"Have a chair," I said.

"Sir," he replied with a bow and remained standing.

"Okay, then," I said. "What now?"

"Sir?"

"Am I going to be interrogated again?"

"I wouldn't know, sir."

Loiosh stumbled on my shoulder, then caught himself.

"Loiosh? Are you all right?"

Rocza stumbled.

I looked at Gormin. "You son of a bitch," I said, and let a dagger fall into my hand, which then continued unceremoniously onto the floor, where it stuck. *Nice point on that one*, I thought.

He took a step back and the light from the candles on the mantelpiece got in my eyes expanded turned thin and became strips turning back on themselves brush of cloth over my face a soft breeze makes the hiss of wet charcoal as the lines go sideways now and maybe I can control them make them slow slow a voice a yell steel screeches a piercing sound that turns blue in the bitter taste of coffee that's too old and too strong and too busy to sort things out make the lines change wider or thinner still nothing voices all blending maybe if it would just go dark yes yes dark working quiet want quiet voices fading *no!* Verra leave me alone alone just me not just me why is my heart pounding head pounding are my eyes even open foul stench of jhereg shit Loiosh! *"Loiosh!"* *"We're okay."* "What . . ." What was I saying thinking doing seeing no it was okay Loiosh was fine something there focus concentrate concentrate focus focus focus.

There were four of them. Three of them. Four of them. It was hard to tell with the room spinning so hard. I tried again to pull a dagger and succeeded in holding on to it, held it out in front of me as menacingly as I could manage. I tried to say something threatening, but realized that the only thing coming out of my mouth was saliva.

Two of them. There were two, and they were both standing there, armed, but hadn't attacked me yet. Why? My head was a little less fuzzy, but my eyes and hands didn't want to do what they were told. No, there *were* three of them, but one was the officer, standing in back, waiting.

She said, "Can you take him?" but she'd said it seconds ago, and it was only now penetrating my brain. I felt myself getting dizzier and thought I was going to pass out, and somewhere in there realized I was still in the chair.

I dropped the dagger—this time on purpose—and drew Lady Teldra. I felt an odd jolt travel up my arm to my head and then it seemed like there was a sparkly, bright blanket being thrown over me and—

Loiosh was nuzzling my ear.

"*Boss?*"

"*Are you okay?*"

"*We're fine. It made us woozy for a bit. And incontinent. And they had to clean it up.*"

I opened my eyes. I was in the same room, the same chair, but the dishes and the wine bottle had been taken away.

"*How long was I out?*"

"*A few hours.*"

"*What did they do?*"

"*Nothing.*"

"*Nothing?*"

"*Boss, your hand?*"

I looked at it, blinked, and then started to re-sheathe Lady

Teldra, then stopped because holding her made me feel better. "*What—*"

"*They wanted to question you.*"

"Oh. *How did that work out for them?*"

"*They eventually decided to just let you sleep.*"

I felt stiff and uncomfortable, like I'd fallen asleep in a chair, maybe because I had. Also, my head felt like it wasn't fully connected to my body. After a few more minutes, I went ahead and sheathed Lady Teldra, and it took work; my hand was shaking. I wanted to get up and escape, but I was in no shape to walk, much less fight if—

"*Anyone guarding the door?*"

"*I've heard some shuffling and throat clearing. It sounds like there are two of them.*"

I closed my eyes and tried taking a few deep breaths to see if that would clear my head. I woke up sometime later after a confused dream in which it was very important to light some charcoal on fire and it was raining.

"*Loiosh?*"

"*A couple of hours. There was a guard change outside the door. Definitely two of them.*"

I tried standing up, keeping a grip on the chair. My knees were a bit wobbly, but they held me, so I tried a few steps. Not bad. I went back and forth a few more times, and started feeling like, if there came an argument, I would have at least as good a chance of hurting the other guy as myself.

I quickly ran through the list of poisons I knew about. I didn't know all of them, but I knew many; had even used one once. I don't care for poison: people react to it too differently for it to be reliable, and it's much too easy to accidentally poison the wrong target. To the left, however, it has the advantage that you can be leagues away at the time of death. So, let me see: joflower requires much stronger-tasting food to hide it in. So do cyanide and sandsnail venom. Buttonweed was possible, except I'd still be waiting for it to work. I tested my tongue to see if there was any aftertaste. There wasn't, so that eliminated a few others. Hmmm. Strange.

"Maybe they weren't trying to kill you?"

"Then—oh. Yeah. Good point."

There were things I'd heard of, though never used, that could supposedly make someone drowsy and pliable and willing to answer questions. I should have thought of that right away, and probably would have if whatever was used on me hadn't fogged up my head. Still, a gutsy move to try it on an Easterner; they can't have known if or how well it would work on me. There must be something they wanted to know very badly. Well, okay, there were things I wanted to know very badly as well.

"You two sure you're all right?"

"We're fine, Boss."

"Okay. This might be boring, but it might not be."

His only answer was to squeeze my shoulder.

I checked that my rapier was loose, tapped Lady Teldra's hilt, and opened the door.

Yes, there were two of them, just across the hall, facing the door. I recognized them from earlier: one was the guy who'd been eyeing me curiously, the other was Trev, who said, "My lord, if you would care to wait, I'll fetch someone."

"And if I don't?"

"Then you're welcome to leave. We have no orders to stop you."

"Maybe I want to explore."

Her eyes darted to Lady Teldra, but it was only a flick, then she said. "If you go beyond the limits, I'll stop you."

"Think so?"

"Yes."

The guy was playing the "solid, silent partner ready to assist" bit, right down to the set of his jaw and the puffed-up chest. It was obvious that they'd both been in the room when Lady Teldra was out, and they'd both wear Purple Robes before they'd let me see how terrified they were.

"Okay," I said. "I'll wait."

I went back into the room, moved the chair so it was facing the open door, and sat down. The guy went off to get someone while Trev waited. I was bored and, yeah, I admit it, a little nervous for about ten minutes, then I heard the gentle tromp-tromp-tromp of many people in heavy boots. Either things were about to get interesting, or things were about to get interesting.

I stood up as Gormin appeared in the door—I confess, he wasn't who I expected. I saw the lieutenant over his shoulder, and there were a few others. Gormin turned, nodded to the lieutenant, then came in and closed the door. I sat down again and said, "Have a seat."

"Sir," he said, and remained standing.

I crossed my legs. "Why do you call me sir?"

"Sir?"

"Why 'sir' and not 'my lord' or something?"

"Sir? I don't—"

"There's obviously a subtle difference. I was called 'my lord' by someone else. Yet another said, 'm'lord' like it was all one word. Why? What does it mean?"

"I hardly know how—" He stopped and looked puzzled. It was like I'd asked him how he managed to move his arm.

"Okay," I said. "Skip that. Why are you dressed as a Teckla?"

He stared at me.

"Oh, come on," I said. "You think I can't tell an Issola when one is being polite to me?"

"I am," he said slowly and distinctly, "of the House of the Teckla, sir."

"But you weren't born into it."

"Sir, may I request we speak of other things?"

I shrugged. "Suit yourself. Who is Klaver?"

I suppose it was a cruel game I played with him, but he'd tried to drug me, so I wasn't overwhelmed with sympathy. He was by this time so confused he said, "A Vallista, sir. A rival of Lord Zhayin's, who is determined to learn Zhayin's secrets."

"But Zhayin hasn't solved his problem yet, so how can he?"

"Sir—"

"Well?"

"I don't know. I imagine he can't."

"Then it would be stupid to think I'm working for him, wouldn't it?"

"I don't—I suppose."

"Am I going to meet Zhayin?"

"I don't think so, sir. He's very—"

"What of his wife?"

Sweat appeared on his forehead. "His wife, sir?"

"Yes. Perhaps I could meet the Lady Zhayin?"

"She—I—sir."

"Yes?"

"She is no longer with us."

"I'm sorry to hear that. What happened?"

"There was an accident."

"Involving Tethia?"

One way I'd known he was an Issola was the way he stood: like someone had shoved a stick up his ass but he'd learned to relax that way. Suddenly the relaxation was gone, and he was standing even straighter. "How do you know of her?" he said, his voice a hoarse whisper.

I shrugged. "You know. Word gets around."

"Sir—"

"What sort of accident was it?"

"I could hardly say, sir."

He was recovering.

"Where did it happen?"

He stiffened again. "Why would you ask that, sir?"

"Just curious. The bedroom? The bath? Out riding?"

"I really shouldn't say."

"The Halls of Judgment?"

He started coughing.

"Careful, mate. Don't hurt yourself. Want some water? Maybe some wine? I can leave the drugs out of it if you'd like."

He turned and left, looking like he was about to get sick. I guess Issola, or Issola-turned-Teckla, don't like to do that in front of people. And actually, I'd lied to him: I didn't have any wine to offer.

"Boss? How did you know she died in the Halls of Judgment?"

"I didn't. It was a guess. Sort of. But if I ask about Tethia, and I'm answered about the death of her mother, then time is doing something weird. So, where does time get weird?"

"Okay. But I don't see how that makes sense of things."

"It doesn't. It makes even less sense now."

"*Oh. Good. As long as we're making progress.*"

I considered whether to wait for Gormin, or maybe someone else, or whether I should just set out and explore, or maybe
just leave. I mean, the whole "sixty hours" thing went under
the hill when they drugged me, right? I didn't know what to
explore for anyway, and if I did set out, things would likely get
bloody. How weird would it be if I killed Gormin, whom I'd
met, I don't know, some few hundreds of years in the future? I
hadn't even thought about that until now, and I *had* actually
thought about killing him when I realized what he'd pulled on
me. Now, though—yeah, maybe just leaving was the right
move. What happens when you make something impossible
happen? Is that how you make a path through time? I shook
my head. That didn't seem likely, but neither did I have enough
information to make a good guess about how likely or unlikely
something was.

I stood up and walked out the door, nodded to the two
guards. They nodded back, looking wary but determinedly not
frightened. As I was making up my mind what to do, three
Teckla in Vallista livery, none of whom I recognized, walked in
front of me holding covered trays. I smelled strong spices and
something that reminded me of watermelon. They continued
down the hall, unlocking a door just before the lieutenant's
office, going through it. I heard it lock behind them.

"What's through there?" I asked.

"Couldn't say," said Trev.

"Mind if I look?"

"I'm afraid that's not permitted."

I thought about making an issue of it. At a guess, Zhayin
and perhaps Discaru and maybe a few others were in a dining
room that way. But I wasn't sure what I could learn from them

now that I couldn't learn just as well later. And I was getting a little tired of wandering aimlessly around hallways.

"Maybe you should escort me out and I'll be on my way," I said.

"We'll be happy to," said Trev, which I was pretty sure was just honesty.

She took the lead, the guy followed me. "Watch your distance," said Trev.

I was shown out the door, feeling like I'd missed a chance to learn some important things, but not sure what I should have done differently. I wished I could have explored the place a little more. I looked around, noting what I could about the area and the castle. Even the outside might have told me something.

It still might.

"*Loiosh?*"

"*Yes!*"

"*Then . . . now.*"

I let a dagger fall into my hand and reversed it. There was flapping and cursing behind me. Trev was already drawing when she turned, and took a backward step; but I was moving by that point. I closed the distance and caught her on the chin with the pommel. I turned to see Loiosh and Rocza in the other guy's face, biting at him, flapping their wings, staying out of the way of his flailing steel. They were both pretty good at this game by now.

"Drop your weapon," I said. "Or die. I'm good either way."

He called me a bad name, still swinging his weapon.

"*Back off, give him a chance to surrender if he wants to.*"

They returned to my shoulder. At the same time, I dropped the dagger and drew my rapier, then advanced so that by the time he faced me I was already inside his guard. He froze, I froze, and he called me another bad name.

He dropped his sword.

"Kneel, hands behind your back."

I sheathed my rapier and picked up the dagger I'd dropped, reversed it.

Okay, let's stop and talk about knockout points for a minute. Years ago, Cawti and I saw *The Falling Damps* at Axon House. We had excellent seats (five rows back, just off center) thanks to Morrolan, and we had a wonderful time. We especially loved the banter and the fights (when Highrunner picks up Rakkos and throws him into the Baron's men, I cheered like everyone else). But on the fourth day there was a sequence where Atasu, in sneaking into Valguard, knocks out three guards with three perfect shots to the head and then knows exactly when they'll wake up. Mostly what this did was provide a lot of conversation between Cawti and me that night, because she didn't buy it either. Yes, you can knock out a Dragaeran (or, presumably, a human) with one good, hard smack, especially on the chin (Cawti explained it in terms of smashing the brain against the skull, which sounds sort of reasonable). There are other knockout points as well. But the thing is, none of them are reliable or predictable. Sure, if I hit a guy perfectly, I can be pretty sure he'll be out— for five seconds, or maybe ten minutes, or maybe a day, or maybe forever. And I said *pretty* sure, not absolutely sure.

Point is, if you'd rather knock someone out than kill him, that's fine, but don't bet your life on getting him in one shot, and don't make predictions on how long he'll be out.

Okay, so, where was I? Right. The guy was on his knees. I walked behind him, wound up and swung with the dagger hilt like I was serving in courtball (I've never played courtball, though I've seen it), and he went down. I took the time to see if they were both really good and out. I couldn't be sure, but from their eyes and their breathing I was pretty confident. I put my weapons away and looked up at the top of the castle; no one seemed to be watching us. Good, then.

My plan was to take a walk around the place, noting what I could, until either I attracted attention, or the strange properties of the manor told me I'd reached some sort of boundary by transporting me to somewhere. In fact, I didn't get very far: I was maybe a quarter of the way around what I guessed was the back of the place, walking just to the side of a narrow cart road, when my eye was caught by an odd door: It was almost parallel to the ground, angled up just slightly. I'd seen a door at just that angle.

I made sure no one had spotted me yet, and approached it. It was a single door but nearly as wide as two, and secured by a padlock. If we were to rate padlocks by time, this one was only about ten seconds. I did the thing, it made the click, and I removed it. I put it aside, pulled the door open, and descended three steps into the same wine cellar I'd seen at the manor.

12

The River at Housetown

I stood for a minute at the bottom of the stone stairway, looking around to convince myself that, yes, this really was the same wine cellar, and trying to figure out what it meant. Same size, same number of racks, and what sealed it was the drip of water in the corner exactly where there had been a brownish stain in the manor. As I stood there, it occurred to me that I might as well steal a bottle. And my thought after that was, what if I took a bottle that still existed back where I was going? What would happen if two wine bottles from different times existed together? How often have you had to worry about that?

I poked around a little more, enough to convince myself that the hallways and storage rooms—now full of fruits, vegetables, bolts of cloth, and boxes of nails—were also the same. I stopped short of going through the door out of the cellar, but I looked through it, and there was a wide stairway.

I went back the other way, and eventually found the stairway that, in the manor, had gone down to a cave. Here, too, there were torches, but they weren't burning. I stopped and lit one with the flint and steel they sell in the Easterners' quarter, and without which I don't know how I'd have lived for the last few years. Once the torch was burning well, I followed the stairway down. In the manor, this had let out into a cave, here it was—

A cave, but a completely different one. Lower, narrower, a lot sandier. For a minute I was completely disoriented, I guess because my brain wanted to orient itself by a sea that wasn't there, but then it gave it up and got back to work. I went left, and the cave unceremoniously ended after a dozen paces; there were no marks on the wall. I turned and went back. As I passed the door, I thought for a moment I was smelling the ocean-sea again, but no, it was all wrong.

It was a long walk, and at times I had to turn sideways when the walls narrowed. What makes caves? Why do they behave like that? Someone must know.

I saw light ahead of me, and took some consolation that at least the back of the cave and the front went in the directions they were supposed to. I stepped out of the cave and into the fading light of early evening. Not the ocean-sea, it was a river, the cave opening onto its bank, perhaps thirty feet from the water, flowing from my right to my left. It was not a big river, and not a fast river, certainly puny compared to the one that cut through Adrilankha, but I could tell it was navigable because I have a good eye for such things and because there were a couple of small barges poling their way along it, both heading downriver.

I waited until the barges were past, just out of habitual sneakiness, then walked down to the edge.

There were tall weeds growing almost up to the water, but right on the bank was sand. It was soft, but not wet. As I said, it was slower than the Adrilankha River, and that meant quieter. I studied it as it went by. The day was still bright enough that I was able to locate the Furnace, and I concluded that, as before, it was late afternoon, which was what it had been when I left the cave, and made sense for when I'd last been outside of the castle. That meant I might still be where I had been, in what was the past, walking around merrily a few hundred years before I was born. What could possibly go wrong? I watched the river, speculating. I kept wanting to make a connection between the river and the fountain, but the source of the fountain was Dark Water, water that had never seen the light of day, and this river was exposed to the daylight.

I knelt down, scooped up some water, let it dribble through my fingers. Another barge came around the bend upriver. I thought about hiding, decided I didn't care. I watched it as it went by. They came close enough so I could see the features of the bargemen, and they stared at me as they passed; one of them almost went into the water from staring so hard, and the others laughed at him. The barge was full of casks; I had no idea what was in them, but that was okay because I had no idea where they were going, either.

There were a few trees of a kind I didn't recognize—short and spindly, with few branches—amid clumps of reeds. The water was a dirty brown. I turned back, but I couldn't see the castle, although my guess was that I'd only walked around fifty rods. I turned back to the river as if it could explain what was going on, make sense of the whole thing. I walked with the water, caught a hint of motion from ahead of me, and stopped. The motion continued, too small or too far away from me to see anything but a sort of darting movement on the other side of the river, near the bank. I got closer, and it didn't stop. Still closer, and about the time I was directly across the river it stopped. I froze and waited, and in a minute or so it started again.

As I watched I picked up more detail, until I was able to make sense of what I was seeing. It was a vallista, of course, because how could it not be? On a riverbank, just where it belonged. As I watched, it would tear off the top of one of the reeds with a quick motion, then chew it for a while, and set it down. At some point it stopped, fiddled around with something—presumably the chewed reeds—then went down to the water holding something in its mouth. It transferred what looked like a box of some kind into its paws, set it carefully in the water, then returned and began chewing more reeds.

I watched, fascinated, for at least a quarter of an hour until the fading light made it impossible. I looked around, and there was a glow coming from behind me. It took a while to realize that it had to be coming from the castle. They must have lit the place up for the night. The light dispersed well enough that I was able to pick out general features of the area, though I couldn't make out details. Loiosh and Rocza had better night vision than me, so presumably they could keep an eye out for anything that needed eyes out. What now? Find a place to sleep, try to make it back to my own time, or wander around aimlessly until something ate me?

All right. Wander aimlessly it is, then.

I continued farther downstream since I'd been going that way to begin with.

"*Do you know what it was doing, Loiosh?*"

"*The vallista? Fishing.*"

"*Fishing.*"

"*Building a fish trap.*"

"Oh. Hmmm. I'll bet that's significant or something."

"What?"

"I don't know. The whole manor is a trap? There's a trap in it? I've fallen into a trap?"

"You think?"

"I don't know. Devera's trapped, anyway. I don't think anything. I'm guessing, trying to plug meaning into things to see if an answer pops out."

Loiosh shut up. I continued downriver, thinking. There was a lot of truth to what I'd told him: there was something about this whole mess, the manor, the movement through time, that felt like there was a clue I wasn't seeing, some key that would explain everything. But while you're waiting for that flash of inspiration, keep picking up pieces. T-A-L . . . never mind, that one wasn't that good. My point is, keep learning what bits of information you can while you wait for it all to make sense. Or, in this case, keep walking down the river.

"Okay, fly around, keep an eye out for anything unfriendly or interesting."

They took off, I kept walking, taking it slow, looking around as well as I went. It was becoming dark, though the process seemed slower than it did in Adrilankha. Probably my imagination.

"Nothing so far, Boss. Think we should go back to where we arrived here and see if we can get back?"

"Think you can find it?"

"Not sure."

"Let's stay with this for a while longer."

My mind kept coming back to Dark Water, and trying to make sense of the river having something to do with it—the cave emerging right on its bank had to mean something. Well, probably meant something. Might mean something.

One of the dangers in trying to solve riddles is a temptation to force answers where they don't belong because things would look neat and pretty that way. I'd been aware of this since I started exploring the manor, but I kept falling into it, or nearly falling into it, anyway.

I made a point to note the softness of the ground, the sounds (more varied than near the ocean-sea, with the lapping of the water only the smallest part), and the complex mix of scents, with the smell of fish predominating.

I hadn't walked that far from the cave—half a mile at the most, perhaps less—when I came to a curving bridge made of stone and wood. I crossed it, and continued in the same direction I'd been going. A few minutes later, Loiosh said, *"Boss? There are buildings, people."*

"Where?"

"Just ahead of you. You'll reach them in a few minutes."

"Anything obviously threatening?"

"You mean, are there a bunch of Dragonlords hiding behind a wall looking like they want to jump out and cut you to pieces? No. I'd have mentioned that."

"Sorry."

A few steps later, following the river around a bend, I saw lights. There was a road not far from the river, so I followed it into the village. For reasons that I'm sure would make perfect sense if I knew more, the village was built on one of the steeper hillsides, rather than the relatively flat areas nearby. There were a couple of dark structures right on the bank, and a small pier, although no boat, extending out into the river itself.

The other structures were placed at various points up the

hill, purely by chance as far as I could tell. Most of them were dark; a few showed faint flickering light, like maybe a candle was going, or there were the embers of a fire. The one exception was about halfway up: there was a lot of light coming from it, and as I got closer I saw there was a sign hanging in front of it, though I couldn't read the sign at all. But I know what a peasant inn looks like; I've been in enough of them over the last few years.

I made my way up without meeting anyone. Now I could see the sign well enough to identify a painted ring of gemstones: diamond, ruby, emerald, sapphire, opal, pearl, and another one that I think was supposed to be a beryl. The paint was fresh enough to make me think it was renewed often, which meant the house was prosperous.

As I reached the door, Loiosh said, *"With you, or wait out here, Boss?"*

That was always the question. Walk in to a Teckla public house with two jhereg on my shoulders, or without? Intimidate, or try to go for the harmless and friendly approach?

"Windows?"

"Plenty of them."

"Then wait outside for now."

He didn't say anything. I knew he didn't like it, and he knew I knew, and he accepted it as part of the job.

I opened the door slowly, entered, and tried to make myself small. The place wasn't as big as I thought it would be, so it probably had back rooms. There were about a dozen tables of various sizes and different kinds of construction, and what decoration there was consisted of poor-quality landscape drawings: a coastal scene, rolling hills with sheep, mountains. The kind of art you like if you want to be anywhere but where you are. At the back was a small stage, hardly big enough for two people to stand on, and I suddenly thought of Sara.

Three of the tables were occupied: all Teckla, of course, and varying ages. It wasn't very busy, but that could be because it was still early, or because . . . that was when I realized that I had no idea what day of the week it was. I don't know why that was so disorienting. I should probably have asked Gormin.

Of course, all the patrons were looking at me. I smiled and bobbed my head a little, and tried not to look too intelligent. The host was a tiny woman, for a Dragaeran, who looked like everyone's grandmother.

I found a table in the corner near the door and sat down with my back to the room. It made me a little nervous without Loiosh and Rocza watching for me, but it's how you invite the room to look at you. The grandmother hesitated, but eventually decided my money was good. I asked for wine and was brought a bottle I didn't recognize. It was already opened, and she poured some and waited while I dug out a coin.

She left, and I drank and wished I hadn't. It was all aftertaste, and none of the aftertaste was taste you'd want to be tasting either after or before anything. If I were a good person, I'd give you the name of the wine so you can avoid it, but I'm not, and also I don't remember. I'm going to bet it was local, and that this was a terrible area for grapes.

I sat there and pretended to drink my wine for half an hour or so, and no one came to talk to me. To the left, no one tried to hit me over the head with a chair either, so we can call it even. I shifted to another chair at the same table where I could get a better view of the room. No one was looking at me, and everyone was engaged in quiet conversation, though what they had to talk about other than me I couldn't guess. That's not true, actually. I'd been around Teckla before, and I knew what they talked about. They weren't talking about how the weather would affect the crop of—I don't know, whatever they grew here. They also weren't talking about how His Lordship treated them, or the share he took. They weren't talking about how much better that plow was now that it'd been sharpened. No, they were talking about what their youngest had been up to, and about that project for the fair, and about how the local merchant had raised the price of dreamgrass and wouldn't he be surprised when no one bought it anymore, and about that funny thing that had happened when the cat got too close to the mama goat as she was giving birth. I didn't need to overhear them, because I'd been in a score of places just like it. The hostess watched the place like a mother bear, occasionally venturing out to fill an order.

The nearest table had two middle-aged women and a young man. I stood up and drifted over. "May I?"

It was obvious that none of them liked the question much. They didn't know what to make of this guy—this *Easterner*— walking around openly armed, and, after all, Easterners were the only people below them socially. Tough decision for them. I put on my best non-threatening smile and waited.

Eventually, one of the women grunted and nodded, which answered my first question: which one of them was in charge. She had almost perfectly round eyes, pale skin even in the dim light of the house, and I've had daggers duller than her nose.

"I'm Vlad," I said.

They rattled off odd-sounding names. The one with the nose I caught as something like a cough. Ouffach, or something like that. I said, "What do you drink here? I tried the wine."

They all laughed, the way you laugh when someone has just discovered what you've known for years.

"Beer," she said. "Stay with the beer." She waved the hostess over and ordered one for me. I made a gesture indicating I wanted to buy a round, and she nodded. I'm not much of a beer drinker, but it was all right.

"What are you doing here?" said Ouffach.

"Just passing through," I said.

"Where are you going?"

"Where? I'm not even sure what direction I'll head in. Whatever I can find. Is there anything to see around here?"

The other woman, whose name I hadn't quite caught, said, "Just a few miles west of here are the fairgrounds."

"Is there a fair?"

"It ended eight days ago."

"Okay."

The younger man said, "The ribbons are still up."

The other woman shook her head. "No, they're gone now."

"You sure? I was by there day before yesterday and—"

Ouffach cleared her throat, and the other two stopped. She turned back to me. "Are you looking for work?"

"I'm not much for farming."

"They hire servants at the castle, sometimes."

"Oh? Did you ever work there?"

"My youngest did."

"And my sister," said the guy.

The other woman said, "When I was a little girl I waited on Her Ladyship."

"Her Ladyship," I repeated.

She nodded.

"I've heard she passed away," I said.

The other two nodded, but Ouffach squinted at me and said, "How did you hear that?"

Her face was wrinkled, and her skin looked like it would have the consistency of leather.

"I pick things up here and there."

She wasn't having it. "You were at the castle."

I nodded.

"Who?"

"Gormin."

She nodded slowly. "He talks too much."

"For a Teckla, or an Issola?"

"He's no Issola anymore."

"Why not? What happened?"

"None of your business, or mine."

Well, that didn't leave a lot of room for discussion. When discussion fails, try negotiation, that's what I always say. Sometimes say. Have said at least once before.

I reached into my pouch and found three imperials. I passed one to the woman whose name I didn't know, and one to the young man. "Take a walk," I said. Their eyes widened, they took the coins, then they looked at Ouffach. She nodded. They got up and moved to a table on the other side of the room. When they'd left, I pushed the third coin over to her.

She picked it up and studied it, tapped her fingernail against it, then frowned. "Who is this?" she said, pointing to the portrait of an Empress who hadn't yet taken the throne. Oops.

"I don't know," I said. "But it's gold."

She tapped it again, nodded, and set it down.

"Why do you want to know?"

I fished around and found another imperial, set it next to the first. "Good enough reason?"

She smiled. She didn't have many teeth, and the ones she had were yellow. I suddenly realized that, during the Interregnum, Dragaerans' teeth looked like the teeth of Easterners in my own time. I couldn't decide if that was funny or sad. I also wondered how much the blacksmith would charge to make her some new ones.

"I don't know a lot," she said. "I know it happened a hundred years or so after the Disaster."

She drank some more beer and wiped her lips with the back of her hand. I nodded and waited for her to continue.

"There's a dancer, also an Issola. Hevlika."

I nodded, but inside, all of my ah ha's were going off.

"It seemed that she and Gormin were sweeping the straw."

That was an expression I'd never heard before, but it was easy enough to figure out. "Involved," I said.

She squinted at me with one eye, I guess to see if I was only pretending to misunderstand in order to embarrass her, which I was, but it didn't work. I flashed her a smile and nodded.

"Of course, they were discovered."

"Pardon the ignorance of a poor Easterner, but was such a dalliance forbidden?"

For a moment, she looked at me as if I were an alien species, which I was. Then her face cleared and she said, "At the time, Gormin was His Lordship's steward."

"Is that like seneschal?" I asked, thinking of Lady Teldra.

She nodded. "He was in charge of the household."

"Which means?"

"The dancer was part of the household. Surely such a thing is improper among your people?"

"We don't have stewards. At least, I've never met one in an Eastern household."

"Then who is in charge of the servants?"

"Who is in charge of your servants?"

"The steward, as I said."

"Yours? In your house?"

"My house?" She laughed. "I don't have servants."

"Exactly," I said.

She glanced at the two imperial coins in front of her, then back at me as if she didn't entirely believe me. I guess I could see her point: how could someone who could toss around imperials like copper not have servants? Fine. Let it be a mystery.

"So, they were caught, and he was booted out of his House."

"And ordered into the Teckla."

"Heh. I'll bet you made him feel welcome."

Her lips twitched. "We didn't make it pleasant for him. But he took it well, and never got above himself, so we stopped. Eventually."

"And now?"

"Beg pardon?"

"What is he doing now?"

"Oh. The same as he did before, only as a Teckla."

"And the dancer?"

"She is still there." Some expression crossed her features too quickly for me to read.

"What?" I said.

"Hmm?"

"What was that look for?"

She looked down. I waited. After a moment, she said softly, "It was cruel."

I drew circles on the table in the condensation from the beer. "What was?"

Her head came up. "You don't see? He made Gormin stay there, where he saw her every day, only now he was a Teckla."

I put that together with what I knew of Dragaerans in general and Issola in particular—he was no longer an Issola, or even an aristocrat. She wouldn't have anything to do with him, and he'd never consider asking her to. Dragaerans are idiots. "He did that just to be cruel?"

She nodded.

"This was Zhayin?"

She winced a little—I guess the local lord is too important to be called by his name—but then she nodded.

"I'm starting to take a dislike to this guy," I said.

"He's been through a lot," she said.

"You mean his son."

She nodded.

"And then, his daughter."

She frowned. "His daughter? He has no daughter."

"Ah," said. "My mistake." And let's have another "ah ha!" In case that went too fast for you, I'd just learned that her mother was already dead, but the woman who was an adult and a ghost in my age had never been heard of by the townspeople. I didn't know what that meant, but it meant something.

A few people came in and found tables; I guess it was still pretty early as Teckla saw things. And then, a number of them probably had to walk in from miles away once the work was done. I remembered from my travels that Teckla did a lot of walking. So far, all of them were Teckla; I had the feeling that if an aristocrat were to walk in here no one would know what to do.

I cleared my throat. "We were talking," I said, "about Zhayin's wife. What was her name?"

"Her Ladyship."

"That was her name?"

"The only name I knew."

I nodded. "So, what happened to her?"

"I don't know. We were never told."

"What was the gossip?"

She laughed. "That one of His Lordship's experiments had gotten out of control. That she had killed herself in despair at his violating the laws of nature. That a god had appeared and taken her to be his bride. That he had killed her when she threatened to go to the Duke about his illegal magic. That he had sacrificed her to gain power. Would you like me to go on?"

"No, no. I get the idea. Who would know?"

"His Lordship."

"Thanks so much."

She shrugged.

"All right, who else would know?"

She considered. "Maybe Hevlika."

I nodded. "Maybe there's some way I could meet her."

"She should be along soon."

"What? Here? She drinks here?"

"She dances here, two or three times a week."

"Oh. I thought she only danced for Zhayin."

She frowned. "Why would you think that?"

"No reason."

She gave me a look and grunted, and a few more people came in. I'd been at events—plays and concerts—where there was a lot of excitement as the opening drew close, and this didn't feel like that. It was more relaxed, like, what was going to happen was a part of the evening, less a special event, more like an Endweek dinner: anticipated, but nothing to burn the chairs for.

I got us another round of drinks. I should add that the hostess collected from me when she brought the drinks; for everyone else, she just made marks on a board behind the bar. To be fair, I don't know if that was because I was human or because I was a stranger.

I waited for the show to start.

13

THE STAR OF THE SEVEN JEWELS

A few more people came in and found seats; then a few more, who stood against the wall because they'd run out of chairs. The hostess was moving like a Dzur in battle getting everyone drinks.

And then she arrived: Hevlika, looking just as I remembered her. She smiled and nodded as she walked toward the stage. A man was with her, a Teckla, and he carried an instrument I recognized as a *lant*. He found a stool that had been set aside near the side of the stage, and began tuning while Hevlika went around the room saying hello to people and generally being gracious as only an Issola can. I touched Lady Teldra's hilt and remembered things I don't feel like talking about.

Eventually she made her way to the stage, had a whispered conversation with the *lant* player, and started.

I've described her dancing before, I won't try to do it again. I will say it wasn't until she was done that I realized she'd done all of that on a stage barely big enough for a full split (that's what they call it when they spread their legs and smack their crotch on the stage; I know stuff). Just the fact that I never noticed how cramped she must have been is a testament. I wish I knew more about dance so I could describe it better. I'll say the Teckla liked it: they all seemed to be holding their breath, and everyone's eyes got as big and round as Ouffach's. I think Hevlika must have danced for an hour or more without a break, although it didn't seem like it at the time. When she was done, they all yelled and cried and stomped their feet, and I did, too, and I sat there wondering how many thousands of hours it takes to get every little muscle in your body to be able to do exactly what you want, down to the tiniest flutter, and then to coordinate it to music. You want to talk magic, that's magic.

It calmed down, and they left the stage, but no one left— it seemed that after the show they went around and talked to everyone again, saying hello, laughing and smiling a lot. She was an Issola; I should get used to it.

As she finished speaking to people, the ones who had said hello to her would slowly say their good-byes and make their way out the door, like this was a regular part of the festivities. Eventually, Hevlika and the Teckla made their way to our table. They looked a little startled to see me, but smiled, and then greeted Ouffach by name. They received our compliments on the performance with modest grace, and made sure we understood how much they enjoyed it.

When they moved on to the next table, Ouffach stood up with a grunt and said, "Have I earned the coins?"

"Oh, yes," I said.

She nodded. "Then I'll bid you a good evening, Easterner. I have kethna to feed in the morning."

" 'Or there will be no bacon for Endweek.' " I completed. Her lips twitched. I stood up and bowed, which seemed to charm her. It's what comes of hanging around with Issola. She left; I sat down and waited.

"*How long, Boss?*"

"*A while yet. Sorry.*"

"*All right.*"

I ordered another beer. Compared to the wine, it was spectacular. I waited until Hevlika and the musician had spoken to everyone, by which time the place was empty except for them, the tired-looking hostess, and one old guy snoring behind a wall of empty cups. As Hevlika went by me, I said, "May I trouble you for a moment's conversation, my lady?"

This is not the kind of question an Issola finds it easy to say no to; she nodded with no hesitation and sat down. The musician picked up that I was interested in talking to *her* rather than *them*, so he smiled to both of us and headed out, instrument over his shoulder like a Dragonlord carries his pike.

"Can I buy you a beer? I'd offer you wine, but believe me, you don't want it."

She smiled and turned to the hostess, who nodded and returned with a wine bottle and two glasses. She poured it for us. It was a very, very dark red, but after raising a glass in thanks to Hevlika, I tasted it, and was pleasantly surprised. The hostess stood there and waited until I paid her, then grunted, left the bottle, and shuffled off.

"I guess they keep this around for you," I said.

She smiled. "I'm Hevlika."

"I'm . . . Szurke."

She caught the hesitation and I shrugged. "I pick among several different names," I said. "I decided you deserved the best."

"You're very kind. What did you wish to talk about?"

"The late wife of Lord Zhayin."

There should have been at least a small sense of triumph in shocking an Issola, but in fact I felt sort of bad. I waited while she drank some wine and recovered.

"Her Ladyship," she said at last. I guess that really was her name. Must have been interesting when she was a child.

I nodded. "I've heard that something happened to her. What was it?"

"May I ask why you wish to know?"

That's the thing about Issola: because you know how hard it is for them to say no, you have just as much trouble saying no to them. "It's complicated," I said at last. "It involves a big house near Adrilankha, the Halls of Judgment, passages through ti—"

"The Halls of Judgment," she repeated.

I nodded.

She drank some more wine. "That's where it happened," she said at last. Her eyes lost focus.

"What happened?" I said after a moment.

She shook her head. "I don't know. No one knows, exactly."

"But Her Ladyship visited the Halls while living?"

She nodded. At one time I had thought Zerika and I were the only ones. Now it was starting to seem like an official Imperial pastime.

"And she was with child at the time?"

The dancer tilted her head curiously. "I hadn't heard that."

"Ah," I said. "Perhaps I was misinformed."

"You are well spoken," she said.

"For an Easterner, you mean?" She nodded. "I read a lot," I told her. "You see us as like Teckla, but we're really outside of the rules."

"I see. Of course, most of what I know I've picked up from poems, folktales, the theatre. It's one thing to know those are unreliable, it's another to know what to put in their place."

"Yeah, I get that."

"I hope I didn't give offense."

I laughed. "I get offended when people try to kill me. And it hurts my feelings when they swing blunt objects at me. Other than that, I don't worry about it."

"I understand. Do you have love poetry?"

"Me? No."

"I mean your people."

"Oh. Sure. Also love songs, erotic paintings, and ribald stories."

"We have those, too."

"Issola? I find that hard to believe. I mean, ribald stories."

She laughed. "You should hear us when no one is around." She winked.

"I'd give pure gold to."

"I'll keep that in mind if we meet again."

"Oh, we'll meet again."

"Oh?"

"I'm an Easterner, we can tell these things."

She smiled politely without making it look like she was smiling politely. "You should try your hand at love poetry," she said.

"I don't think so. There's enough bad poetry in the world without my contribution."

"Very well."

"Why, though?"

"It'll help."

I snorted. "Help with what?"

"Your grief."

"What grief?"

"You know what I mean, Lord Szurke."

"I really don't."

"You mean you don't keep composing letters to her in your head? You don't keep wanting to tell her how wretched you are, but then you don't send them, because what if she took you back because you were wretched? How terrible that would be, you tell yourself. When something happens—something funny, or interesting, or sad—you look around to tell her about it, then you remember. And you want to tell her *that* is going on, but you don't, because you don't want to add to her burdens, only you do want to add to her burdens, and you hate that you want to add to her burdens. You wonder if she's seeing someone else, and you hope she is, and you hope she isn't, and you hate that it matters so much. And maybe you've found someone else yourself, but you worry that it isn't fair to her, and then you worry that you shouldn't worry about that, and then it infuriates you that you're spending so much time thinking about it, and so it all turns into aimless grief."

"Oh, *that* grief."

She nodded.

"*Loiosh, you didn't hear any of that.*"

"*Any of what?*"

"*Exactly.*"

"How did you do that? Also, why?"

"How is easy, Szurke. You carry it in how you walk and in the set of your shoulders, but mostly in how you watched me dance."

"Bloody Issola."

"Pardon?"

"Nothing."

"As for why, because I can, and because I felt I owed it to you for my rudeness."

"Heh. Thanks *so* much."

"You'd really have preferred I said nothing?"

"I'll tell you something," I said. "You people live thousands of years. We live fifty or sixty. And I'll bet you couldn't find any one of you, or any one of us, who didn't have something like that going on. It's just what happens when you live. Spending all your time worrying about it just means getting so wrapped up in your head that you never do anything. Yeah, sad sh—sad stuff happens, it hurts, and you move on."

"And what are you doing?"

"Hmm?"

"Of what does your moving on consist?"

"At the moment, I'm trying to solve a puzzle. It distracts the mind."

"Maybe I can help."

"You have helped. Twice now."

She gave me a look that invited me to expand on that.

"It's complicated," I said.

"Yes, that's why it's called a puzzle."

"Let's speak of other matters."

"Certainly."

"Do you write poetry? I mean, about Gormin?"

She looked away, then looked back. "I dance," she said. "And Ouffach has too much air in her lungs."

"I'm sorry," I said, and cleared my throat. "I wouldn't ask if it didn't matter, but this might tie into my problem."

"What makes you think so?"

"Because as far as I can tell, everything ties into everything else, and half the time does so in perfectly straightforward ways, and half the time in ways that make no sense. But I'm going to just assume that everything connects. And, after all, you brought it up."

"I?"

"Yeah."

"What did I bring up?"

"Love, romance, the breaking of hearts, all that crap. You're an Issola, and an Issola would never just start in on a stranger's personal life without a good reason."

"You think you understand Issolas?"

"Better than I understand Vallistas."

She laughed then; she had a nice laugh. I smiled, waited, then said, "So, what is it? You had a reason for bringing that up."

"Insistent, aren't you?"

"Somewhere a little girl is trapped in time, and I'm trying to set her free."

"I'm afraid I don't know the reference."

"It wasn't a reference, it's what I'm trying to fix."

"Oh." She frowned. "Trapped in time? That doesn't make sense."

"Yeah, that's why it's so tricky."

"I don't understand."

"Neither do I. It's necromancy, and I know nothing about necromancy, and it has to do with another structure built by—crap, by someone, sometime, that connects to the castle here, and if I could explain it any clearer I would. But there is something going on, and I'm set on figuring out anything I don't understand, and right now the top of the list of things I don't understand is why you gave me that lecture about love and heartbreak, all right? Of all the things that have happened to me over the last two days, that's the strangest."

She said, "It isn't that complicated, Szurke. I brought it up because you asked me to."

"Because I . . . all right, go on."

"Do you think I'm not aware of the audience when I dance, that I don't pay attention to them?"

"Hadn't given any thought one way or the other."

"Dancing has meaning, it has substance. It reaches into people. Something in me reaches something in those who watch, and sometimes the connection is so strong it can't be mistaken."

"Sounds like magic."

"Not really."

"So, the way I reacted when you danced is how I said I wanted to talk about all sorts of private and personal crap that I don't even like to think about?"

"Exactly."

Most of the responses that came to mind I couldn't make to an Issola. After sitting for a bit, with her refusing to say anything, I settled for "I suppose you're right. But it still doesn't explain about you."

"As you said, we all have those heartbreaks."

"Most of them don't have to do with an Issola being expelled from his House."

"There are always reasons."

"In your case, it's a little more than that, I think."

"What do you mean?"

"Let me review, and you tell me if I'm missing anything. Gormin was in charge of the household. He met you, and developed an attachment. As you were, at this time, associated

with the household, this was deemed improper, and it was decided he'd failed in his duty and was expelled from his House."

She nodded, her eyes locked on mine.

"But not from the household."

"Lord Zhayin was pleased with his work."

"Yeah. Nonsense."

"My lord?"

"There was more to it than that, and, what's more, you
know there was. He comes on to you? Maybe winks, maybe lets
you know he is if you are? And things go as things will with
people who are attracted to each other. So, then the House
finds out about it, and it's improper. Fine. What do they do?
Normally, he gets a letter or something that says cut it out.
That's it. They don't kick him out of the House for that."

"You are an expert on the workings of House Issola?"

"I'm an expert on the workings of Dragaerans. It's a natural result of not being one."

"That almost makes sense."

"Thanks. The point is, either he did a lot more than that,
or there's something else entirely going on."

"Both," she said.

I nodded. "All right. Don't stop there."

"We were lovers."

I nodded.

"It began when I was visiting, before I was attached to the
household."

"How long? I mean, how long were the two of you involved
before Zhayin hired you?"

"Forty-one years."

"And how long after that until he was—"

"A year and a half."

"Um. I see. So, how did the House find out?"

"I don't know."

"Zhayin?"

"I asked him directly, to his face. He denied it, and I think I would have known if he'd been lying. And why would he care?"

I shook my head. "I'm nowhere near looking at whys yet. I'm still on whos and hows."

"I don't know."

"And you haven't had anyone, uh, make advances since then?"

She shook her head. "I've made a few, but only on my travels. There are no Issola here."

"Wait, you mean, you're the only Issola in the castle, or the town?"

She nodded.

"Well. Isn't *that* interesting."

"My lord?"

I shook my head as things danced through my brain and I tried to make sense of them.

"What is it?"

"Harro."

"Who?"

"An Issola named Harro."

"I don't know him."

"Yes. Exactly. That's what's so odd. How could you not know him? The timing doesn't make sense for you to not know him."

"Who—"

"He helped take care of Zhayin's son."

She shook her head. "No, no. The nanny's name—"

"Not the nanny. She was ill the day it happened."

She frowned. "That's right. How did you know that?"

"I've been looking into this for a while."

"What else can you tell me?"

"About your problem? Nothing. I don't know. I'm busy being puzzled about things. But I can tell you one thing: If you meet someone named Harro, don't trust him."

"Harro," she repeated, as if committing it to memory. "That's all you can tell me?"

"I may be able to tell you more next time we meet. No, the time after. If there is a time after."

"I don't understand any of this."

"Welcome to my life. But let me ask you one more thing."

"Of course."

"Do you really think writing bad poetry would help?"

She smiled again, and reminded me of Sara. "Yes. But burn it after you've written it."

"That sounds like good advice."

"I have all sorts of good advice."

"Any on finding out what happened to Her Ladyship in the Halls of Judgment?"

"It's that important to you?"

"Yes, it is."

"I don't know what to tell you. I'm no one's confidante. I knew Her Ladyship, briefly, a little—she and His Lordship were patrons of my troupe before the Disaster. After that, I only know what I heard."

"From Gormin," I said.

She gave a quick nod.

"You were here when the Disaster happened?"

"Not far from here. Lord Zhayin had sponsored us on a

tour. We were lucky to be out of the city." She sighed. "I miss the stage at the Rock Garden, in Dragaera. It was built on layers of sanga wood, dozens of layers, so when you landed on it, it gave. And the house! The seating went more up than out, so the worst seats were so close, they were almost onstage."

"You said 'us.' Your troupe?"

"Yes."

"What became of them?"

"They let me go and continued without me."

"That's when Zhayin hired you?"

She nodded.

"I apologize for continuing to bring up those aspects of the past," I said, "the ones that revolve around Gormin. I know it must be painful. But I'm trying to understand."

"Why?"

I took a breath. Fine, then. If she was going to be that insistent. "I've explained some of it. Because something has set off a necromantic event and a friend of mine is caught in it."

"A necromantic event?"

"That's the only way I can describe it, yes. And I don't understand it, but I think it has something to do with the Halls of Judgment, and with Her Ladyship, and her daughter, Tethia. Okay, let me be more precise. Something happened during the Inter—no, let me try again. Something happened at some point that had to do with Her Ladyship, and the Halls of Judgment, and the new manor they're working on. I have a friend who's trapped in that manor, and I need to figure out how it works. I know it has something to do with Her Ladyship, and her daughter, Tethia."

"Tethia," she repeated, then shook her head. "I know of no daughter, and no one named Tethia."

"And you don't know how she came to be in the Halls of Judgment?"

She shook her head. "I know little of necromancy, I'm afraid. I don't know any way to the Halls of Judgment, except to walk the Paths of the Dead, or be taken by a demon—what? What did I say?"

"Son of a bitch," I observed.

"Pardon?"

"Do you know someone named Discaru?"

"Athyra? His Lordship's sorcerer? We've met."

"Of course you have."

"What is it?"

I shook my head. "Nothing, nothing. I—"

"*Boss! Trouble!*"

"*What?*"

"*An even dozen heading toward you at a trot, swords out.*"

"*Oh, good.*"

"What is it?" said Hevlika.

I stood. "Thank you for the delightful conversation. You've been extraordinarily helpful. But I'm afraid it's time for me to scamper."

She smiled. "Just as well. I believe our hostess would like to close up. Best of luck to you."

"Thanks."

I stood, took a last look around, and gave Hevlika a last smile, a little sad that, as it turned out, she wouldn't remember me very well a few hundred years from now.

14

A Short Fatal Hate Chase

I stepped out of the door. Fortunately, the house had been dark enough that I wasn't too night-blind.

"Where are they?"

"Two minutes, Boss. Coming from the castle."

Hide, or run? The area was dotted with small structures, shacks, up and down the hill, but this was their home ground; they'd be better at finding hiding places than me.

"Let's go the other way," I said.

I set off running. I wondered if the strange magic that had brought me here would snap me back at a certain point; but if it did, that was just as likely to help me escape as to hurt me. I reached the riverbank and cut right.

Rocza landed on my shoulder. *"They're pretty close,"* said Loiosh.

I kept moving—not running, but walking pretty fast. I kept wanting to break into a run, but they could run faster than me, and I didn't want to be exhausted if they found me. There were a lot of them; even with Loiosh, Rocza, and Lady Teldra, I didn't much care for the odds.

There were no more lights off to the side, so I figured I was past the village, such as it was. The river curved gently to the right. I moved away from the bank to avoid growing things, but kept following the curve, and I came upon a structure, a large shed or a small cottage. It seemed there were no windows. If I hid there, might those chasing me go past? If they decided to search, I'd be nicely trapped for them. I hesitated, then tried the door. It was unlocked. All right, then. I stepped inside and shut the door behind me, then bumped into something. I felt around, and it proved to be a stool. At shin height, of course. I don't want to talk about it. I couldn't see a bloody thing, a problem I solved by not moving. I just crouched down near the door and waited.

I heard footsteps outside, getting closer, then—"Look!" "Duck!" "They're his, he must be nearby." "Follow them!"

"*Good call, Loiosh. I should have thought of that. Where are you leading them?*"

"*Back toward the village.*"

"*Perfect.*"

I remained still for a long time, though I'm sure less time than it felt like—if you want to screw up your sense of the passage of time, sit in a dark room with no sound except the very faint lapping of water some distance away. When I felt like it was safe, I opened the door again.

My eyes had adjusted more than I thought they could: I was able to make out objects now. There was a large bench, some casks, some boxes, ceramic bowls, glass jars, some empty, some stoppered and full of liquid that, from what I could tell, was clear. Against one wall was a stack of what I at first thought were planks of wood, but after checking proved to be sheets of glass—beautifully made, too: flat and smooth and even. They couldn't have been made here; I didn't know of more than two or three glaziers who could do that kind of work even in Adrilankha in my own day. I at once thought about the windows in the manor, and wondered if this is where they were processed, made unbreakable. That meant that construction on the manor had already started.

There was a lantern hanging by the door. I pulled the cover off, managed to get it lit, covered it again, and looked around some more. A ceramic jar held fine, white powder. I don't recommend tasting every random white powder you come across in a building where magic or construction or something is taking place, but it looked so much like well-sifted flour, I just had to know. No, it wasn't flour—it was sugar, ground down to an incredibly fine consistency—that kind of work is why bakers' apprentices have such powerful shoulders. But—sugar? I couldn't make sense of it. At the back of the room was a large brick oven, a smokestack leading up from it; next to the oven was a cauldron no bigger than a cooking pot. The incongruity of size between the cast-iron cauldron and the massiveness of the oven was at least as strange as the sugar. I studied it a little more, and realized that, no, it wasn't an oven, at least not the way I thought of an oven; it was more of a kiln. Next to it was charcoal; someone needed to get something very hot for some reason. I felt the brick and it was cool to the touch, so whatever it was hadn't been used for a while.

A little more exploring revealed a crate with two shiny bricks. I picked one up, tapped it, tasted it, weighed it in my hand: silver. I set it down after only briefly considering stealing it and looked around some more. I had even less idea what the other things were: one jar was full of some kind of crystals, and yet another, a glass jar, had the unmistakable and not at all pleasant odor of ammonia. Maybe you can put all this together and make sense of it, but I couldn't.

"Boss!"

"What is it?"

"They haven't given up; they're starting to head back toward you. I think they might have figured out what we're doing."

"All right. I'm going keep heading along the river the way I was. Catch up when you can."

I put out the lantern and hung it up again, stepped back into the night, and pulled the door closed behind me. That place had to have something to do with construction, but I sure couldn't think of what it might be.

I made my way back to the riverbank and turned to continue following the long curve. I was just in the process of asking myself how far I was going to go when, just like that, it happened: it didn't feel any different, but as I crossed some invisible boundary, my next step took me back to the other side of the river, just before the bridge, with the river on my right and the castle somewhere out of sight over the hill to my left.

"Loiosh, where are you?"

"Heading back to you now."

"No, continue the way you were going."

"Oh. All right."

He sounded dubious about it, but a moment later he appeared and landed on my shoulder.

"That's a little strange."

"Tell me about it."

Rocza appeared then and landed on my other shoulder. Her wings continued flapping.

"She's upset."

"Yeah."

"*She thinks that's kind of weird.*"

"*Me too.*"

She settled down and I studied the area and considered my options. I was assuming that since all the nice people chasing me belonged here, they wouldn't be subject to whatever boundaries I was. I hoped I wasn't wrong; it would be embarrassing. But assuming I was right, I could head to where I'd first entered this, uh, this area, and maybe somehow find my way back.

"*Loiosh?*"

"*I'm not sure, Boss. We noted it, but we've moved around a lot. I guess sort of back toward the castle, kind of?*"

I'd been very clever, you see, in memorizing the exact spot where I'd appeared, because I'd realized I might have to find it again. It hadn't occurred to me that I'd have to find it coming from some whole other direction, and in the dark at that. I didn't like my odds.

"*See what you can do.*"

"*Right.*"

"*And let me know if you see those guards coming back.*"

"*Oh, good thing you mentioned that. Otherwise, I'd have kept it as a surprise.*"

They took off from my shoulder again. I took my best guess as to the direction of the castle. A couple of jhereg passed overhead, wild ones, none of my business. Loiosh had a sort of superior attitude to them. There were also a few nocturnal birds flying low above the river, but I couldn't see them well enough to identify them.

I set off, Loiosh guiding me with instructions like "*I think it might be more that way,*" and "*that kind of looks familiar,*" and other confidence-boosting remarks. I still wasn't sure we were even going generally the right way when I saw a figure looming up in front of me. I stopped, waited; whoever it was, was also waiting. I tried to make out details, but it was too dark. I took a wild guess.

"Hello, Discaru. I was wondering if I'd see you again."

"I was hoping you'd find your way here."

"Right. If I die in the past, I just vanish, right? I mean, no body to worry about."

"You're very clever."

"Why haven't you transformed?"

"It seems we can't communicate when I'm in my natural shape. And I wanted to make you an offer."

"An offer? Why not just kill me? Not sure you can pull it off?"

"Exactly. I think I can, but I'm not certain, so why take the chance?"

"How very rational of you."

"Do you want to hear my offer, or am I wasting my time expecting sense from you?"

"Oh, this is bound to be good. All right, I'm listening."

"First, let me explain your position."

I looked around elaborately. "You mean, lost in the past, unsure if I can find my way home, and with a batch of angry Dragonlords chasing me? I'm kinda used to that."

I took a step closer. The issue wasn't killing him; I was pretty sure I could do that. The issue was how to get information out of him.

"No," he said. "I mean the shield that's gone up around us, so your friends can't help you."

I gotta give the bastard credit for good timing. As he finished saying that, there was a scream in my mind.

"*Loiosh?*"

Nothing.

"*Loiosh!*"

"What did you do to him?"

"Easy, little man. I doubt he's harmed. He just flew head-first into the shield. I'm sure he's only stunned. And he won't come to any further harm, as long as you behave yourself."

"As long as I—Discaru, or whatever your true name is, you are really stupid."

"Your pet is surrounded by magical energies, and I can pour as much energy into it as I wish, or collapse it. So, if you care about its life at all, you'll be very polite to me, and do precisely as I say."

Even in the dimness, I could see Rocza, about ten feet away, trying to get closer to Discaru, unable to, as if there were a sort of invisible bubble around him.

"This demonic plane you're from," I said. "Is everyone there a complete idiot, or is it only you?"

"Curb your tongue. You can't harm me."

"Oh?"

"I exist here, in the past, in another form. Do you know what would happen if you were to kill me here?"

"No, but I'm really close to finding out."

"Two of me cannot exist at the same time. My existence here is already causing necromantic disruptions. Sooner or later, probably sooner, the platform that permits this access will collapse on itself. At best, you will be trapped here in this time. More likely, you will be caught in the collapse and destroyed."

"Sounds grim," I said, and took another step forward. "Is that what happened when you brought Her Ladyship to the Halls of Judgment?"

"One more step, and I destroy your pet."

I stopped.

"Do you understand what I'm telling you? Destroy me, and you destroy yourself."

"Yeah, yeah. I get it. But you haven't answered my question. I know you brought her to the Halls, and she gave birth there. But was she already pregnant at the time? Did you know it? Did you bring her daughter back out? How did that all work?"

"If I were you, I'd forget about—"

"You are so very, very much not me. You are nowhere near being me. I can't even begin. Now, are you going to answer my questions?"

"Of course not. If you care to get out of here alive, you have one chance."

"Oh, good. I was getting worried."

"Here is what you're going to do. I suggest you listen, and quickly, because I can already feel the pressures building, and I honestly do not know how much time there is."

"All right, tell me," I said. "This is bound to be good."

There were two long steps between us.

"I'll create an opening to your own time, to the road outside of Precipice Manor. You'll go through it, after giving me your word that you won't try to come back or interfere in any way. Then I'll let your pet go through."

"Uh-huh," I said. "Can I make a counter-proposal?"

"You're in no position to—"

I drew and moved, as fast as I ever have. From fully relaxed, to draw and move and strike; to be honest, I wasn't sure I could pull it off until I felt the contact. Lady Teldra came up under his chin and into his head.

Yeah. Feed, Lady Teldra. Take it. Take whatever grotesque

ugliness he uses for a soul and chew it up and digest it and make him gone gone gone—

His scream was a thing of agony and despair and I relished every lingering note, and it continued in my ears after that and I didn't mind a bit. At one point, his eyes met mine, and past the hate I felt a jarring contact that formed into the words *I will remember this, and you will regret it.* I have to admit, as dying words go, they aren't bad. I was not, however, excessively impressed. The last thing he did was start transforming, but he didn't get very far, so he was a sort of strange misshapen mostly-human partly-demon object. Students of sorcery may draw whatever conclusions they wish from the fact that, on death, he didn't return to his native form.

Rocza settled on the ground. I jumped over what remained of Discaru and found Loiosh. I picked him up; he didn't seem colder than usual. Rocza fluttered and flapped and half flew and settled again, and eventually landed on my shoulder.

I felt for a connection to Loiosh. *"Hey? You there? Hello? Loiosh?"*

There was something; not a conscious thought, but something, and my knees almost gave out with relief. Now all I had to worry about was the minor issue of, what if the demon had been telling the truth? I looked around. Everything *seemed* normal. Not that I had any idea what to look for.

I tucked Loiosh carefully into my cloak, then grabbed hold of Discaru's legs and began pulling in what I hoped was the right direction. That was my clever plan, you see: if I could get his body back to the other time before everything collapsed or he met himself, then, even if the bastard had been telling the truth, it wouldn't matter because they'd never meet.

Pretty smart, huh?

The question is, how can a guy make a living as an assassin for the better part of a decade without ever learning how bloody *heavy* a Dragaeran is? I managed about a foot, then stopped, panting.

Well, I could always hope he'd been lying—that's what I'd sort of counted on in the first place. I mean, he was a demon, right? Being a demon meant being able to manifest in two places at once, which ought to mean that two of him could exist at the same time without everything collapsing. Maybe. And for the hundredth time, I wished I could consult with the Necromancer. I wondered if I could bury him, or maybe sink him in the river, when the air sort of shimmered in front of me—getting wavy, like how on a hot day you see waves go up from the water, only it wasn't hot, it wasn't day, and there was no water. My stomach dropped, and my first thought was *Oh, crap, it's happening.* But no: a figure came through the shimmering, and for the second time in as many minutes, my knees got weak with relief. Or maybe I'm just getting old.

"Hello, Devera," I managed.

"Hello, Uncle Vlad. We shouldn't be here."

"I know. Can you get us out?"

She nodded and held her hand out. "Come with me."

"What about him?" I said.

She looked at the remains of the demon, her expression, from as much of it as I could see, mostly one of curiosity.

"He doesn't belong here either," she announced.

"Yeah. What do we—"

She reached out, and he began to dissolve. I don't mean, like, melted, or turned into something; it was more like the whole area he was in turned two-dimensional and wavered, became indistinct, and faded. Or it might be that my mind filled in a lot of that. It seemed like I saw, at the last moment, a vaguely human shape kneeling over him, holding a sword or a wand, but it was just for an instant, and may not have been real, and then that, too, was gone.

"Can you teach me that?"

She gave me a look I can't possibly describe.

"Never mind," I said. "I suppose we should get out of here. Tell me though, the Halls of Judgment, that's where you were born, right?"

She nodded.

"And would someone else who was born there be able to do what you do?"

She frowned. "You mean make spinnysticks?"

"Um, no. I mean walking around in different times."

"Oh! Maybe. Is this about why I'm stuck here?"

"I think so. A demon seems to have arranged for someone named Tethia to be born there, and Tethia did something, made something, that permitted that kind of travel."

"Where is the demon, Uncle Vlad?"

"He's gone."

"Gone where?"

"Um. I killed him, and you just made him vanish."

"Oh!" Devera nodded, the expression on her face incongruously mature. "She'd have had to raise it up above the normal plane of existence, so it could reach other places."

"I don't understand."

Her face twisted up, and it reminded me of Loiosh once when I'd asked him to explain how he flew. "The world is a place, and there's another place next to it, okay? But you can't get from one to the other unless there's a way to get to somewhere else that you can get there from."

"Uh, yeah," I said as if I understood that. And then suddenly I did. "Yes, she made something above the normal world. A platform."

Devera nodded. "So that—" She stopped and looked around and above her. "It's collapsing," she said. "We need to go."

"All right."

"*Boss?*"

"*It's okay, Loiosh.*"

"*I ran into something.*"

"*I know.*"

"*That guy—*"

"*He's dead now.*"

"*Oh. Good.*"

Some distance away, I heard a shout of "What's that? Over there?"

"Come on, Uncle Vlad," said Devera.

How could I refuse? Still holding Loiosh, I followed her through the shimmering area, and found myself, once more, back by the fountain—not the one in the Halls, the one that looked like it.

"Thank you, Devera. Now maybe you can explain—"

I was talking to the air. I should have seen that coming.

Part Two

SYNTHESIS

15

THIS SMOOTH MAGIC

Since I'd left the castle, it had gone from afternoon to dusk and now it was back to evening. All of this random messing around from night to day and back was going to do serious damage to my sleep cycle. The drugs they'd given me probably wouldn't help much either. I was probably going to have a long, long, nap after this was all over; maybe a couple of days' worth. For now, though, I didn't feel tired. I did feel warm, however; I shrugged my cloak back off my shoulders, only now realizing that it'd been colder at the other place. Temperature is one of those things I notice when I'm not busy with anything else.

Loiosh stirred in my cloak, then, without saying a word, made his way up to my shoulder. I felt him grip and flap as he nearly lost his balance.

"*You sure you're all right there?*"

"*I feel better here.*"

"*All right.*"

"*What now?*"

"*I think we backtrack, and keep an eye out for Discaru.*"

"*I thought you killed him.*"

"*In a different time. He's a demon, remember? I only banished him from that place.*"

"*But it's connected, and—*"

"*Yeah, I know. And maybe he's gone from here. I just don't want to count on it and be surprised.*"

"*Yeah. Good thinking, Boss.*"

To be clear, I thought he was probably right—I was pretty sure Discaru was gone from this world; but if I was wrong, things could get ugly. One reason I'm still around to tell you these stories is because when I'm doing big things that are crazy, I try to play it safe with as much of the little stuff as I can. It's worked so far, right? Of course, "It's worked so far, right?" do pretty well as last words, so let's not get cocky about it.

I took a look around the courtyard area in case there was anything I'd missed, but if so I missed it again. And then it was back into the passage, and back around, making tedious but necessary stops to pick the locks on the other doors just to make sure that, yes, they really did lead back into the same courtyard, just like they appeared to.

Eventually I came back to where I'd first entered the passage. What now? Retrace my steps the whole long, bloody way? To where? To do what? I had my answers now, at least some of them, but I didn't know what to do with them. I know what I wanted to do: go find Zhayin and smack him around a little just on general principle. But that probably wasn't the best way to get my answers and solve Devera's problems. What was?

Okay, I'd start by retracing my steps, just for lack of a better idea.

Once more, then, into the bedroom. I frowned at the strange window-doors; I wasn't sure that was the way I'd come in, but how else?

I tested the doors, they opened, and I stepped through.

And I was back on the cliff. I didn't think I'd ever get used to this.

I took a few steps down, and I was outside the cave again. There was an extinguished torch at my feet. I picked it up, tried to light it, failed, then stepped into the cave out of the wind and managed to get it going. The stairway was where it was supposed to be; I followed it up and was back in the cellar beneath the manor. I deliberately avoided looking around too much as I went through it; I didn't want any more distractions. It was a long walk, all in all, up and down, and through scary rooms of sorcery and boring hallways, but then I was back to—

There. That was the room where Discaru had brought me to the Halls of Judgment. Would it work without him there? Or was he still there, waiting for me, really annoyed at me for having shoved a Great Weapon up under his chin? There was also the question of did I *want* to visit the Halls of Judgment again. That was easy: no, I didn't. I like it when there are questions I know the answer to.

I went farther down the hall until I stood in the room with the fake wall, with the *thing* on the other side. It didn't come bursting out while I stood there, which I thought was kind of it. I stared at the wall. *One way or another, I don't think you and I are done with each other, my friend.* I turned and went back through the door and continued down the spiral stairway that emerged—I'm tempted to say as usual—on the wrong side of the hall.

I walked down the hall, remembering where things were, or should be, or might be but probably weren't. Like, directly above me *should* have been the room where I'd reached the Halls of Judgment, the little room where I'd seen Discaru, then the hidden cell that contained the beast. Like I said, that should have been above me, but where was it, really, relative to where I was? It was slightly crazy-making. I kept trying, pointless as it was, to fit it all into my head. What was past the beast room? The balcony above the ballroom? No, that should be farther back. The armory, then. No, the mirror room.

The mirror room.

A workshop cabin full of glass sheets, silver, an oven, and a bunch of things whose use I didn't understand. Put them together, and what do you get? Mirrors. Lots of mirrors.

Use of mirrors is one of the few things Eastern witchcraft and sorcery have in common. Glass with a silver backing reflecting light is used in all manner of things. For necromancy? Well, form a connection with the Halls in order to create a link with a higher plane, then bounce it off mirrors to symbolically reflect it through the manor; the odd backwardness in places, where things were on the wrong side of the hall, or up when they should be down, was just a side effect of the spell.

Well, so what? I mean, I'd already tried to hit one of the damn things, and all I'd gotten was a numb hand.

"*Lady Teldra, Boss,*" said the brains of the outfit.

Damn.

"*That could be interesting. When did you think of it?*"

"*First time you hit the mirror.*"

"*Why didn't you mention it then?*"

"*Because it could be interesting.*"

Straight ahead to the ballroom, then up—a stairway up that actually went up. Around the edge of the balcony, and there was the mirror room. I pulled the door open.

Was I really going to do this?

"*Ready, Loiosh?*"

"*Not really, Boss.*"

Of course I was going to do this. I drew Lady Teldra. She had her most usual form, the thin, very long knife or very short sword. Without giving myself time to consider consequences, I picked out the nearest mirror, thought, *Verra, I hope this doesn't kill me,* and gave it a good, hard, backhand cut right across the middle.

This time, the transition was *not* smooth. It wasn't subtle, either. I felt like my teeth were about to rattle themselves out of my head, the room spun, there was a roaring in my ears, and then I was facedown, still holding Lady Teldra.

I opened my eyes. The floor was a hard, manufactured substance of pure white. I turned my head, and there was a wall next to me that seemed to be made of the same thing.

"Hello, my dear. Would you mind terribly putting that away?"

I knew that odd, weird, echoey voice.

I raised my head. "Goddess?"

"Whom were you expecting?" said Verra. "Please be so kind as to sheathe your weapon, my love."

"Where are Loiosh and Rocza?"

"They didn't come through whatever strange device brought you to me."

I got up on my knees, stared at Lady Teldra, then sheathed her.

"Thank you," said Verra. "So, little Vladimir, what brought you to me today?"

"Yeah," I said. I stood up slowly. I seemed to be all right. "Yeah, that would be my first question. But don't worry, there are others. A lot of others."

"Goodness," she said. "Well then, be comfortable."

We were sitting—her in a big chair on a raised dais, me in something padded and comfortable. I'm not even talking about the sudden travel without teleport, just suddenly appearing somewhere else. I was getting bored with it.

"Let's start," said my patron goddess, "with how you got here. What happened?"

"I hit a magic mirror with a Great Weapon in a house that travels from the past to the future and contains halls that exist necromantically across worlds, including the Halls of Judgment—you know, like you do."

"Ah," said Verra. "I see."

"Good. Then explain it?"

"You refer to a magic mirror. What is the enchantment?"

"Goddess, what in the world would make you think I'd know that?"

She nodded. "Of course." She looked thoughtful. "You meant it, when you said past and future?"

"I know about the past, I'm pretty sure about the future."

"Connected by hallways."

"And doors, yeah. Mostly doors."

"So someone did it."

"Yeah, someone did it. Did what?"

"Something the Vallista have been attempting for thousands of years. Tens of thousands. But someone managed it. Now, of all times. Was it a Vallista?"

"Yeah. What do you mean, now of all times?"

"I've suspected, my beautiful young Vladimir, but I didn't know." She smiled. "We should celebrate."

"Celebrate. Right. Yes. Let's celebrate. What are we celebrating?"

A table popped into existence next to me, then a glass cup formed like a flower. She also had one, and a bottle.

"Come," she said.

"All right."

I got up and went over to her, climbed the dais, and let her pour the wine, then I went back and sat down again.

She raised her glass. "The end of an era."

"What era?"

"A very, very long era."

"And, it just ended today?"

"No, no. It ended more than two hundred years ago. I just wasn't sure until today."

"Well, good then. I guess all of my questions are answered."

"Vlad, your sarcasm grows wearisome. If you continue, I won't give you any more wine."

"Fine, fine."

I raised my cup and drank some. "Dear Goddess!" I said.

"Yes?"

"Uh, this is, this is really, really good."

"Yes. I've been saving it."

"I mean, *really* good."

"Shut up and drink."

"Yes, Goddess."

I drank some more, trying to commit it to memory. It was sweet, very sweet, but without the annoying too-much that usually comes with sweet wine. It was like drinking light, like drinking purity, and all of it was doing a dance on my tongue that defied me to pull the pieces apart.

"That is, well, thank you."

"You're welcome."

"So, ah, just what are we celebrating?"

"Don't think, Vlad. Concentrate on the wine."

Yeah, that was a good plan. I did that. I would kill for wine like that. Okay, I guess that's not saying much, what with all the things I've killed for. But you know what I mean.

The wine took up all of my thinking for three cups, at which time, alas, it was gone. But if I die tomorrow, I've had that. It was almost enough to make me forgive the goddess for, well, everything else she had ever done.

"All right," I said, putting my cup down. "What exactly have we just celebrated?"

"The end of an era, as I said. And that, I'm afraid, is as much time as I can spare. This is big, my dear Vlad. There are things I must do, things I must prepare, gods in whose face I must laugh while crying in my best theatrical voice, 'Told I thee not so?'"

"Uh, what?"

"I should bring you back to where you were. Mmm. That may be difficult. I think I can manage it by—"

"Goddess!"

She tilted her head and looked at me. "Yes, little one?"

"What is going on? How did I get here? What's Devera doing there? Why—"

"Devera?" she said sharply. She had been half out of her chair, now she sat down and looked at me. "What has Devera to do with this?"

"She's the one who got me into it."

"Into what, exactly?"

"Brought me to the house, the place, the"—I coughed—"*platform* where all of this happened."

"Why?"

"She's trapped there."

"Trapped? Impossible."

"Uh, if you say so."

She settled back fully into her chair, the way you do if you plan to be there for a while. "Tell me everything," she said.

I glared at her. "You first."

She stood up. "Vladimir—"

I didn't stand up, but I touched Lady Teldra's hilt and said evenly, "Do not threaten me, Goddess."

"You would draw that, on me, in my own home?"

"Only if I have to."

"You're a fool."

"Is that why you picked me? I mean, the first time. When I was Dolivar. You needed some idiot you could wield like a tool, who'd be too stupid to know he was being played? Was that it? All the way back, the first time? I'm stupid, Goddess, but maybe not as stupid as you think I am."

She slowly sat down again, and I let go of Lady Teldra's hilt.

"First of all," she said, "I didn't pick you, Devera did. Second, it wasn't because you're a fool, it was because she thought you'd be willing to stand up to her grandmother when it was needed."

"So, in other words, a fool."

She chuckled, and I relaxed a little more. If Loiosh had been here, *fool* would have been the kindest thing he'd have called me.

"One thing," I said.

"What?"

"When I was remembering that, that life with Dolivar when you and I first met—at least, I assume it's the first time."

I paused, but she didn't choose to comment. "I remember thinking that Devera must have been around nine years old."

"What of it?"

"Well, Dragaerans grow slowly, right? I mean, by the time they're grown up, a human would be dead."

"Yes, that's true, now."

"Now?"

She nodded.

"When did it change?"

"Gradually, over an immense length of time. You know how long the Empire has existed."

"Yeah, but—"

"Yes?"

"That seems an odd thing to happen."

"A natural side effect."

"Of what?"

"Of the way the Jenoine tampered with the world."

"I don't understand."

"It was a result of their whole effort. No, not effort. Experiment."

"Experiment?"

"They live a long time, Vlad. Long by Sethra's standards, long by mine. And they're observers, and they are absolutely heartless, at least where other species are concerned. This world is an experiment to see if a society can be made to stagnate."

"I am lost."

"Societies develop and change, Vlad. There are inventions, and inventions have repercussions throughout society; associations among people grow and become different."

"If you say so."

"You've never seen it, because, for one thing, you don't live long enough, and for another, that hasn't happened here. Or rather, it has, but it has been very, very slow. The formation of the Empire, from scattered tribes, took tens of thousands of years. Without the interference of the Jenoine, it would only have taken hundreds."

"That's—I don't know what to say."

"I was one of their servants, and I didn't enjoy it. My sisters and I took offense at the whole idea, not to mention how they treated us, so we took action."

"The Great Sea of Amorphia."

She nodded. "It didn't undo what they'd done, but it introduced a certain amount of slow, gradual progress. Between that and our efforts to keep them from interfering, things have moved. A little. But now . . ." She smiled.

"Now what?"

"I should have realized it, of course. Adron's Disaster. That was it. Seventeen Cycles. They built in their stability, and I destabilized it. That was the proof it worked. I should have recognized my own handiwork."

"Um. I have no idea what you're talking about."

"I'm talking about Devera, my granddaughter, my little seed of catalyst thrown into the swamp of stagnation. Catalyst, yes, the silver tiassa. How did I not recognize it?"

"Goddess, I have no idea—"

"Devera. A product of the Interregnum."

"That makes no sense. Her mother wasn't even around during the Interregnum. I know, I rescued her myself."

"Yes." She smiled. "From the Halls of Judgment. Where she came in a disembodied form because of the actions of her father. It was, after all, why I introduced that ability into the e'Kieron line so long ago, though I had no idea in what way it would bear fruit." By now, I was generating questions faster than I could even remember them. She kept talking. "But there it is, time out of time, stretching from the first disaster to the second, and the second brought everything—even you, my oh-so-tough Easterner—together to create little Devera, the perfect catalyst to unlock—everything. This is splendid. I should open another bottle of that wine."

"Yes, that would be—"

"Tell me everything that happened."

I was done trying to fight her on it. I gave her a more-or-less complete version of events, leaving out things that were none of her business, or that I'd promised not to mention. She listened, nodding occasionally, her eyes fixed on me like they'd keep me pinned to the chair.

When I finally stopped, she sat back and rubbed her chin with one of her weird fingers. At length she said, "What aren't you telling me?"

"Stuff," I said.

"How did she end up trapped there?"

"I don't know."

"You didn't ask her?"

"Our conversations kept being cut short by her vanishing abruptly."

She nodded. "Of course, yes, that would happen."

"Why?"

She brushed it aside as if it didn't matter, which, with my luck, meant it was the key to the whole thing (it wasn't, but I didn't find that out for a bit).

"All right, then," she said. "It makes sense now."

"I'm glad it makes sense to someone. Can you explain why, when I struck the mirror, it brought me here?"

"I am certain," she said dryly, "that if you put your whole mind to it, you can work out why it was that when you, in your typical subtle, discreet, and nuanced way, blasted a big hole in the fabric of the universe, you happened to come here."

"Uh . . ."

Verra, I hope this doesn't kill me.

"Right," I said. "Got it."

She shrugged. "That's a relief. Come with me."

I followed her down a narrow white hallway, trying to organize my questions into something coherent. The hall ended in an arched opening, with a large room on the other side, also white, except that it didn't. I followed her through the arch, and we were in an entirely different room, circular, not especially big, with windows looking out—

"Hey," I said. "This is Morrolan's—"

She unceremoniously pushed me. I fell backward into one of the windows, and ended up—

Of course. In the manor, on my back, just outside the mirror room.

"Boss?"

"*Loiosh, you wouldn't believe—*"

"*I think you should get up.*"

I know that tone. I did so. "*How long was I—*"

"*Not long, just a couple of minutes. But just as you vanished, there was that sound.*"

"*What sound?*"

"*You know, like, stones rolling?*"

Crap.

"Yeah, I must have set off an alarm."

"Uh-huh. Should we run?"

"To where?"

I glared at me in the mirror I'd just tried to break, and I glared back.

That's when I heard a scuffling sound behind me, just as Loiosh said, "Boss!"

I turned around, and there was the big, ugly, misshapen thing making its way toward me from down the hall. As far as I could judge, it wasn't coming to raise my Imperial county to a duchy.

No messing around this time; I drew Lady Teldra.

"Plan, Boss?"

"Can you distract it?"

"Maybe."

"Let's go for that."

It was coming very fast, and it was very big.

Okay, thing. Let's do this. I dropped into a crouch, watching how it moved, gauging distance. Loiosh and Rocza were on its back, biting it, filling it with venom that none of us expected to have any effect, at least not soon. It didn't even seem to notice them, and I could tell that Loiosh was offended. As the thing got up to me, Loiosh left its back and flew into its face; I rolled to the side as it continued right up to where I'd been and stumbled into the mirrors, which caused nothing whatever to happen, unfortunately.

But it did leave the thing's back exposed.

I struck, and it twisted like it could feel it coming and I missed, and at the same time it lashed out at me and I caught a hand to my head and saw spots in front of my eyes and felt a little sick. I backed up as fast as I could, but it was faster; at the last minute I rolled forward, scampered between its legs without a shred of dignity, and came up behind it, but I didn't even try to take a shot; I just put some distance between us. Loiosh and Rocza landed on its back again and bit it some more, and it still didn't seem to even be aware of them.

It was really fast, that thing. Inhumanly fast. I scrambled to the side and ducked, avoiding another great thump—I swear the air of its fist passing almost knocked me down. I looked for an opening, but it stopped and turned too quickly for me to do more than gaze wistfully at its exposed back before its teeth were in my face again.

Rocza flew close enough that I felt the psychic equivalent of an indrawn breath from Loiosh, but the thing stopped long enough to swipe at her, and that gave me a moment to pull a shuriken from my cloak and—here's hoping—whip it at the damn thing's eye.

Almost. It hit it where its eyebrow would have been if it had one, which caused it to flinch for a second, at which time the shuriken fell to the ground; it didn't even stick. Really? I backpedaled, pulled another, tried again, whipping it like a throwing knife, overhand, which sacrificed a little accuracy for force.

The shuriken went flying over its shoulder and I turned and sprinted down the hall. Was the armory near by? Was there anything in the armory that would help? I could see the advantage of having a halberd, I just couldn't see the possibility of finding it and taking it and positioning it before that thing crushed me.

I tossed a knife over my shoulder and heard it clank. Stupid—the thing wasn't smart enough to slow down. There were more flapping sounds. Then I had a great idea: there's a pocket that I had tailored in the back of my cloak to keep various odds and ends, and one of them was a small vial of oil that I'd use to keep doors from squeaking, and I realized that I might be able to spill it on the floor and make the thing slip. Two problems: one, pulling something from the back of my cloak without slowing down enough for it to get me, and two, I no longer carried the oil.

But it was a really good idea, wasn't it?

When I felt its breath on the back of my neck I stopped and dropped to the ground, fully prone, fists clenched against my head, elbows locked at my sides, then I said something like "Ugh" as its foot hit my left arm enough to numb it and make me wonder if I'd broken it. It went sprawling. I didn't even wait to stand up, I just sort of got to my knees and leapt on top of it, Lady Teldra first.

It was already rising, but Lady Teldra went into its side nearly to the hilt, and then I was flying through the air, and I swear to you by my hope of rebirth, I hit the Verra-be-damned *ceiling.* Then, presumably, I fell to the floor, though I don't exactly remember that part.

Some time later—Loiosh says about ten minutes—I sat up and looked around. I knew I'd been in a fight, and I figured I'd probably won, but I couldn't make it come together. Eventually I spotted the big, ugly thing with Lady Teldra sticking out of it just above where people have a hip, and I wobbled over there and drew her, and cleaned her off on the thing's body as my brain reconstructed the events.

I stared at it. At him. Poor bastard. Toddler goes wandering off, gets possessed by a demon, or maybe just warped by one, I don't know, and then spends I don't know how long locked in a little room and then ends up like this. I felt bad for him.

Then I ended up needing a minute for introspection. I felt bad for him? Since when did I start feeling bad for people I had to kill? Well, yeah, but this wasn't the usual thing. Other times, what led me to kill them was a result of their own decisions. This thing, this person, had never made any decisions. It had all happened to him, and then I had happened to him. A lousy way for a life to go. And there wasn't even, really, anyone to blame for it. I hate it when I don't have anyone to blame. I usually get out of it by blaming Verra.

Verra. Sheesh.

"Boss? What happened when you vanished?"

"Loiosh, when we get out of this, you and I are going to have a long talk about it, and maybe you can make sense of it."

"Uhhh. I can't wait?"

I took a last look at the poor creature I'd just killed, then turned away.

Well done, Vlad. You lived. You've also almost certainly pissed off a few people as soon as they find the big white naked, ugly dead guy. I wasn't sure there was anyone left in the place I had any reason to be afraid of, but I couldn't be completely sure there wasn't either.

I went back and stood in front of the mirrors. I had dried blood on the side of my face, and it looked like I was developing a black eye.

"Boss, you're beautiful."

"Shut up."

I checked to see if my hands were shaking. Is it strange that I needed to look? Anyway, they weren't shaking much. I was convinced these mirrors were the answer, or at least a big part of it. That when I'd struck one with Lady Teldra I'd been transported to Verra's Halls, and that the beast had come after me, seemed like good evidence that I was right.

"*Boss? Any ideas?*"

"No. You?"

"*Yeah. Let's just kill everyone we meet and see if that does anything.*"

"Not the dancer. I liked her."

"*You're getting soft.*"

I looked over at the body. Did I need to hide it? I wasn't sure how I could, but did I need to? No, I guess of all the ways things could go down, being arrested for that particular murder was the least likely.

And no one was here anyway—

The door I'd just closed opened. I pressed myself against a wall and let a dagger drop into my hand, and I waited.

And stick me with flags and call me a fair if three servants, each holding a tray of food, didn't come walking out, cool as you please, as if emerging from a room full of mirrors were the most natural way in the world to serve dinner. They didn't turn around, they didn't appear to see the dead lump of monster not twenty feet away from them; they just went down the spiral stair, not marching, but walking at the same pace; there was almost an air of ritual about it. I moved so I could keep watching as they went out the door of the ballroom.

"*Boss? What—?*"

"I have no idea. Don't even ask."

"*But you remember those three—*"

"I remember."

I went back down the stairway and out the door, catching

sight of them as they turned a corner. I stayed a good distance back and followed the long twisty path. Two of the servants stopped in the kitchen; the third continued on. As I passed the kitchen I heard voices: the servants, then, taking their meal. I reached the passage to the first corridor I'd come to and stuck my head around as the servant went into the room where Zhayin had been.

So, that's why the kitchen was empty: the food was brought in from the other place. From the past. They cooked food in the past and brought it to the present. Sure, why not? Why had I never done that? Everyone should do that.

"*Loiosh, have I gone completely down the well?*"

"*Maybe.*"

"*Thanks.*"

I tried to put the stuff Verra had told me out of my head, because it wasn't helping me with this.

It was tempting to just go rushing in and have a talk with Zhayin, demand some answers. But I wasn't sure he'd give them to me, and then I'd probably get mad and kill him, and besides, it's rude to interrupt someone's dinner.

I went back to the little room just before the ballroom and shut the door behind me. Finally, I was doing something I was good at, had done before, and was confident I could do with quiet competence: waiting. It was most of an hour, but then I heard the footsteps, the same slow, deliberate pace.

I waited until they were past me, then stuck my head out, and, yes, all three were there, bringing the dirty dishes and leftovers back to the past, to clean the dishes and give the leftovers to the kethna or the other servants. Once they were past me, I waited for another minute, then followed them from a good distance. I was just coming up the stairs when they coolly disappeared once more into the mirror room. They still hadn't realized there was a body there.

I hesitated after they'd passed; there were a couple of ways to play this from here, but I knew what I wanted to do. There had been something nagging at me for a while, and, even if it wasn't part of the big picture, I wanted to get it settled.

I gave myself some time to come up with reasons not to— almost a whole second—then I went back and around and poked my head back into the room where I'd gotten my meal the day before. There was a rope hanging there, vanishing into a hole in the ceiling. I pulled it.

In under a minute, Harro appeared and bowed. "My lord," he said. "How may I serve you?"

"Just a little conversation, if you wouldn't mind."

"Not in the least."

"Would you like to sit?"

"I should prefer to stand, if I may, my lord."

"That's fine."

I sat down and stretched out my legs.

"What did you wish to discuss, my lord?"

"Hevlika."

I was watching closely; there was definitely a tightening around his jaw as he attempted not to react.

"What did you wish to know, sir?"

Remember when I was talking about how you need to use different means to get different people talking? Well, sometimes you need different means to get the same person talking, if it's on different subjects. Let's take Harro, for example: an Issola, a butler; he was all about duty. He'd rather die than violate his duty, which made it a question of turning it around, so that one aspect of his duty required him to violate another. When it was a personal matter, and didn't violate his duty, that was entirely different, requiring an alternate form of negotiation.

I drew the dagger from my right side. It was big, as knives go, really more fighting knife than dagger, what with the wide blade curving wickedly down to the point for the last four inches—it's the sort of knife that makes one think of long gashes in the torso with entrails falling out of them. Most of us don't care for images like that applied to our person.

I held it loosely in my hand, thumb and forefinger at the crossguard, letting it bounce up and down like a snake looking for where to strike.

"Tell me about you and Hevlika."

His eyes were wide, and on the knife, which was where I wanted them. I waited for a little while as his mouth, which seemed to have lost all connection to the rest of him, did a credible imitation of a fish.

"Maybe you'd like to sit down?" I said.

He sat on the bed and continued looking at the knife. At last he managed, "How did you know?"

I shook my head. "You're confused about who is asking questions and who is answering them. I"—I pointed the knife at my chest—"am asking. You"—I pointed the knife at him—"are answering. Start answering now."

"I . . ."

"Yes. You. Good. Good start. You and Hevlika. What's the connection?"

"I'll . . . I'll call for help."

"I don't think I believe you, Harro. I don't think you're capable of generating a sound much louder than a whimper. But if you want, sure. I'm not sure who you're expecting to rescue you, though. That monster that used to be Zhayin's son is lying up on the balcony above the ballroom, getting cold and waiting for the excitement of its body getting rigid. As for Discaru, I believe I managed to send him back to whatever strange, unreal place spawned him, although I could be wrong. But if you want to try anyway, go ahead. I'll only cut you twice for each scream, and only one of those will be on your pretty face."

He stared at me.

I tapped the flat of the blade against my palm and gave him a few seconds to consider his options. He looked at the door and I chuckled. "No, I don't think that's a good idea." He turned his attention back to the knife.

"We were. . . ."

"Yes. You were?"

"I'm in love with her."

"Yeah? How'd that work out for you?"

"She hates me."

"Where'd you meet?"

"I had occasion to accompany my lord to the dance, and I saw her."

"Uh-huh. You saw her. Onstage."

He nodded.

"And then, what? You decided she was destined to be your true love?"

"I—you make it sound pitiful."

"No, pitiful is how you arranged for Gormin to be expelled from the House, just to get him out of the way."

"Out of the way? I had no idea they were involved!"

As he said that, he took his eyes from the knife and looked at my face. I believed him.

"So, it was just to get his job? You made up the part about

them being involved, had no idea it was true, and used it so you could get his job to be close to her? Really?"

He looked down again, at the floor now, not the knife. I took it as a yes.

"How long have you known that you're a complete moron?"

"About two hundred years."

"Here's what I don't get—no, here's one of about a thousand things I don't get. How is it that, back then, after you'd managed to get Gormin's job by being a slimy worm with no more decency than your basic suckerfish, Hevlika never saw you? I mean, never even knew you were there?"

"How did you—"

I smacked the flat of the blade against my hand. He swallowed and changed his mind. "That was at Lord Zhayin's orders, my lord."

"But how?"

"It wasn't difficult. I stayed away from the theater, and from her chambers. She never mingled. Back then, she either saw Lord Zhayin, or she'd visit the village."

"That's it?"

"Yes, my lord."

"How long did that go on?"

"It wasn't long, my lord. Only until the manor could be occupied, which was less than a hundred years ago. Most of the time has been spent working on the sorcery, you know, not the construction. Once the household—that is, Lord Zhayin, and Lord Discaru, and Gormin, and Odelpho, had taken up occupancy here, he no longer minded. That's when Hevlika and I actually met."

I nodded. "Good. Down to nine hundred and ninety nine."

"My lord?"

I shook my head. "Then answer me this: Why?"

"Why what, my lord?"

"Why didn't Zhayin want the two of you to meet?"

"I don't know, my lord."

"Um. Humor me. Take a guess. I won't hold it against you if you're wrong. I'm holding so much against you now there's no more room anyway."

He spread his hands.

"Why?" I repeated.

He looked thoughtful. "I don't know, but, well, he was very secretive about everything in those days. He was always careful who spoke to whom, and we suspect that Discaru would sometimes cast listening spells on us. Perhaps it was part of that?"

"Huh," I said. "And he isn't like that anymore?"

"It's different now," he said.

"Go on."

"Now he just tries to limit the intercourse between here and the old castle. The servants who bring the food are all deaf, and those of us here are forbidden to journey back there. I wouldn't know how to, but I know it's done, because of the food."

"So, that's why there are no guards here. He doesn't want to bring them from the past. But then, why not hire some from here and now? And cooks as well?"

"I don't know, my lord. Maybe he will. It's only just been finished."

"All right," I said. "I think I've gotten as much from you as I can."

"What are you going to do with me, my lord?"

I shrugged. "I should probably kill you, you know. Just to put you out of your misery."

He made no response whatsoever.

"Are you inclined to live, Harro?"

"My lord?" He swallowed. "Yes, my lord."

"Good. Because I'm not going anywhere. Well, I mean, I am, I'm leaving this place as soon as I figure out how. But I'll still be in the area. And if, by chance, someone starts taking legal action to become reinstated in his House, and if in the process you're questioned, you'll cooperate, and you won't lie. Because if you lie, you die. Is there an understanding between us?"

"Yes, my lord."

"Good. Okay, tell me something else, then. Why did you stay? To be near her, because you liked the work, or just inertia?"

"All of those, I think," he told the floor between his feet.

The floor didn't seem impressed.

I looked at him; he avoided looking at me. "Never mind," I said. "I think you've managed to make yourself more miserable than anything I could do. Go be miserable. Don't say anything, just get out of here, and do whatever it is you do. If I want anything, I'll ring."

He didn't even say "Yes, my lord," which might give you an idea of what kind of shape he was in.

The door closed behind him. I hoped this would all be over soon; I was hungry.

16

ON THE NIGHT OF THE SURLY MOOD

I gave Harro time to get clear, then left the room and made my way back to the ballroom, then up to the balcony, and to the door to the theater. I stood in front of it, took a breath, and opened it.

And I was sitting down.

That transition was one of the hardest to get used to. I wasn't in the same seat as before, but almost; maybe one forward and two to the side or something. That, by itself, would mean a great deal to someone who wasn't me.

There was no sign of Hevlika, so I settled in to wait. I'm not sure why I was so convinced that sooner or later she would show up, but I was, and in maybe a bit less than half an hour, she did; just walking onto the stage. She noticed me at once, because she always noticed her audience. She'd said so.

She jumped down from the stage, walked up, and sat down in the chair next to me. As per protocol, she stared straight ahead.

"You really don't recognize me?" I said.

"Of course I do. You were here yesterday."

"I mean from before."

"I don't understand."

"We met before, at a house called the Seven Jewels."

She frowned for a minute, then turned and looked at me. "That was you?"

I nodded.

She scrutinized my face with no sign of recognition—maybe we really do all look the same. Then she glanced at my left hand, and said, "Yes, I remember."

I nodded.

"How is it possible?"

"It's complicated."

"But Easterners—"

She broke off.

"Yeah," I said. "We don't generally live that long. I cheated."

"I don't understand."

"I don't either, entirely. But that conversation we had a few hundred years ago? That was a few hours ago for me."

"The manor."

"Yeah."

"Who *are* you?"

"Vladimir Taltos, Count of Szurke by the grace of Her Majesty, former Jhereg, current traveler, *nehixta*, and connoisseur of fine food and drink."

"I don't recognize that one word. Is it Serioli?"

"No, one of the languages of the cat-centaurs. I was called that once. She translated it to 'one who cuts himself twice on the same knife.'"

"It doesn't sound like a compliment."

"I got the feeling it was mostly used of children who won't learn to stay out of things they should leave alone. Somewhere

I'm sure there is a desecrator who could explain the full cultural significance and get it entirely wrong."

"I don't recall much of our last conversation. Just that you asked a lot of questions."

"And I warned you not to trust Harro."

She frowned. "Yes, I sort of remember that. I know I don't trust him."

"He's the one who got Gormin expelled from the House of the Issola."

She turned and looked at me again, and this time didn't look away. "Why would he do that?"

"He's in love with you."

The look on her face was mostly disgust, with an overlay of disbelief. I turned my head so I was facing the stage and waited while it sank in.

"Why are you telling me this?"

"To be honest, I'm not entirely sure. It seemed like something you should know. Besides, I sort of liked Gormin before he drugged me and tried to interrogate me."

"I can't believe he'd do that."

"He was acting under orders."

"When did this happen?"

"A few hundred years ago. Or earlier today, depending on how you look at it."

"Gormin," she said. "He . . ."

"Is it hard, living under the same roof as him?"

She cleared her throat and turned back to the stage. "That's a little personal."

"We got more personal than that, back before."

"Did we? I don't remember. And I can't think why I would."

"Neither can I. It didn't seem very Issola-like."

"Perhaps that was close to"—she looked for the words to get around saying what she didn't want to say—"to when things happened with Gormin. I wasn't myself, then. What is it?"

"Hmmm? What is what?"

"Your fingers are twitching."

I looked at them and made them stop. "I feel like killing someone, but there's no one I'm sure needs killing. Harro's a bastard, but not enough of one for me to put a knife into his eye."

"I . . . can't imagine what that must feel like."

"Really? You can't? You've never been angry?"

"Well, yes, of course I've been angry."

"That's what it feels like."

"All right."

We didn't speak for a little while after that.

"Back then," she said at last. "Did you ever explain what you were doing?"

"Sort of."

"Want to try again? If I can help you, I will."

"All right. Do you know about the mirrors?"

"The practice room? Of course. I work out there every day."

"No, the other mirror room."

"Oh. I'm not to go in there."

"It's pretty much the magic focus for the entire place."

"I guess it could be. But I don't know any details. I haven't made much of a study of sorcery, beyond what everyone knows."

It's hard to explain to someone what you don't understand yourself. "Okay," I said. "I've got some of it. The manor wasn't built here, it appeared here. I put that together when I saw all the dead plants—never mind. I found a cave, with sorcerous markings on it, that was, well . . . think of it as an anchor, all right? They built it, and one of the parts of it had to—"

I broke off.

"What?" she said after a moment.

"I think I have it," I said. "Paths, hallways, doors, necromantic mirrors. The mirrors provide a way to turn physical motion into motion through worlds, which sometimes means through time. That's how it got here. There are places it is anchored—like the cave under the cellar, and the Halls of Judgment, and the place in the past where they started construction. The mirrors work like Morrolan's windows—"

"What?"

"Uh, never mind. The thing is, all the pathways in the manor, controlled by the mirrors, are sort of, well, think of it like they're stacked on top of each other. Zhayin's idea is to be able to make additional pathways to different worlds, that you can reach just by opening a door or walking down a hall."

I felt myself frowning. "Only, he hasn't done it yet. All he has is a way to reach the Halls, the future out from the courtyard, and the past—the anchors. He hasn't built any of the pathways, just a lot of places where they can go, which is why right now they turn into just odd rooms placed in strange places; it's like he set up a bunch of sheaths but hasn't put the daggers in them yet. Why hasn't he? Oh, right. Harro said the manor had just recently been completed.

She nodded. "Two days ago is when we shifted. I've been living in the manor for years and years, but it was next to the old castle, by the river, and then we were suddenly here."

"That's it, then," I said. "Time."

"Pardon?"

"Pathways in space are pathways in time, when you're going

between worlds. I'm sure if the Necromancer were here she could explain it so it made sense, but that's the best I can do."

"I don't—"

"It's all about Tethia, and you, and Harro, and Gormin."

"I've never met Tethia."

"Yes, exactly. Because she died, you see."

"When?"

"Yes, exactly. When. When and where. That's the part that's hard to wrap my head around, but it sort of makes sense."

"You've lost me."

"Tethia died here, in the manor, in the past, but was trapped in the now."

She shook her head.

"Try it this way: Tethia was involved in casting those spells for a couple of hundred years. You never met her, because her part of things involved being in the future."

"The future?"

"Uh, the *then* future, the now now."

"I don't, wait, I think I see what you mean. She did her work here, near Adrilankha, in the time and place where the manor was going to be."

"Yes, casting the spells that would allow it to exist."

"But how did she get here? How did she move through time that way?"

"My head hurts."

"Sorry."

"No, it's okay. I'm working it out, I think. Try this: She didn't really move through time. In the Halls of Judgment, there are a lot of times and places to choose from, maybe an infinite number, I don't know. But while Zhayin was overseeing the building of the physical structure, Tethia was spending her time in the Halls of Judgment, making the magical connections that corresponded to it. When they were both done, the manor appeared here."

"But Tethia was . . ."

"Yeah, okay. She was in the Halls of Judgment, with her spells following pathways to here and now, and she was here and now, with spells sending pathways to the Halls."

"But you said she wasn't traveling in time. That's where I'm lost."

"Yeah, me too."

I really did feel like I was on the verge of a headache. You know that feeling that hits you when you put the pieces of a puzzle together and it all instantly makes sense? I like that better. "Okay," I said, speaking slowly as it worked its way through my skull, "In the Halls, in the travel between worlds, time and place are part of the same thing. So, if she was in the Halls, she could find a *place* that was a *time*. That's what she was connecting the manor to. You can think of it as a place and a time above us, that touches our own. That's why she kept calling it a platform."

"That sort of makes sense. But then, what happened to her?"

"That's what I'm going to find out."

She nodded. "There's a sorcerer here. Maybe—"

"Discaru. Yeah. He wasn't helpful. And I'm pretty sure he's no longer around."

"Oh?"

I took that as an invitation to tell her more and declined by not saying anything. She seemed to think that was an excellent choice, and did the same. I broke first. "How are you?"

"M'lord?"

"With what I told you. About Gormin and Harro. How are you doing with it?"

"It'll take some time to settle in."

"Will it be hard to act normal with Harro? I mean, if you even want to?"

"I don't know."

I shook my head. "I just don't understand it. I can't wrap my head around it."

"Around what?"

"You two. You and Gormin, I mean. You're together, all is well, then his House changes, and, boom, everything's different. It isn't even that his station changed, because it didn't. It's just his House. How can you let that—"

She was quiet for a few seconds as I broke off and stared into space. Then she said, "What?"

I shook my head, my brain spinning. "That's it," I said finally. "It all ties together. The Houses. The Cycle. The Empire. The Disaster. Stagnation. Catalyst. All of it."

She waited patiently until I started to get up, then she said, "Vlad, you can't just leave it like that." Her tone was one of amusement, but she had a point. I sat down again.

"Sorry. Too much, too fast. And, yeah, this affects you."

"How? What?"

"I don't think I can explain it, except to say that you—I mean Dragaerans, all of you—have been fu—messed with. And it permeates everything you do, even who you let yourself love, and it was done deliberately by the Jenoine because they wanted to see what would happen."

"Ah. . . ."

"You're very nice. You don't want to say 'You're crazy.' That's sweet."

She put on an Issola smile, but didn't say I was wrong.

"Okay, believe it or not, whatever. A lot of this I've known for years, some of it is new and I'm putting it together, and my head is spinning. But just tell me this: why is it so unthinkable to marry someone from another House?"

"Well, because . . . you wouldn't understand."

"No, I wouldn't. But the odd thing is, you don't either. You know it, you feel it, but you don't understand it."

She looked at me, then slowly returned her eyes to the stage.

"Sorry," I said. "This must be making you uncomfortable."

She said, "Maybe we should talk about your problem."

"Sure."

"Maybe if you explain it? I mean, what exactly you're trying to do."

I shrugged. "All right. There's a girl named Devera. She was born in the Halls of Judgment. Her grandmother is a goddess, her—"

"Which goddess?"

"Verra. Her father is the shade of Kieron the Conqueror."

"Go on."

I blinked. All right, well, if she was just going to accept all that as if it were reasonable, I might as well tell her the rest. I went through the conversations I'd had, the things I'd seen, the oddness of the room design, my conclusion about Lady Zhayin, and about the mirrors. She didn't say anything, but nodded at a few of my conclusions, and winced when I spoke of killing Discaru and the thing that had once been Zhayin's son.

When I'd finished, she was quiet for a long time, then she said, "Devera."

"What about her?"

"You described Devera appearing and disappearing. Why does she keep doing that?"

"Um. Yeah. I guess I just thought, well, because of her nature."

"That doesn't answer the question though, does it?"

"No, I suppose it doesn't. You're right."

"So?"

"So, you've got me asking the right question, now how do I figure out the answer?"

"I can't help you with that."

"Every time you say you can't help me, it means I'm about to learn something."

She smiled at the stage. "I think that's more you than me."

"Maybe. Well, okay. It isn't just her nature, or she'd do it all the time. And it isn't just the manor, or it would be happening to everyone."

"Which means?"

"It's the interaction."

She nodded.

I laughed. "Well, good then. In order to understand how the place works, I need to figure out why Devera keeps disappearing, which I can do as soon as I've figured out how the place works."

She smiled at the stage again. I wondered if the balcony was getting jealous. She said, "Well, none of the rest of us vanish. That gives you lots of people to talk to."

I chuckled. "That's true. Polite of you. Except . . ."

"What?"

"Tethia."

"What about her?"

"She also vanished abruptly."

"But, isn't she a ghost? You said she was a ghost. I mean, ghosts do that, right?"

"I don't know. I've only ever met one before this."

She nodded. "And I've never met any."

"And I think she's pretty much confined to that one room, whether she's a ghost or whatever else she is."

Hevlika nodded. "That makes sense."

"So I guess I'll go talk to her."

She nodded.

"I doubt I'll run into you again."

"It's been a pleasure."

"Thank you. For dancing."

She smiled and nodded, and I went through the door.

I had a theory.

I returned to the room where I'd slept, grabbed the rope hanging from the ceiling and pulled it twice, and waited. The wait went on far longer than it should have; I was about to conclude that my theory was wrong, or else you just can't find good servants, when Gormin appeared, looking hesitant.

"Sir? You rang twice."

"Yeah."

"The call for Harro is once, and for me it is three times, so I was uncertain—"

"My mistake. I meant you."

"Very good, sir."

"Who is two?"

"No one, at present."

"Of course. I'd like to speak with you. Want to sit?"

"I'd prefer to stand, sir."

I knew he'd say that, but I had to ask. I sat down in the chair. It was like a repetition of the little drama I'd played out with Harro just an hour before. Or maybe that was the rehearsal, and this was the performance.

I said, "You remember me, don't you?"

"Yes, sir."

"I mean, from before, when you drugged me and tried to interrogate me."

He stared over my shoulder and was silent.

"Answer," I said. "Do you remember me?"

"I didn't recognize you at first. And then I wasn't sure."

"But now you do, and you are."

"Yes, sir."

"Good. I'm not altogether pleased about that, you know. Especially because to me it was only yesterday. But you suspected that, didn't you?"

He did his "staring over my shoulder" thing again. If he kept that up I was going to get irritated.

"Answer me," I said. "Did you suspect that?"

He nodded.

"So you know about paths through time."

"I—know there are odd things. There are rooms we are not permitted to visit, and restrictions as to with whom we can speak. And I've known for a long time that my lord Zhayin was working to solve the problem of a structure that could reach other worlds."

"But not that he'd solved it?"

"Not then," he said.

"When?"

"Two days ago, I heard a scream. I tried to see where it

came from and became lost. Eventually I reached a window, and we were on a cliff."

"And that was your first clue that the entire manor had moved?"

"Yes, sir."

"Who screamed?"

"I don't know, sir. I asked Discaru if he knew anything and he told me it was none of my concern."

Well. Salute me and call me General. I hadn't expected that. A mysterious scream, just as the manor is appearing at its new location. Another piece fell into place. I let it buzz around in my head for a minute, then I said, "Well, interesting as that is, it isn't what I wanted to talk to you about."

He cleared his throat. "No, I imagine not."

"And it isn't about the unpleasantness when we met before, either."

"Sir?"

"It's about Hevlika."

His jaw clenched, and he again fixed his eyes over my shoulder. I waited it out, and he said, "What about her?" His voice was a lot smaller.

"I know what happened. I know who had you expelled from the House."

"Yes," he said. "Harro. He was in love with her."

I blinked. And there was another surprise. "Okay," I said. "I hadn't expected you to know that. When did you find out?"

"When he appeared. I suppose a couple hundred years ago."

"Have you talked to him?"

"There didn't seem to be anything to say, sir."

"And you never spoke to her about it?"

"How could I?"

"Yeah, how could you. Tell me something else."

"Sir?"

"The food. It comes from the old castle, doesn't it?"

"Yes, sir."

"The servants cook it, bring it through the mirror room?"
He nodded.

"Why?"

"Sir?"

"Why not bring staff here? There's a really nice kitchen, a big pantry. Why not use it?"

"I don't know, sir."

"Good. Yes. Perfect."

"I don't understand."

"No, but I think I might be starting to."

"What—?"

"No, don't ask. It's bubbling around in my head, and there are still things I don't get. But it's the mirrors, and it's Discaru, and it's Zhayin. And it's the front door."

"The front door, sir?"

"When I first spoke with Zhayin, he was surprised that I was able to get in, and he was surprised that the front door wouldn't open. Had you ever gone in or out of that door?"

"Of course. Many times."

"I mean, since the manor arrived here on the cliff."

"Oh. No, I haven't had occasion to."

"Right. And what about the other door?"

"Sir? What other door?"

"Exactly. A house this size with only one door to the outside?"

"Well, there is the door to the courtyard."

"Yeah. And there's one on the side that goes to—have you ever gone out that one?"

"No, sir."

"Don't. It's disturbing."

"Yes, sir."

Necromantic paths to alternate worlds, doors that opened to different times but not really because you couldn't go anywhere—

"Are you all right, sir?"

"I think I'm getting a headache."

"Would you care for some springroot tea? It has been known to be efficacious—"

"No, no. I'll be fine."

"Yes, sir."

"I will figure all of this out."

"Yes, sir."

"Adron's Disaster changed everything."

"Sir?"

"I'm just starting to realize what that means. You wouldn't, because you're living it, it's part of your life. But I'm getting it."

"I don't—"

"Dragaeran history, as it was, started with the explosion that created the Great Sea of Amorphia, and it ended with Adron's Disaster."

He got that look you get when you don't want to rile up the madman. I ignored it and kept going. "Right now, you're operating on inertia. But none of the old rules apply. Everything's changing. The Houses. The Cycle. All of it. And you could be part of it, old guy."

"Yes, sir, no doubt—"

"All you have to do to be part of it is walk up to Hevlika

and say, 'I love you.' See, I'm the most romantic assas—
Easterner you'll ever meet. But it's true. That's how this
place, Precipice Manor, came to exist. Part of that same dis-
ruption, knocking holes in things. It's shaken up everything.
And one thing it's going to do is change the Houses. Go ahead.
Do it. Just go up to her—"

"I could never."

I looked at him. I thought about Cawti, and the way she
used to look at me, and the way she looked at me now, and I
wanted to hit the idiot over the head with a chair. I knew it
was none of my business, but I wanted to.

"Fine," I said. "Tell you what. How about you just go watch
her dance. See where it leads from there."

He sighed. "If only I could."

"Why can't you?"

"My duties—"

"Right. I have the feeling your duties are going to be considerably lighter soon. I'd go and watch her when she dances.
She likes having an audience."

"I—all right. And sir?"

"Hmm?"

"I'm sorry."

"About?"

"Drugging you."

"Oh. I never blame the dagger for where it's pointed. Well,
almost never."

"Thank you, sir."

"Look, I'm not trying to tell you your business—no, wait,
I am. I just want you to know that I had a talk with Harro,
and if you go to the House and claim it was all a lie, he'll
admit it."

"Sir? He will?"

"Yeah. If you go to the Iorich Wing of the Palace, there's an advocate named Perisil who can either help you, or point to someone who will. If he's willing to deal with an Easterner, he'll be willing to deal with a Teckla. So you can probably fix all of this without ignoring the House thing. But I still think you should. Anyway, think about it, and do whatever you bloody want to."

"Thank you, sir."

"That will be all," I said, because I've always wanted to say that to a servant, and I don't dare say it to Tukko.

Gormin didn't appear to find it odd; he just bowed and went about his business. I sat there and considered. What I really wanted to do now was ask Discaru a few questions. Unfortunately, I'd made that impossible.

"*Boss? Is there a plan?*"

"*Getting there.*"

"*I was afraid of that. It worries me when you have a plan.*"

"*Yeah, me too.*"

17

Zhayin's Heir

I made my way back to that room with the long table and didn't run into anyone. I walked in like it was no big deal, sat down, and waited. There was some of the emotional deadening I'd felt before, but not as intense—which is an odd word to use about something that removes intensity, but you know what I mean. I waited, and eventually even that passed, and then I said, "Hey, Tethia. It's Vlad. Got a minute?"

I waited, and after a while my glib words didn't seem so clever. I was in the middle of trying to come up with some other way to perhaps reach her when Loiosh said, *"Boss!"*

I turned around and there she was, sitting in a chair on the other side of the table. I looked closely, and from what I could see, the padding on the chair wasn't compressed the way it would be if she were really there. But I could see her, and presumably we could hear each other, so who cared about the rest? Corporeality is overrated. Taltos. You remember the spelling.

"Hey there," I said. "Remember me?"

"Vlad," she said.

"Good. That means time isn't—never mind. Can we talk?"

"We are talking now."

"Yeah. You say you built this place. This 'platform.'"

"No, I designed it. My father built it."

"Right. But you figured out how to anchor it in the Halls of Judgment so it could cross worlds."

"It isn't anchored in the Halls, it only passes through them."

"Okay. But tell me something: why is it you keep disappearing?"

"I don't know. Is it important?"

"I want to understand how this platform works. And that's part of it."

"You're a necromancer?"

"No."

"Then I don't think I can explain."

"Try?"

She nodded. I thought that would be an appropriate, or at least an ironic, moment for her to vanish, but thank Verra, for once the world withheld its irony. "Let's try it this way, then. You have a familiar. Do you understand the mechanism for how you communicate with him?"

"No, but I'm very curious."

"Ah. Well. All right, then. Another way: You say I vanish. I don't vanish, and I don't even move, really. Not much, at any rate. I turn."

"Turn. All right. You have my attention."

"That's why it happens so randomly. Right now, I'm working very hard to hold myself still, because the least shift in position"—she smiled—"I almost moved just now to demonstrate it, will bring me to another state."

"I'm still listening."

"Time and space seem like distinct things, but they're not. They're the same. This matters because, where I was born, places and times come together as—" She looked frustrated, then she vanished, but reappeared just as I was preparing a good curse. I didn't tell her that at least some of that I'd figured out, because I didn't want to interrupt the flow. She said, "Do you understand what it means to be a god or a demon?"

"Yes. It means you can manifest in more than one place at the same time. Oh. Are you a god or a demon?"

"No. If I were, I would have control of this process, and I wouldn't shift the way I do."

"I don't get it."

"I know." She frowned. "All right, I think I can explain it. To acquire powers of a god or a demon means to gain the awareness of the connections between different worlds, and to be able to move among them, and to control that movement. If you do not have these powers, but were born in a place where they meet, you can always see them, sometimes move among them, and only occasionally control the movement. Does that help?"

I nodded slowly. "Yes. Yes, that helps."

She was silent while I compared this with what I knew about Devera. Yeah, it made sense. But—

"Okay, here's what I'm not getting. How is it you ended up being born in the Halls of Judgment?"

"I don't know," she said. "I wish I did."

Me too. "Maybe I'll find out," I said.

She smiled a little. "Maybe you will."

I wondered what all of this had to do with how I communicated with Loiosh. I wondered how Devera seemed able to move where she wanted to—except here. I wondered how—

"I have another question," I said.

"I'm still here."

"This room. The effect it has. How is that possible? It's not sorcery, because I'm protected from sorcery. It feels like a psychic effect, but I'm protected from that too. Before you said it was the nature of the room itself, but I don't understand how that's possible."

"There is an art to it," she said. "It has been studied by the Vallista for thousands of years. The windows, the color, the tilt of the chairs and their height: all work to produce the effect."

"There's more to it than that, I think."

"Oh, yes. But you see, that's the heart of it. Those feelings become part of the designer of the room, and part of every craftsman who works on it. You draw it into yourself, like inhaling, and then you exhale it in your craft."

"Um. Sounds like witchcraft."

"The Eastern art. I've heard of it, but know nothing about it."

"I'm not saying that's what it is, it's just, it sounds like it. Or I guess feels like it would be more accurate."

"It is as much art as it is sorcery, but the result is that the feelings become inseparable from the room. As I said before, the effect on you was more pronounced than it would have been on a human." She was polite enough not to add, "because your brain is weaker," or something.

"I think I kind of get it," I said, though I didn't really and I still don't. But with any luck, I wouldn't need to. I'd gotten the answer to the question I'd come for, and that by itself made this an occasion for celebrating if I'd had anything to celebrate with. I needed more of Verra's wine.

"What do you know of your state?" I asked her.

"I don't entirely understand it. I feel like I died. But I'm here."

"What do you remember?"

"Running."

"To something, or from something?"

"From something, I think."

"From what?"

"I don't know."

"All right. You don't seem exactly like a ghost."

"How much experience with ghosts do you have?"

"A little. Tell me something. What do you want?"

She was silent for a long time, then she said, "If I am dead, then I'd like to be free so I can move on, or rest, or reincarnate, however fate should decide."

"But what could hold you here?"

"I don't know. It would have to be necromancy."

"Discaru," I said.

"Who?"

There's a particular kind of annoyance that comes when you realize you've killed some bastard before you know all the stuff he'd done that would have given you even more satisfaction in killing him. I'd never had that happen before. Oh, well. "Never mind," I said. "A demon. It's gone now. The question is, why?"

"I don't know."

"I think I do," I said. "And I think I know why I'm here."

"That's something many of us never learn."

I snorted. "I meant it in a slightly more practical sense. I think you did it."

"Did what?"

"I think as you were dying, you reached out to the Halls, and got some help."

"I don't remember that."

"Yeah, you don't remember dying. But I think you were asking for help from a god, and managed to reach Devera instead."

"Who is Devera?"

"Not a god."

"Oh. So it didn't work."

"I think it sort of did. And I think I'm on track for fixing the rest of it now."

"I don't understand."

"Good. We're even. Tell me something else?"

"Anything I can."

"What does the guide look like for your House?"

"Guide?"

"I don't know what to call it. The Dragons memorize a book so they know how to navigate the Paths of the Dead. The Hawks have a signet ring that acts as a guide. The Jhereg wear a pendant that works like the ring, and the Tiassa get a tattoo that works like the book. What do the Vallista use?"

"Oh. Our key. It's a piece of linen, usually dyed yellow, with purple threads that indicate the proper paths, usually made into a dress, or a toga, or a sarong."

"Does it appear with you when you die, like the ring, or do you have to memorize it, like the book?"

"You're dressed in it when you go over the Falls. You re-move the thread as you progress, and it gradually falls apart, so that you arrive in the Halls naked."

"That's how you established the connection with the Halls, right?"

"Yes."

"Was that the only one your family had?"

"I don't know."

"Yeah," I said. "I believe I do, however."

She nodded.

"All right, I think I have what I need. Thank you for your help."

"Good luck," she told me.

This time, because I was looking for it, I caught the slight turn in her chair she made just before she vanished. I drummed my fingers on the table. I wanted to find Lord Zhayin and have it out with him, shake him until I'd squeezed the answers out, but no, there was something else I needed to do first.

I stood up and headed out.

I emerged from the cave, went up the path, through the bedroom, and out, then to the nursery. She was sitting in a rocking chair, her eyes closed. I watched her for a while, trying to interpret the expression on her face as she dreamed, then it started to feel creepy so I cleared my throat.

She opened her eyes, took me in, and stood up. "My lord?"

"Hello, Odelpho."

"Hello, my lord."

"May I trouble you with another question?"

"Yes, my lord."

"Why did you lie to me?"

"My lord . . . I . . ."

"About the kitchen, and the cooks there. That's nonsense. You knew that didn't happen. It seems an odd thing to lie about. Why?"

"My lord, I—"

"Stop it. Answer my question."

She was scared, but I figured that was because, well, I'm scary. The question was, was she also scared of someone else? If so, who and why and how much? "If you're worried about Discaru," I said, "he's not going to be around anymore."

She tilted her head. "Are you sure?"

"Yeah," I said. It wasn't a lie. I was pretty sure. And turned out I was right, so no harm.

"I . . . may I sit down?"

"Of course," I said. Where were my manners? What would Lady Teldra say?

She folded her hands in her lap and said, "What happened to him?"

"He had an accident," I said.

She studied my face as if expecting me to wink or smile or something. I didn't, so she just nodded.

"He's the one who wanted you to lie about the kitchen?"

"Yes."

"When did he tell you to do that?"

"Just before we spoke, my lord. Perhaps an hour?"

"So, it was me in particular he didn't want to know about it."

"Yes, my lord."

"Why?"

"He didn't say, my lord."

Yeah, he didn't have to. He'd have known when he saw me that I shouldn't be there. He couldn't have known about Devera, but he must have realized that Tethia had done something that resulted in me being there, which meant that I had to be prevented from learning about the manor until I could be disposed of, because—

Tethia. It all came back to her, and to what she knew and what she could tell, and what had happened to her, and why. I studied Odelpho and considered.

She looked uncomfortable with me staring at her. She shifted and said, "Will that be all, my lord?"

"Not quite. I'm curious about something. It isn't terribly important, but do you go outside at all?"

"Sometimes."

"And pick apples?"

She nodded, then frowned. "Is there something—"

"No, no. You just set me a little mystery, is all."

"I like apples."

"Yeah, me too."

"You had one?"

"I had two. They were good."

"I'll be tending the trees myself from now on."

"There's no gardener?"

"At the old castle, not here."

"Of course. There were lots of things Discaru didn't want known, weren't there?"

She nodded.

"Such as Lady Zhayin's visit to the Halls of Judgment."

She looked down.

"Were you with her?"

She nodded.

"You took care of Tethia, there, in the Halls."

She nodded again.

"Odelpho, how did Tethia die?"

"Her mother died during the Interregnum."

"Odelpho!"

She jumped a little, then looked down again.

"Tell me what happened. It can't hurt you now."

She remained still, eyes fixed on the floor. I was getting tired of people staring at the floor or over my shoulder.

"Odelpho, tell me how Tethia died."

"It was the monster," she said.

"The monster? That, ah, I mean, Lord Zhayin's son?"

She nodded. "It chased her. I don't know why. She couldn't get out, so she tried to escape to the roof. In the end, she threw herself off it into the ocean-sea. She had only returned that day. I hadn't seen her since she was a child, when she went off to, well, I don't know. But I hadn't seen her in so long, and an hour after she was back, she was dead."

She looked like was about to cry. I said, "How?"

"My lord?"

"How could she get off the roof?"

"I don't understand."

"Have you ever been up there?"

"Only that one time. I saw her jump. Lord Discaru came up behind me, and he was able to control the beast. He said I must never speak of it. Is he really gone?"

"Yeah."

"Good," she said, like she meant it.

"How did it get loose?"

"My lord?"

"You said it was chasing Tethia. How did it get out of its cell?"

"I don't know. It was just after the completion of the con-

struction, when we first appeared here, so perhaps something
went wrong."

"Or something went right."

"My lord?"

I shook my head.

"Thanks for your help, Odelpho. What did you say your
name means?"

"Delpho means 'home of the bear' in the ancient language
of the Lyorn, my lord."

"Nice name," I said. "Take good care of it."

I bowed to her because I felt like it, and went on my way.

Time to end things.

Zhayin put his book down as I came in. "Well, what do you—"

"Shut up or I'll kill you. Is that clear enough? I hate killing
people for free, but I'm already inclined to make an exception
for you, so don't give me any more reasons."

"I'll—"

"You'll what? Discaru is gone. That monster of yours is
dead. Who—"

"Dead?"

"—is going to protect you? The dry-nurse or the butler?"

He glared at me. The news that his son was dead seemed
to affect him not at all. Maybe I shouldn't let that bother me,
especially with what else he'd done, and the fact that his son
had become an inhuman monster hundreds of years before. As
I said, maybe I shouldn't have, but I thought about my own son,
and I liked him even less.

He reached for a pull-rope next to him. I said, "You don't

want to do that. Your guards are in the past, and in the old castle, and they have to go through the mirror room and down stairs to get here. By the time they've done that, I will have sliced open your belly to see how many times I can wrap your entrails around your neck." Hey, look: if you're going to threaten someone, making it graphic is always better. I wouldn't really have done that, but it was effective, all right? Don't judge me.

"And you don't even want to, do you? You want as few people from the past here as possible, because the more who know about it, the more chance someone will figure out what you did, and find a way to get the message out, even from two hundred years ago. But I still want to see how much your entrails will stretch. Or maybe I won't even bother. Maybe I'll just stick you. With this." I drew Lady Teldra. She appeared as I'd first seen her, a very long, thin knife, slight teardrop shaping along the blade. She was beautiful.

I once had someone explain to me that we don't have real interactions with people, we have interactions with the image of those people we carry in our heads. I don't know. Maybe. But I figure if I stick a Great Weapon into a guy's eye, it's close enough to a real interaction for most purposes.

"What do you want?" he said. His voice was hoarse.

"Take your clothes off," I said.

His eyes widened.

"What do you think—"

I walked toward him until the point was inches from his face. "Take. Your. Clothes. Off."

He was shaking. He had every right to. He stood up, undid the belt of his robe, and let it fall off his shoulder. He wore thin yellow pants under it. I let him keep those.

"Hand me the robe," I said.

He stared down the length of Lady Teldra, then picked up the robe and handed it over.

"Sit down," I said.

He did.

I sheathed Lady Teldra, and he visibly relaxed. "What are you—"

"Shut your mouth or I will cut out your tongue," I suggested.

I drew a small throwing knife from inside of my cloak, found a piece of purple thread on the robe, and cut it. Then I looked Zhayin in the eyes, and started pulling on the thread. He swallowed. It all came out in one long tear; it took maybe a minute. When I was done, there were pieces of yellow silk on the floor, and a length of purple thread in my hand. I dropped the thread, and as I did so I heard, as if from far away, a deep metallic "click."

"There," I said. "Now the door is open."

He started to speak, but someone else did first. "Uncle Vlad!"

"Hello, Devera. This is Lord Zhayin, who murdered his own daughter and trapped you here."

She turned and looked at him, then turned back to me. "I don't like him very much," she announced.

"Yeah, that's two of us. But you're free now."

"I know."

"And so is the woman who brought you here."

She nodded.

"I should get going now, Uncle Vlad. I need to go back to yesterday and find you."

"Of course you do," I said.

"Are you, are you going to hurt him?"

"I haven't made up my mind yet."

"Maybe you shouldn't."

"Maybe I shouldn't."

"Well, thank you, Uncle Vlad."

"You're welcome, Devera."

She vanished, like she does. I moved a chair so it was facing him and a little too close. Then I leaned forward. I said, "I know what you did, I just want to know why you did it. I have a suspicion, but I hope I'm wrong, because I don't want there to exist anyone who—never mind. Start talking."

He didn't speak.

I said, "Tethia solved the problem, didn't she? She figured it all out, how to cut through the Halls of Judgment to permit travel to other worlds."

He grunted, which I took as a yes.

"But you're not there yet. You just put the touches on the basics of it, and now you're ready to extend the *platform* to wherever you can find access points. And you had a friendly demon lined up to help with that, except now you'll have to find another, because he accidentally fell on my Morganti knife when he was trying to kill me. I feel bad."

He went back to glaring.

"Or maybe I'll kill you, in which case you won't have to worry about it. But, here's my question: Why is Tethia dead? And not only dead, but trapped here, locked into this place? Oh, I know *how* you did it. You bound her to the Paths of the Dead with your key, that robe. I get that part. But *why?* Did you need a soul in order to make it work? No, you didn't. Was it a tragic accident that the monster you accidentally created happened to get loose just at the point when her work was done? No, it wasn't. Was it some fluke of her having designed the place that, after she died, she was unable to leave? No, it wasn't.

"You control the door to the thing's lair, don't you? You released it first when I showed up, but—and here's the part that took me the longest to figure out—you failed to tell Discaru, so he thought it escaped and recaptured it. That's pretty funny, when you think about it. You're really bad at this stuff. Then you released it again when I started messing with the mirrors, only this time there was no Discaru, so I put it out of its misery. If that makes you sad you're the worst hypocrite this sad Empire has ever produced. You used your son—what remained of him—to kill your daughter, didn't you? Only this time your friend the demon was in on it with you. You'd sealed the entire structure so no one could leave, but he opened it up just enough for her to jump off it, didn't he? That way she'd be dead and you wouldn't even have a mess to clean up. He was a good friend to you, always ready to do your dirty work. I'd say I'm sorry I dispatched him, but I'd be lying.

"Only that wasn't the end of it. After she died, Discaru bound her to the manor, so you could keep her here. He used the front room to contain her soul, to keep her trapped. I know he did it, and I know he did it for you, but why? That's my question. Why did you kill your own daughter, and then prevent her soul from moving on? What did you get out of it?"

"If you're going to kill me, just—"

I pulled the dagger from my boot. Not Lady Teldra, not this time, but a nasty stiletto. "Answer the question."

"I don't like answering people who are threatening me."

"Okay, fair enough. I won't threaten." I transferred the blade to my other hand, then slapped him across the face. His head rocked, and when it came back, I transferred the dagger again and slapped him with the other hand. He put his arm up and slid forward and I gut-punched him. He doubled over on his knees on the floor and started retching.

I sat down again and waited. After a minute, I said, "There. You see? No threat. Would you like me to not threaten you again?"

After a minute he looked like he could maybe form words. I got up and assisted him back into his chair; he flinched when I moved, but sat down.

"I'm listening," I said.

"What do you want?"

"Why did you have your own daughter killed?"

He raised his head and looked at me. "I'd been working on it all my life."

"It? You mean—"

"Creating a crossplanar platform. A place to live through which one could walk the halls and visit worlds as if they were rooms."

"Well, at any rate, you've managed a place where you walk into rooms and end up in places that make no sense."

He shook his head. "That is nothing, trivial. A matter of adjusting the mirrors. The principle is there, it works; that is how you can reach the Halls of Judgment, and the Housetown castle. It works."

"Okay, I believe you. It works. And?"

"All my life. More than three thousand five hundred years I devoted to this. That is a hundred times as long as your kind lives."

I didn't correct his arithmetic, or comment that it explained why he was having trouble adjusting the mirrors. I said, "Okay, whatever. That doesn't explain—"

"Three thousand, five hundred years. And after all of that, *she*, my own daughter, would get all the credit."

"But she solved the problem, didn't she?"

"No! I did! I solved it by bringing her to the Halls to be born! That was *my* idea! I arranged for her to have the power, to be able to walk from world to world, bringing reality with her as if it were a length of string, tied in one place, carried to another. The House gives an award, you know. An award for superlative design, for building something no one else has been able to build. For all time, that award—"

"Which you'd cheated to get?"

He snuffled like a puppy. "Cheated," he said. "I didn't cheat. I restored things to the way they should have been."

"Fine, you did all that amazing stuff," I said, "I'm sure if I were an Athyra I'd understand that, and if I were a Vallista I'd care. But I'm just a humble, simple Easterner. So I just say, so what?"

"So what? So what? Didn't you hear me?"

"Yeah, I heard you. You had the bright idea to forge your daughter as if she were a tool, and it worked, and all you care about is whose name gets in which history books. I heard it, I just don't believe it. What sort of worthless waste of skin and bones cares more about that than his own daughter? Not to mention your wife; you got her killed too, didn't you. Because of reasons that are none of your business, I get to see my son every month. Maybe every week if I'm lucky. Those are the best days I have. And, hey, maybe family isn't the most important thing to everyone. Fine. But you had your own daughter killed, and are now trying to erase the memory of the thing she . . . you know, you just might be the most disgusting, worthless specimen of a Dragaeran

I've ever seen, and I've killed dozens of you guys, all of whom deserved it. I'm impressed."

I might as well have saved my breath for all the effect it had on him. "There's no point in trying to make you understand," he said.

"No," I agreed. "There isn't."

"What are you going to do now?"

"I'm going to go home, find someplace where they let Easterners stay, and take a long bath and try to scrub your filth out of my soul."

He couldn't come up with an answer to that, so he just looked disgusted.

"And that isn't all, is it? You sealed the place. No one can get in or out? You kept all of your servants in the past, where there was no one to tell, except three, and your pet dancer who is too good for you. And you sealed the doors to make sure they couldn't leave. Only I got in, and you never could figure out how that happened."

"Tethia—"

"She'll be fine," I said. "As for you, I'm not so sure."

"Do what you will," he said. "The manor still stands. I accomplished what no one else has before."

"Yeah," I said. "And if that had been enough for you, I wouldn't be standing here deciding whether to kill you before I leave."

Epilogue

Reader, I murdered him. I know I'd said I might let him live, but I meant that *might*. I hadn't made up my mind. The smug look on his face made it up for me.

He seemed more offended than frightened. I think he was going to say something, but I put the dagger into his left eye and twisted, and the sounds he made had no more significance than an award falsely given. He stopped twitching and I left him there to rot and stink up the place; they could move him if they felt like it. For all I know, he's still sitting in his chair, my knife in his eye, and some justification still on his lips.

As for Precipice Manor, well, it's still there, overlooking the ocean-sea. Back in the past, servants still prepare food, and, not knowing what they do, carry it forward into the future, then clean up the trays. An empty wizard's chamber collects dust, and wine that is already bad becomes worse. On a stage that is on the first floor but reached by the second, an Issola still dances, and a Teckla who was once an Issola watches her as she spins, jumps, and with every movement, gradually allows her body to injure itself more and more, in the name of art, in the name of love. Whether it is worth it is none of my business, or yours.

I walked down the hallway to the entry. I still had to deal with all that crap Verra had laid on me. But no, forget it. Not now. Now was the time to just concentrate on surviving, because the instant I left the place, I'd be back in a world where people were trying to kill me, and for now, that was enough to worry about. If the Mighty Hand of Destiny had something planned for me, it could either squash those who were threatening my life, or make itself into a fist and strangle itself. Ideally, both.

The doors opened for me, and I began the long walk back to Adrilankha, the pitiless ocean crashing in my ears.